2029

A tale of love and betrayal in a dys

By

Michael Fitzalan

A tale of post-Brexit smugglers, love and betrayal in a dystopian society

THIS IS A WORK OF FICTION

Copyright © 2020 by Michael Fitzalan

All rights reserved. No part of this book may be reproduced, stored, or transmitted by any means—whether auditory, graphic, mechanical, or electronic—without written permission of the author, except in the case of brief excerpts used in critical articles and reviews.

Prelude

Momentarily, I was the happiest person on the planet; I even joined in their splashing of each other and swam around a bit. Their bay etiquette was spasmodic splashing followed by swimming around in circles and starting the splashing again; mine was flicking water and floundering around in a circle.

They swam like professionals, performing the Australian crawl in slow languid movements, I could only do breaststroke. When particularly high waves lifted me up, I resorted to the safety of doggy paddle but only if I was sure they were too immersed in their swimming to notice me.

When I finally thought about clowns, I remembered my mother's music. One song's lyrics said: 'the tears of a clown when no one's around'.

My emotions were up and down like a yoyo. If this was love, I did not think much of it. I was ecstatic one minute, morose the next. I shook off all negative thoughts, determined to spend the last few hours in Cornwall enjoying myself with my new friends. I would deal with my heart another time.

Thankfully, splashing each other lasted only a few minutes. Adel was the first to leave the water. I tried to watch as she emerged from the sea, but Freddie was talking to me and it would have been rude to turn my head around.

'Are you having fun?' he asked, swimming towards me.

'Yeah, but the water is so very cold,' I replied, treading water.

'I'll do a few more minutes, you go in.'

'I'll do a few strokes with you if you like.'

'I think I might go in myself; I'm feeling a bit woozy all of a sudden.'

'So am I. I thought it was the cold.'

'You make me laugh.'

'That's good.'

'Have your legs gone numb?'

'No, I just feel a bit sleepy.'

'Let's go back, I feel like I've been drugged.'

'Ha, your body's closing down with hypothermia. I told you it was cold.'

'No, I've been drugged before.'

'You're kidding.'

'No, I'm not, help me get to shore.'

'How?'

'Please, just do it. My arms are going numb, now!'

'Okay.'

'Help me, I'm going under.'

I swam towards him, confused.

It was incredible.

A strong athletic youth was losing consciousness. He was not fighting to stay on the surface. He was letting the water swallow him up. I snapped out of my daze.

His head had slipped under the water.

I had to do something. I grabbed for him ,– his arms were slippery. I tried to get a grip on his shoulders, but he sank further; I had dived under the water and grabbed his biceps, lifting him up as best I could. Kicking wildly, we broke the surface.

'Help me,' he whispered.

I had a chance; he had not swallowed any water.

He was so heavy, and I was feeling weaker and weaker.

'Help me, Freddie!' I begged, 'Kick your legs.'

'I can't,' he sighed, 'Adel?'

'She's on shore!'

He was lucid for the time being, but he was falling in and out of consciousness.

'Adel,' I shouted, turning around, I could not see her on the beach.

Freddie's head lolled forward into the water.

I pulled his face out of the water pulling his head up by his hair. He did not so much as wince.

'Freddie, you're too heavy, wake up, I need you to help me!' I screamed in his ear.

No response.

I pushed my nails into his arms.

No response.

I kneed his leg.

No response.

Willing myself to be stronger, I pulled Freddie towards the beach; we were too far out for me to touch the bottom.

He was under the water. I had to get his head above the surface.

Why had we followed Adel so far out?

I was not a strong swimmer at the best of times, I should have told her; I thought I had in conversations before the meeting.

'Come on, Freddie,' I hissed, impatiently, as I brought his head above water again. I supported the back of his head, keeping his nose and mouth above the surface.

A huge wave lifted us up, I lost my grip and water gushed over Freddie's head. He choked and came around. Shaking his head slightly, trying to get the sea out of his ears.

I thought we could make it, but his eyes were still closed. It was like he was asleep. I held his head and kicked for shore. Now I was feeling weak. His head was heavy, and kicking was exhausting. I turned my face to shore; no sign of Adel but there were people on the shore.

'Help, help!' I shouted as loudly as I could.

No response.

Luckily a wave came and pushed us towards the shore.

I let go of Freddie's head and started waving both arms while I was treading water.

No response.

I grabbed Freddie's head. Another wave came and pushed us towards the shore.

'Hey,' I screamed at the top of my lungs reaching out for Freddie's head as the third wave came.

No response.

No Freddie.

He was gone.

The undercurrent in the last wave must have taken him under. I swam around in a circle, dived under the water and searched around.

Nothing: no head, no body, no arms and no legs. I was feeling weaker and weaker; I had to get myself to shore; I had to get help.

Swimming as fast as my breaststroke allowed, I saw a crowd gathered on the shore.

As I neared them, I heard raised voices.

'I heard cries for help, are you okay?' asked a man dressed in a wet suit, standing next to a surfboard.

'It's not Freddie,' the woman announced.

She was similarly dressed and similarly equipped.

'Where's Freddie?' Adel asked, her voice slipping between the shoulders of the surfers as she arrived.

They parted to allow her to slide between them so that I was facing her; she was searching my face for answers.

'I lost him.'

'No,' she cried, stepping around me, she ran into the water; she had dressed, and the water lapped over her fresh pair of beige tailored trousers, but she pushed on through the waves.

As she waded in her white shirt became transparent, clinging to her back and then she was under the water and swimming out to sea. The surfers followed her. When they had reached a suitable depth, they crawled onto their surfboards and paddled out behind Adel.

Adel duck-dived twice, and then swam on.

She arrived at the exact position where I lost Freddie; it was uncanny that she had the sense to go to that spot. Was it female intuition? Diving down again, she surfaced and spoke to the surfers. I distinctly heard her asking for help. Yet, they seemed not to have had heard me. Like a magician, she pulled Freddie's head from the water, her hand resting under his chin.

In a flurry of activity, the surfers slipped Freddie's body on to the nearest surfboard, kicking for shore. Adel took the far surfboard and slipped on to it, paddling behind. I was standing in the warm breeze, still frozen like an ice cube, helpless but relieved. I loved Adel even more at that moment; she was a heroine. I had missed the first aid course at school, but I felt sure she could perform mouth to mouth or CPR.

She could bring Freddie back to life. As they neared the beach, I braved the frozen water again and tried to help but they ignored me all three of them; they had gone into rescue mode.

The three of them manhandled him off the board and on to the soft sand of the beach above the waterline. Freddie looked white like marble; his eyes were closed he looked like he was asleep. Adel knelt down next to him and felt for a pulse, she bent down and put her ear to his chest. Then, she shook her head.

That was that.

'You killed him,' the woman said.

'No, I was trying to save him,' I argued.

'I heard him crying for help,' she protested.

'That was me,' I explained.

'You deliberately drowned him, we saw you,' she insisted.

'Adel, you don't believe, that do you?' I appealed to Adel.

'Freddie's dead,' she sighed.

Those were the last words I heard from her that day; the day Freddie died.

'Murderer,' cried the man, taking up his girlfriend's chant.

He lunged at me but even in my drowsy state, I was able to step back and out of his grasp. Adel was on her haunches hunched over the body; the woman was trying to comfort her while looking at me with daggers. The man was floundering in the sand. He would be on his feet beating me to a pulp in a few seconds.

Adrenaline kicked in and I was off.

I have never run so fast in my life. I could feel the man running after me, hearing his panting as he gained on me.

Everyone was so damn fit; it was sickening. I pumped my arms and kicked my heels up, heading for the car. I was going to be accused of murder and, running around the country in swimming shorts I was going to alert the police to my presence in any area. The boot was still open, the man was still gaining, he wasn't as tall as me and I had longer legs, but he was far fitter.

Just as I reached the car, he put his hand on my shoulder. I slipped from his grasp, but he came at me again, gripping my shoulder so that I almost passed out with the pain. I looked down into the boot, grabbed the bottle of champagne and twisted my body.

The swine did not let go but I biffed him on the head with the bottle, which sent him flying and magically made him release his grip. He was lying right in my path, if I was going to reverse the Maserati out, I would have to run him over. So, as he staggered to his feet, I lured him away from the car.

As I fully expected, he grabbed for the bottle. He did not want to get another bruise on his noggin. I could see the bump already forming on his temple. He had expected me to struggle but I just let him take and as he did so, I planted my knee in his crotch.

I felt a squidgy contact, heard a groan and watched as the poor man dropped to the ground and curled into a ball. The pain was obviously agonising; he wriggled like a worm that had salt poured on it.

I raced to the car, threw open the door, jumped in and pushed the starter button. Nothing, the fob was missing. I had no idea how the man broke through the pain barrier, but he was at my shoulder again and he grabbed the sore flesh and bruised muscle once more. I winced in pain and roared in frustration. I threw the door open, knocking him off balance, and stepped on his toes, jabbing down hard.

As he hopped on one leg, I opened the door fully, knocking him to the ground. If he could worry my shoulder, I could worry his crotch.

As he tried to clamber to his feet, I planted another kick between his legs with the arch of my bare foot this time. I think it had more power this time and was more effective because I felt a spherical mass on the end of my foot. My assailant went down again, curled into a foetal ball, moaning in pain.

At the back of the car, I scoured the boot; the fob was lying in the hamper. Why, I could not tell. Returning to the driver's door, I checked that my assailant was still down; he had got to his knees but was still doubled in pain. I had time.

I slipped into the driver's seat, started the car; reversed out of the parking space, avoiding their black car-club rental Jaguar F-Pace and headed for the border.

I was leaving Poseidon Bay forever.

As I turned on to the main road, I saw a Toyota Hi-Lux pick-up in the distance. I knew it was packed with Lawless's security men, armed to the teeth, speeding up the hill towards the point.

They were coming for me.

Chapter One

Falling in Love

The first memory I have of Poseidon Bay was the bar called The Captain Benbow. It was a maze of rectangular rooms with cream matt paint smeared over roughly plastered walls. Ceiling fans were spinning overhead, wobbling on their black metal stalks, wafting the smell of steam perfume and Lebanese Red about the place. All the tables were small and round.

Couples dressed in Parisian designer clothes that had been bought from containers standing in the docks sat drinking strong English craft ale in pint jugs and staring into each other's eyes. Their dresses were black, their suits were black, and my mood was black.

Women wearing elegant, figure-hugging, dresses smoked from long elegant cigarette holders, the roaches stuffed deep into the stem and the liquorice black, Rizla papers sizzling quietly. Wisps of thick cannabis smoke snaked to the ceiling.

What else would you expect?

Every single person there was a smuggler. They either drove the boat, or they processed the manifests, or took stock or lugged the gear themselves. Like any other business there were a myriad of disciplines. Despite this, all of them looked the same.

The women had all crossed their elegant, long legs, leaning forward on an elbow to get closer to their men. Their loyal men, mirroring their women, were leaning forward on crossed arms, casually lifting the top arm to drink or smoke.

Not one of the women was under five foot nine and not one of the men under six feet. It was the land of the giants. Giants in well-fitting and expensive designer gear but giants, nonetheless. These were obviously the ones in charge, the organisers.

I surveyed my pint. I was alone, a stranger in town. I dared not stare at any of the pretty women, a grockle eyeing up a local girl was likely to be dealt with severely; a glance at a man would be seen as an invitation to fight. I looked at my shiny shoes.

I hated drinking beer from a glass with a handle and dimples. It reminded me of my father – not a pleasant man, he had been all anger and fists before he left; he always drank his beer out of a jug.

He was also the genius who chose my name, claiming it came from the Germanic name Alberic who was king of the elves in German mythology; he looked that up. I wished he had called me Alberic. The truth is he had a crush on Audrey Hepburn after seeing her in a rerun of *Breakfast at Tiffany's* on television and he wanted a daughter. That was how I got a boy's name that could be turned into a girl's name with the flick of a pen, a reversal of one letter.

My school years were miserable especially as my mum let my hair grow and I was considered a bit of a pretty boy. I became a lonely boffin and only got to be a salesman after a steel mill took me on as an apprentice; they sent me on the road when times get hard and the sales team dwindled. I had to pretend to be confident. They called me Biddy at the works. Get it? 'B', 'D'; they were not sure if I was male or female or 'trans'. Nor was I by the time they had finished bullying me.

I sipped the cool beer; the bitter hops from Kent could not hide the inferior malt. They had added rice and sugar to the mix; that never worked, but it did not stop them from trying. I felt depressed by that. Smugglers even adulterated their own beer. I heard that you could get good craft ales in the big cities, but I doubted it.

If you could it would be the preserve of the rich; they got all the good stuff but at a price. Banks and financial companies and institutions held normal people's pensions. These quaint gentlemen's clubs packed full of the brightest and best graduates believed that the casino, which was the stock market at that time, would provide such riches that all the problems of shortfalls would be solved in no time.

Everyone waited while the bankers paid themselves three-figure bonuses and the shortfalls in profits grew and grew as the economy plummeted like a pigeon shot from the sky.

I could do nothing about the financial situation in the country, so I went out to work. I was young, single and careworn; it should have been carefree but two out of three was a result in those days. I should have been chatting to girls; I looked handsome and smart in my grey flannel trousers, blue blazer and white open-necked shirt. Shiny shoes in black leather with laces completed the suave look.

I looked sophisticated and clearly my conversation would match my clothes. When I spoke to the gorgeous, young, lovely ladies of Poseidon Bay, they would all fall for my easy charm, my knowledge of books and of science and my great sense of humour. I have an uncanny ability to remember every joke I have heard.

Unfortunately, there were no lovely ladies in that rat hole of a pub, just Amazonian giants with bottle blonde hair and eyebrows plucked within an inch of their lives who looked into the eyes of their thug ugly boyfriends.

I hated my boss, too, Mr Campbell-Lamerton, also known as 'The Silver Ingot Merchant'. Why had he sent me to this godforsaken place? He had call it a 'den of iniquity' and then laughed like an evil genius before driving me to the railway and buying me a ticket to St. German's station. Why was I so desperate for commission that I would mix with smugglers?

I needed to go to the men's room. Annoyingly, I realised after buying my pint. I walked out of my oblong into another rectangle, slightly narrower and slightly longer and slightly shabbier this time.

The clientele were slightly rougher, too. This was where the younger crowd were, mostly men. They wore white suits made from Irish linen with open-neck Britannia blue silk shirts under the jacket. Each breast pocket was festooned with a red silk handkerchief spilling out in a defiant celebration of all things British. It was the uniform of the successful smuggler set.

Finding the 'gents', a huge green neon sign above yet another doorway alerted me to its existence, I pushed the door open. I was surprised at how cavernous and clean the place was.

You can guess the shape of the room by now but there were floor-to-ceiling mirrors, a bank of cubicles on the far wall and, on another wall, a row of huge butler's sinks in heavy white ceramic.

After using the almost completely clean cubical, I dared to approach the sinks. Above them, gold taps protruded from under a shelf laden with fluffy white flannels, which were used for drying hands; it was like an international hotel, not a high street bar.

The soap on the shelf, slotted between each pile of flannels, had a warrant from the king; he still maintained his Duchy of Cornwall Estates brand even if most of his land had been purloined or been squatted on by the fine citizens of that wonderful county.

The soap smelt like camomile and lavender; the camomile reminded me of the shampoo my mother used to wash my hair with when I was a small child and the lavender reminded me of the scent of her wardrobe.

I missed my mother desperately and the thought of her, then, made a lump rise in my throat but I was not about to cry into a mirror in a pub. If someone had come into the privy and found me blubbing, they would have me kicked out of Portwrinkle.

The Lawless family had annexed the whole of Whitsand Bay and renamed it Poseidon Bay.

It was the most lawless and dangerous fiefdom in England and Lawless had given new names to everywhere; the pub had been the Finnygook Inn – less *Treasure Island* and more proper Cornwall.

There was a little wicker basket for the used towels. I tossed two into the bottom of the empty basket; clearly, I was the only one who bothered to wash his hands in this place. I made a mental note to wash my hands back at the hotel; there must be faecal matter on every surface here, I reckoned.

I only trusted the beer glass because I had seen it come out of the dishwasher; although I could not vouch for the barman who touched the handle, at least the matter would be on the outside of the glass rather than on the inside.

On reflection, I decided that it might help to add a bit of flavour; the watered-down beer was insipid, it needed all the help it could get.

Returning to the table, I found that there were two dockers in blue overalls standing next to my empty glass. They had their Union Jack hard hats in their hands and were approached by a tall woman in a black dress, followed obediently by her shorter minder or boyfriend, dressed in the red, white and blue uniform like the drinkers next door.

She handed each of them a wad of plasticised twenty-pound notes, which they openly counted and checked for authenticity. No one trusted anyone in this place. She smiled and they nodded, then she wafted past them leaving a trail of steam perfume behind her.

The two men looked at each other without expression but I could tell what they were thinking about and it did not involve the man who followed the local beauty from the room.

I knew she would have been horrified if she had known what their plans might be. Appreciative but discreet glances from men whose partners were looking into their glasses or ashtrays led me to believe she was considered a beauty in Poseidon Bay. She left the room. She left me cold. It was time for action.

'Which one of you drank my beer?' I asked bravely, rolling my shoulders so they could see how broad they were under my navy blazer.

I wished that I had packed my leather biker jacket and black jeans that I normally wore to look hard in places like this. I breathed in so my grey flannel trousers actually looked like they fitted me; a paunch is never very threatening.

'Not us, guv', we wouldn't drink beer 'Fam'; lager depth charge, that's our tipple isn't that right, Roy?' the taller said, smiling at me.

He was big and broad like a bear. He could crush me without any effort. His partner was short and squat and smiled at me only once his friend had. He wore a very beery moustache; the froth on it smelt of my pint, I was sure, but I let it go. It was not a good idea to antagonise two beefy locals.

It was true, I had been to the gym yesterday but that had been the first time in three months; they were shifting smuggled goods on a daily basis: barrels of cognac, boxes of perfume bottles, which they unloaded by hand; the forklift trucks used too much electricity, so everything was shifted by hand and pure muscle power. The blue overall men did the hard graft of generators.

The tidal boom power station, which was being built for this part of the English coast, was three years behind schedule as well as three times over budget. The regular power-cuts would have brought all the smuggling activities to a halt if it weren't for grafters like these two men. Their tattoos and their bulging muscles put the odds firmly in their favour.

They would get their tips, what they called 'bunts', anywhere they could. Normally it was a percentage of what they were unloading; in my case it was my drink. It had been stupid of me to leave my pint unattended.

They left sharpish; I looked around the room. If anyone had witnessed the altercation, they were doing a very good impression of carrying on as if nothing had happened.

Everyone was used to looking the other way now. I was down to my last tenner, enough for a pint. There was no way I would visit the cash machine at dark around this place; I would get some more money out in daylight hours.

I had been given a company cash card; all the expenditure would have to be accounted for and all drinks would be docked from my wages at the end of the week whether or not I secured the silver deal. My boss was tough.

No one within a seventy-mile radius of the bay accepted anything except for cash. I could use the card to get money out of the hole in the wall at exorbitant rates, twenty per cent of the withdrawal. The only institutions that made money were banks.

I could not use contactless anywhere outside the main cities, Bristol or Southampton, but even then, the outlets charged a fifteen per cent administration fee. Cash really was king, a far cry from the early years of Brexit where no one used folding money or change.

Smugglers only ever took cash.

They were experts at liberating and unloading stolen goods as well; currency changed hands at alarming rates, quicker than a rat across a railway track.

Striding up to the bar, I waited my turn.

There was one barman and only three customers sitting at the bar. You never had to wait long; people nursed their pints these days.

'Another pint of your Pope's Toe, please, someone snaffled my pint,' I complained, hoping he would replace my drink. If I was looking for sympathy, the barman's raised eyebrows did not instil me with confidence.

'Hardly surprising is it? You are in the biggest smuggling harbour in the world, work it out, Einstein,' the barman breathed dismissively.

'How did you know my name?'

'Is that really your name?' he asked flabbergasted, he obviously had no sense of humour and not much common sense either. I had thought my remark might raise a smile.

'No, just kidding. I'm new in town, I heard Poseidon Bay was a tough place, but I thought my pint would be safe.'

The barman looked at me as if I were mad. I stood my ground; I was going to get another pint, even if I had to pay for it.

'No chance. If you've got a complaint, have a word with the manager. Here he comes,' the barman assured me.

'You are over twenty-five, aren't you?'

'Of course,' I lied.

'Good,' he said, obviously not believing me.

The irony in in his voice rang out like a monastery bell. We both knew half the people in the place were underage. He set the three-quarter filled glass jug on the counter and pretended that the froth on top that brought the level to the brim was part of the drink.

I stared at him willing him to top up my drink, we both knew it was a short measure; he stared back at me willing for me to pay up.

I caved.

'How much is that?' I asked.

'Nine pounds fifty, please.'

'Thanks,' I hissed.

I knew arguing in Poseidon Bay was useless.

I was not going to ask for change – he knew it, everyone knew it; fifty pence coins had gone out of circulation six years after Brexit. That was why they set the price like that: 'look after the pennies' so they say. That was their motto. They made a five per cent profit for each pint, not bad for just pouring it into a glass. Add that to the short measures and you had a recipe for a smugglers pub.

No one would argue over fifty pence; I was not going to be the first. They knew that I knew that. The rules of 'The Bay', as the locals called the area; they were tough and had to be obeyed.

Besides, I had spotted the manager wending his way towards me; he slipped past the barman and opened the flap on the bar, walking through the gate, bolting it behind him and deftly putting the flap back. He was safely behind the bar.

He turned to face the throng standing in front of him waiting to be served. There were just four of us and one of them was being served by my friend, the barman. It was my chance.

'Excuse me, landlord, but my pint was just stolen,' I exclaimed angrily; my acting abilities were second to none. I had played Puck like a professional actor; well, that was what Miss Thwaites, my drama teacher, said after my role in the school production.

'Happens all the time here. We sell beer but we don't provide security for it,' he noted as he lifted the hinged bar counter, stepped through the wooden gate and closed the bar flap behind him. 'The police won't come here after one of their squad cars was pushed into the harbour. Those electric cars don't like water; it was a shocking waste of life.'

He walked towards me; he did not look aggressive but four years of being in sales had taught me to expect the unexpected. I put my pint on the cigarette machine in order to talk to him without a pint as a prop.

Even though he was moving through the bar, I was determined to stick with him. I was his shadow; I followed him that closely, talking at his shoulder.

'I appreciate that but what exactly are you doing to keep everyone safe here?' I asked indignantly.

He would no doubt buy me a replacement pint just to get me off his back and out of his hair.

'Come with me and I'll show you,' he replied tersely, surprising me by his reply and by the fact that as he spoke, he was rolling up his shirtsleeves like a street fighter.

I briefly wondered if he were going to have a pop at me. I could see us sparring in the beer garden. I turned around to grab my pint and follow; it was already gone, yet there was no one there.

The Captain Benbow had originally been a fifteenth-century inn; I would have genuinely believed that there was a dipsomaniac ghost haunting the place if anyone had told me.

Hurriedly, following the landlord, I caught up with him at a large rectangular table with bentwood chairs on either side. I noticed a pile of cans and glasses piled up in front of two lovely looking local girls. They were nursing their beer, seemingly oblivious to the mess; everyone nursed their drinks in those days.

Next to them were six smugglers, you could tell. They had their white suit jackets on the back of their chairs, Britannia blue shirts undone so much that wisps of chest hair peeped out from the open neck, royal red braces and Union Jack cuff links.

'Right boys,' the landlord announced with a friendly manner; he was, obviously, used to dealing with characters. 'We can't allow cans brought in and the glasses you've piled up in front of the ladies need to be put back on your side or taken to the bar.'

His instructions were met with incredulity. On the far end was a freckly, fresh-faced teenager who seemed to be the ringleader. He swung back and forth on his chair defiantly. The landlord promptly produced a Phase Three Taser gun from his trouser pocket, no bigger than a pack of cards, and hit the closest of the white suits with a jolt of a few hundred volts of electricity. It was like he had seventeen piranha fish in his white suit trousers. The poor boy went into spasm for thirty seconds, screamed in agony and collapsed back in his chair unconscious.

The silence that followed was palpable. It lasted for a few seconds, no sound.

Gradually, voices began to rise above a whisper and the hubbub of the pub returned. There was a flurry of activity while the other four cleared away, taking the detritus up to the bar. The ringleader still swung on his chair, unfazed by the Taser. Or the plight of his friend.

It was my chance to make a name for myself. He was sullen and uncooperative, obviously a troublemaker and the manager would be grateful for my intervention and impressed enough to replace my beer – in theory.

He was the archetypal pretty boy, tall, dark and handsome. The landlord had shock value; I just had to be brave.

A tough reputation as a salesman was always needed in those days.

'Yeah, those cans need to be recycled and you shouldn't be swinging on your chair,' I thundered like Thor with a headache.

As I passed the corner of the table, I pushed the ringleader's shoulder forcing all four legs on to the floor. He looked up into my eyes, a sneer on his face and a death stare, his lips twitched as though he were going to speak.

I noticed that he was the typical leader: good-looking, tall and charismatic, everything I was not. I was taking on Alexander the Great.

Only, in my rush to make a name for myself, I had neglected to notice exactly 'to whom I was talking and exactly with whom I was tangling' as my teachers frequently warned me.

I am fairly tall, fairly good-looking and fairly good fun to be with. He was the Adonis above all others, the epitome of all three. The presence of the landlord and his electric pacifier may have been the main reason why he did not rip my head from my body.

Perhaps he was polite and kind to strangers, or he was biding his time because he felt revenge was a dish best enjoyed cold, or maybe he was waiting for there to be fewer witnesses around.

'Now, lads, you leave these girls be if you want to avoid a bolt from heaven,' the landlord warned.

He stood, shaking his Taser in the air, like Zeus holding a thunderbolt above his head and deciding which target to hit. The other smugglers meekly sat down, having cleared away, ignoring their unconscious colleague.

He was still out cold; his eyes were still closed, his chin still rested on his chest and his body still slumped in his chair. It was as if he were an old man having an afternoon nap. The girls were talking animatedly, pretending nothing was going on.

That was the way in Poseidon Bay.

'Yeah,' I growled, 'my name is Aubrey East. I'll be in town for a while, so I'll get to know all of you sooner or later.'

I surveyed the faces, looking to see if I had impressed anyone. I got another deadly look from the ringleader. I think one of the girls secretly glanced over at me, sighing with admiration, but she could have been rolling her eyes and groaning, it was difficult to tell. It was time to leave; I was not sure how much charge was left in the landlord's pocket-size electric cattle prod.

I walked out on to the fire escape, my leather shoes tapping out a tune on the metal grid beneath my feet. I trotted noisily down the steps and into the beer garden. To the left I spotted a lane. If the six smugglers were coming after me, they must have completed Ninja training.

I could not hear footsteps on steel. I was assured by the silence behind me but the walk to my hotel was going to be dangerous. I dared not look back.

Far ahead in the lane, within calling distance, was a group of rugby players coming for an evening pint, still dressed in their sports' clothes. I had noticed another team sitting in the beer garden, in rugby shirts, shorts and socks, their filthy boots piled up at the end of the benches.

If I was attacked from behind, it was likely both teams would save me. I was confident of that. I felt sure that a single person attacked by half a dozen wimpy-looking teenagers would be rescued. Rugby players are tough and hate injustice, I know that much.

Luck was finally on my side, but I was still thirsty all the same.

I had taken the train from Bristol to get to Poseidon Bay and had only wet my whistle on a sip of beer. The railways only went to main stations and Campbell-Lamerton had given me a lift to the station to catch a train to Liverpool. Then I had transferred to Bristol before ending up in Plymouth.

From there, I had hitched over the Tamar to this forgotten part of Cornwall. It had been forgotten by the tourist hordes;

discerning travellers had sought it out, apparently. Once smuggling had started again in earnest, it had become a hub.

I would have to buy a litre carton of water at the hotel. Maybe I would eat out tomorrow night, if I could pull off a deal. My boss would not begrudge me a decent meal if I made him so much money.

That night, I had to look forward to half a tin of pilchards and a hunk of baguette. The next day would be my second day in Poseidon Bay. I had finally made it to the most famous den of iniquity on earth.

Poseidon Bay used to be Portwrinkle until Lawless arrived, bought up all the houses on the lower streets and built his empire rechristening the area and the hotel he bought, Poseidon Bay. I wondered what this place must have been like before Article 50 had been triggered and the smugglers moved in.

My boss had helpfully advised me to read *Moonfleet*.

The book was set around here in the eighteenth century when smuggling was civilised. I wondered if I would be able to see the latest wreck, a Czech freighter run aground when the Privateers turned off the lighthouses and blocked the GPS signals along the coast. It had floundered on Seaton beach, only ten miles away.

I might get a lift there after a good night's sleep and a hard day negotiating. There was a good pub according to my boss, and I might pick up some bunts on the shore. If not, if it was a hot day I might go for a quick dip or a little paddle.

With the thoughts of swimming in my mind, I suddenly realised I was at the hotel reception and I was in one piece and I had no trunks with me.

In my room, I laid out a blue, red and white silk tie, my navy suit and a white shirt on the cheap, thin computer desk next to my bed; I slipped a pair of highly polished brogues under the desk. I stripped off my white shirt and slid my trousers over my legs. There was an alcove with a curtain behind which I had stowed my roll-top rucksack and a linen bag. I gathered up my clothes, slipped out of my socks and popped all my dirty clothes in the linen sack. I have to be highly organised, literally living out of a suitcase and visiting people around the country.

Wrapping a towel around my waist, I walked into the shower next door. Travelling around the country necessitates minimising everything: a small sponge bag contained a 100ml plastic bottle of shampoo, 100ml plastic bottle of shower gel, 100ml tube of toothpaste, a 150ml roll-on deodorant and an electric toothbrush.

I had bought my own tiny towel, but the hotel had provided me with one that was a size up, not quite the size of a swimming towel but close. The shower made me feel better, the water was hot; they must have had solar panels on the roof. Finally, I was clean and ready for supper and bed.

Drying my hair afterwards, I thought about the meeting with Lawless. I knew he was interested; otherwise, why would he see me? All I had to do was negotiate a good price if I wanted to keep my job.

I could not blow the negotiations; no matter what happened, I had to seal the deal. If I failed, my boss would sack me immediately. I wrapped myself in a fresh towel – my own – and drew back the alcove curtain again.

Reaching up on to the single shelf above all my gear, I carefully took down a plastic sandwich box, being careful not to tilt it. Sitting on the edge of the bed, I opened it, relieved to see nothing had spilt from the tin.

Pilchards in tomato sauce would not be on my list of final meals before execution, but I was hungry and feeling depressed.

I eat when I feel down; comfort food is my thing. The baguette was still dry; no sauce had sloshed out on to the bread, which was a result. Even the stale, chewy baguette provided some comfort. I went to bed on a full stomach, which put me in the top ten per cent of the population, which made me somehow feel ashamed and better both at the same time. Tomorrow morning, the rest of my baguette would be hard just like my day.

ii

That night I dreamt about the Plague or Virulent Virus, as it was known; the Deportations, the Food Riots and the Flood – snippets of each of the disasters that ripped Britain apart and tore me from my mother came to me in that sinister room. It felt haunted, too; nightmares haunted my dreams, haunted my sleep, haunted my fitful waking moments and stole my repose.

    I woke up seven times that night. I was sweating; it was just like the fever I had when the Plague hit. I dreamt about the Virulent Virus that had swept England in 2023.

    It killed hundreds of thousands; there was no cure and no antidote. I had survived. My mother had survived, but only because she had been sent back to Ireland in the Deportation Wave of 2021.

    I woke up, got up, stumbled into the small shower room, and urinated, then I returned to bed via the gable window. Turning the handle, I opened the window out into the moonless night; a chill breeze cooled my sweaty chest. The night was still, not a sound could be heard but I had no ease.

    Returning to my damp bed, I lay down closed my eyes and tried to forget my worries. Drifting off, I must have fallen into a deep sleep. I had a vivid nightmare as clear as crystal. In my dream, I was feeling faint, I heard a doctor speaking.

    'Wrap him in the anti-bacterial material,' he instructed.

    Then I blacked out.

    Still in my dream, I woke up in the hospital ward at Blackpool Victoria Hospital. Outside, on Whinney Heys Road, black bags lined the street.

    Men in white forensic investigation suits and wearing gas masks, the filter strapped to their hips by a thick, khaki, elasticated belt, moved amongst the body-bags.

In squads of twelve, they were loading dead bodies on to a bus that had been specially fitted with hooks.

Three men had to lift each swollen and corpulent corpse. They manhandled the cadaver on to the bus and holding the body vertical they hung the bag on to the hook that was suspended from the grab handles that ran along the roof of the bus.

There were nurses at the window giving the conscious patients a running commentary. They had little else to do.

My head throbbed and I ached all over, my legs felt sore, as if I had just run a marathon.

The backs of my thighs were telling me that they had been stretched to breaking point; hunger gnawed at my stomach. We had been arranged in rows of three; a normal ward had a row on each wall. Ours was special; we had an extra one running down the middle of the cavernous room. There were no beds, just blow-up mattresses; there was hardly a gap between each patient.

Going to the bathroom necessitated picking your way through the mass of bodies. On my left was a cadaverous figure in his forties whose new nickname was 'Coffin Dodger' and on my right was a corpulent, flatulent, fifty-four-year-old man whose new nickname was 'Silent Slim'.

'Excuse me,' Coffin whispered wearily, 'I need to get to the bathroom.'

I curled up into a foetal ball to allow him to step over my bed, trampling on my sheet in his bare feet. I looked away, he was wearing a hospital gown, tied at the back and I didn't want to see his bits especially not from below.

It was like seeing a skeleton in a dress but animated; I looked for the puppet strings, but this marionette had none. There was no marionettist; he, poor old Coffin, was just a bag of bones floating across the room like a ghostly galleon heading for the rocks. It was a sad sight.

I could do nothing to help him, I was too ill.

Slim tried to roll into a ball but just managed to bring his knees slightly closer to his chin and as he did so, he farted loudly;

it was not the first of the cacophony of sounds he would make during the day.

'Thank you,' seethed Coffin; he sighed heavily, trying to blow away the aroma that was wafting up from Slim's bed as he crossed over. Poor Slim looked suitably embarrassed.

He mouthed: 'Trapped wind.'

Coffin ignored him, choosing the best route through the recumbent throng. I was sweating, my nose was running but I could still smell the dead rat whiff coming from Slim.

'How are you feeling today?' he asked, smiling; he had a friendly smile.

'Terrible,' I moaned, pulling the sweaty sheet over my soaked hospital gown. I was shivering but my head felt hot; my forehead burned, and my cheeks were flushed. I was fed up with being drenched in sweat. 'I think I've got it bad.'

'You'd be out on the street in a body bag, dead or alive if they were worried about you. Never fear, you're over the worst, you're with the weary-well.'

'It doesn't feel like it; how long have I been like this?'

'Here, quivering and quaking?'

'Was I that bad?' I asked rhetorically.

'About a week, I guess, I've been out of it myself. They took you to the bathroom every day, but you were in a daze, I guess dehydration has kicked in now, or do you want to follow the Dodger.'

'I just want to feel better.'

'Don't we all mate?'

'When do we eat? I'm starving.'

'Eat? No fear, eating might cause diarrhoea, they will give you water but no food.'

As if on cue, the nurses who had been at the window shuffled through the foot-wide gap between each patient, dispensing water in cone-shaped paper cups and doling out papier-maché urine bottles, which was the closest we had to bedpans.

Any other business had to be conducted in the toilets at each end of the ward, which was where Coffin Dodger was heading.

'How long have you been here?' I asked. It was only to fill the silence between us.

I could hear 'please' and 'thank yous' being muttered as the nurses approached.

'I was three stone heavier when I came in,' Slim joked. 'Longer than you mate, you're a blow-in. They say we wouldn't have this virus if we had stayed in Europe, but I don't believe that. We've got the country back, now.'

'What you want it all for yourself?' I asked. My body was wracked with pain, but my salesman's shtick and patter was as highly developed as ever.

'We got rid of the Muslims, we got rid of Africans and Jamaicans, we got rid of the Europeans and, now, divine intervention is getting rid of the weak,' he asserted, smiling to himself.

I winced at his enjoyment of his fascistic tendencies. I half expected him to look up to heaven and cross himself, but no Christian would take such delight in the deportation of millions and the suffering of thousands.

'It's just a virus, it's just got out of hand because the hospitals have no funding,' I argued.

'You have been out cold, my boy, the news today estimates three million people dead. I'd put it at more like nine, judging from what I've heard on the grapevine. The amount's been adjusted, I'm sure, to stop panic.'

'You're kidding me,' I stammered, I was genuinely shocked. It did not seem possible.

'Radio Four announced it on the ten o'clock news but you were sparked out.'

'How do you know there's more?'

'I go for a fag break with the porters at four every afternoon, it's their tea break. We're not supposed to smoke but the CCTV cameras in the boiler room have been put on the blink, so no one knows.'

'They've sabotaged the cameras and smoke detectors in an area that's a fire hazard anyhow? Are you all mad?'

'Keep your voice down.'

'Keep your hair on, the nurses are way down the line now. So, these guys know what's going on in the real world, is that what you are telling me?'

'Yes, they do, they're the only one with jobs for a start and their canteen ensures they get good food, not the scraps that you and I eat, that crap contained the bugs that started this plague.'

'Is that what they reckon?'

'In the kingdom of the blind, that's you and me kid, the one-eyed man is king.'

'That has to be them?'

'That's them, they get actual money, real money like the rich folks; they can afford proper cigarettes with filters and all: Marlboro, Fortuna, you name it.'

'They have fags? It doesn't make them gurus and soothsayers.'

'You're more stupid than you look; all these guys are paid by the NHS; they have the only paid jobs left in the country apart from the police and armed forces.'

'I know that, and?'

'They belong to a union, their reps around the country talk to each other.'

'So?'

'They spread the word. Without them, there would be no NHS; your precious National Health Service would have gone the way of all other industry. They reckon it's only the VAT and the public's donations that keep the whole thing together.'

'What about other taxes?'

'You really are as daft as a brush, aren't you? We all barter or smuggle stuff, the rich avoid taxes through accountants and the government refunds corporation tax for the few food manufacturers that are left. Then there's housing; all the letting agencies get tax relief on the mortgages for the properties they let out to us. The few companies that are left in England are being subsidised by the government. The NHS is kept going by goodwill.'

'You're joking.'

'That's not all. The big companies put chemicals in our food and poison everyone. Don't get me started on those killed by pollution. We're the least affected area, mate, you can count your lucky stars you're not in the south-east.'

'That's where the rich are.'

'Oh, the rich can afford to import their fresh pasta and American cereals and other fancy foods.'

'True.'

'I'm talking about the working people, poisoned and dropping like flies. The porters reckon there's a gas-fired power station in Kent being fuelled by bodies.'

In my mind I pictured body bags being thrown into a big furnace and then, to my great relief, I woke up. It was dark and I was sweating. It was a cold sweat and the room was cold, a haunting ghostly chill that made me feel uneasy.

I was anxious enough about the meeting without having dreams like that.

I rose, showered in freezing cold water and shivered back to bed, hoping I would not be too shattered the next morning when I met Lawless. I turned the duvet over and flipped the pillow before snuggling into the bed.

Fortunately, when my head hit the pillow, I fell into a deep but not very contented sleep. The next morning, I awoke with that old hunger gnawing at my stomach, yet again. It was my normal waking state.

I needed to shower again, and my stomach was rumbling by the time I lifted the smelly, fishy lid of the pilchard tin and bit into the rock-hard baguette.

I dipped the 'biscuit-crunchy' bread into the sauce to make it easier to chew but only succeeded in coating it in a gloopy sauce that attempted to drip on to my towel before I could suck it off the bread. As I tried to chew from the short stick, bits exploded all over me, it was like trying to eat frozen caramel or peanut brittle.

Hunger helps you to endure anything and I scraped up the crumbs with my hands, swallowing them down and using my index finger to scoop up the last of the tomato sauce. Licking the remnants from my fingertips, I felt the food bubbling in my stomach. My yearning for food had been satisfied and so I brushed my teeth and drew back the curtains. It was a beautiful day; the sky was a bright blue curtain, and the scorching sun made the whitewashed walls of the houses look freshly painted.

iii

If you go down to the docks today, you're sure to have a nasty surprise. That is unless you have an appointment. All the boats with fast engines were painted black and sat like black hippos in the water.

Amongst these superfast speedboats with their twin propellers, looming over the bay was a red lightship with the legend Poseidon Bay etched in white on its scarlet hull. It was the only other boat in the water. The sailboats clog up the waterway and delay the fast smuggling boats.

Any yachts that could not be sold to Europe were up on the hard, their barnacled bottoms revealing their neglect, their steel stays clinking against their masts in the wind. There were perhaps twenty of them, making a proper din.

All the docks were cordoned off with electric fences behind the main apron. Men in black balaclavas and police marksmen overalls, carrying old Belgian FN self-loading rifles over their shoulders, patrolled in threes. They looked like old-fashioned rifles, but they were well oiled and lovingly looked after.

They might have been old, made in the nineteen seventies, but their accuracy and ability to shatter a kneecap or kill have been well documented on the BBC website.

They were the favoured weapon of British security forces in Northern Ireland and their fearsome reputation had been forged all over Africa as their nations emerged from English domination during the twentieth century. Only four hundred pounds would buy you one; a pint was ten pounds; forty of those and you could have a gun.

It was unbelievable to think that if you saved your beer money, you would have enough money to buy one after forty days and forty nights of not drinking.

Of course, most people around Poseidon Bay drank about a gallon a night. Over forty days that would be the equivalent to forty gallons of beer, just over a barrel. There were thirty-six gallons in a barrel. That was why I was there; I was over a barrel; negotiate a good deal for my boss or join the queues for the food banks.

I walked through the town; my hotel was on the higher of the high streets. My bedroom was like any of the bedrooms in this old fishing village, unchanged since it was built in the 1700s. The bed was comfortable, and my boss was paying so I was in a good mood when I arrived. It was cold in the room, no one heated their homes these days, but the duvet looked warm and there were thick blankets on the bed. That was when I had first arrived, and I had not envisaged my experience at the pub and a fitful night.

Attending an important meeting called for a super smart suit – navy, of course – a blue, white and red striped tie, a white shirt, starched and pressed professionally at the dry-cleaners and my beautifully polished black brogues. I tried to avoid wearing the same shoes two days running to let the leather breathe but apart from two pairs of smart shoes, I was travelling with just the bare essentials.

It's easier when you have to hit the road and you have to hitchhike. My bag just needed to be waterproof and able to accommodate three changes of clothes, two for business, one for leisure, hence the white shirt and grey flannels last night. I had black jeans and a bottle green polo shirt for days off, when and if they came. I had left my hard-man black leather biker jacket at the office. My towel and sponge bag would sit on top of all my clothes. I was good at travelling light; I had to be.

The new harbour was next to the old town and at first, I thought they had fenced off the old quarter from the rest of the town but, in fact, it was the new harbour that was built like a fortress. It reminded me of Dover, high fences and high security.

All they needed was the twenty-two-foot concrete wall that surrounded Dover to make the look complete. I waited at the gate; I noticed the spikes and razor wire on this chink in the compound's armour. They were taking no chances; any vulnerable spot was made as equally dangerous as the other parts.

One of the guards approached me. He was wearing a bulletproof vest and a full-face helmet that looked just like the ones bomb disposal teams use. All the guards looked indestructible. He was pointing a Browning nine-millimetre automatic pistol at my heart, gripping the gun with both hands.

In the past suicide bombers had tried to persuade the smugglers to share their spoils with the poor by blowing them to bits. Naturally, all of the guards were on heightened alert when any stranger threatened their sanctuary.

'Move to the booth to your left,' commanded a booming voice from above my head.

I looked up and clinging to a lamppost outside the perimeter fence was a wireless speaker and, next to it, a rotating closed-circuit television camera. My every movement was being monitored.

'Yes, Big Brother,' I muttered to myself as I walked towards a rectangular Portakabin on wheels; it was a mobile security centre.

'Less of your cheek!' barked the speaker above me. I marvelled at the fact they could hear my slightest sound – or could they lip read?

I shuddered. These guys were good, but I also knew they were all on an illegal amphetamine of some sort. I hoped they were not trigger happy; I was too young to die. I decided to silently comply with all their instructions. The Portakabin could only be accessed by checker-plate steps. I did not touch the metal handrail as I bounded up all six in three strides; fear of faecal matter. It haunted me after I read an article where tube users were swabbed and seventy-five per cent had tested positive for faecal matter on their hands.

The door was open, pinned back to the wall by a single breezeblock. In front of me was a counter and behind the counter was a sign, a white poster with red writing: 'All items will be returned on departure. Ensure all bangles, chains, including ankle chains, ear-rings, watches and shoes are left on the counter.'

I immediately complied; I had made my mind up to do so beforehand. It was going to be my benchmark for behaviour. Deliberately, I slammed my shoes on the counter so their microphone would pick it up. I never wore a watch, who wants their wrist severed by bandits?

I used to have a pierced ear but sold my earring for food last winter; the hole was closing up now, healing nicely. The only other jewellery I had possessed was a discreet, penny-sized gold medallion. My mother had given me a thin gold chain for my eighteenth birthday, three years ago. There was an image of St Jude on the disc.

He is the patron saint of lost causes.

I like to think it was an ironic gift, but I have not had contact with her since she was deported back to Ireland. I went to sleep with St Jude in a hostel in Wales when I went for a job in a mine.

The next morning, St Jude was gone, even the saints had deserted me. They were meant to have more patience than that, weren't they? I lost the opportunity for a job and my patron saint that day, but I at least survived because I was too far from the front of the queue to be involved in the skirmishing. At the mine, there were four jobs going and four thousand applicants. The ones who could beat their way to the front of the queue and who could survive the pounding from those behind them got the job.

The Portakabin was painted the same ubiquitous industrial cream inside. At the bottom of a large poster, it proclaimed: 'Once you have deposited ALL items, including piercings, proceed through the door on your right.'

I had no piercings, so I obeyed the instructions. As there was no door on my left, I proceeded as I had been told.

It was a funnelling operation with no choices except backing out and I had come too far to do that. Opening the wobbly door and stepping through the paper-thin partition between the two rooms, I was confronted with the most amazing, state-of-the-art, body scanners.

It was like the super sophisticated type of whole-body scanner that you used to get in top-of-the-range airports, like Gatwick, or Heathrow, if you accidently set off the standard detectors. It looked like a weird luxury shower in black plastic, shaped like an overgrown almond shell.

It was a distant but powerful reminder of the times before Brexit and global warming scares when I used to fly to Ireland as a young child. Not that anyone but the richest flew once Brexit was finally completed, with few flights, and airport taxes and fares that were astronomically expensive.

I wondered if it would detect the metal fly on my pants. I stood on two light blue footprints in the middle of the device. I felt like I was on some sort of amphetamine while I listened to the machine doing its work.

My heightened hearing detected a weird whirring, a strange clicking and a loud clank. Each sound made me more and more paranoid. I was worried I might be electrocuted or shot should an alarm sound.

'Proceed,' ordered a small speaker clinging like a cobweb to one corner of the roof.

I complied; I proceeded through the machine to another doorway. There were white hotel slippers waiting for someone to step into and a corridor yawning ahead of me. Slipping on the slippers, my feet proceeded as ordered.

Again, it was like the tunnel, the one you used to go through to get from the terminal into the plane back in the days when EasyJet and Ryan Air ruled the skies, and everyone could afford to fly. Now, Administration Airways flew only first-class passengers to international destinations and that was only on government or strictly trade business. Global warming activists were happy.

I stumbled down the incline, willing myself to slow down. My feet inadvertently stomped on the linoleum floor and my pace increased because the corridor went down sharply for five metres.

At the end there was a dogleg corner, and I was out the other side.

I reckoned it must have come from Southampton airport or Bristol when they closed them to passenger traffic.

They only operated freight flights from there. Generally imported food from Europe or America, strictly for the rich; tariffs had priced ordinary people out of eating proper food.

We were the monosodium glutamate generation because food was processed, and you only ever had hot meals at home through pouring hot water over granules.

Outside was another revelation. I was in the biggest room I had ever seen; seriously, I had been on school trips to old castles and palaces, I went to the Tower of London once, but I had never seen anything so huge and opulent in my life.

The ceilings were three times my height; I have to duck my head if I need to pass through a 1.95-metre-high barrier. The room must have been fifty metres long; I know because we had an Olympic size outdoor lido near us when we lived in Mitcham before 'the Troubles'. It must have been twenty metres wide. The whole expanse was carpeted with the softest Junior Wilton; it was a burgundy colour, a rich red, like a carpet at a king's court.

There was a model of the SS *Katherine*, in a solitary display case to my immediate left; it had been one of the largest cruise liners in the world until it was hijacked and scuttled in Cardiff Bay.

It remained there as a hulk, protruding from the sea like a shark's dorsal fin; divers visited its empty shell for fun. It had become a tourist attraction; rumours circulated that several divers had not come to the surface after getting lost in the labyrinth of rooms. All the copper wiring, piping and fixtures and fittings had been stripped from it in Bristol before it was deliberately sunk further up the coast using explosives.

Some of its opulent carpet had arrived here and felt soft under my feet as I tried to walk as confidently as I could across to the reception desk in bedroom slippers.

Behind the model was a massive fish tank with tropical fish swimming around. It reminded me of *Finding Dory*. To my right was a brand-new Rolls-Royce Silver Cloud; its sunroof was open, but the doors were locked. It was royal blue and underneath its wheels was a white dustsheet. It was an ostentatious piece of sculpture.

Behind the Rolls was the most enormous Union Jack the world has ever seen. It seemed to stretch to the ceiling and to the end of the room. I imagined all the care that would have gone into creating all these amazing objects: the model, the car, the flag and the expense of it all. The room reeked of power, the stench of smuggling money.

Suddenly, I noticed a faint soundtrack, which my dazzled senses had not picked up as yet; 'Land of Hope and Glory' was playing almost imperceptibly from speakers high and low in the building's fabric. I felt like I was being both brainwashed and intimidated at the same time. I understood the meaning of awe. I must have looked around like a bewildered tourist for a few minutes before noticing the far end of the room.

A matt black steel wall, which sectioned off this part of the dry dock hangar, was dotted with prints of country life. These were lit up by spotlights that were embedded in the carpeted floor. One depicted a water mill in Lancashire; another, the Vale of the White Horse; there seemed to be one from every county: a windmill in Oxfordshire; a canal wending its way through Shropshire; a church in Wiltshire.

The wall was a tribute to the quintessential English countryside, an idyll that could only be found in the most remote corners of England, which had become even more inaccessible recently. Food tended to be people's main concern; tourism and travelling were very low priorities in the new, 'improved' Britain under The Administration.

I spotted a desk by an enormous sliding door almost in the centre of this wall. I walked towards it.

This took time.

Fortunately, since I had an appointment at ten o'clock, I had allowed for an hour to get through security and it had taken half as long. The receptionist behind the desk was my first point of contact and I did not want to spoil things between us by being late or running towards her at great speed.

She was staring at a monitor before looking down at a small iPad. A wireless keyboard and her paper diary were spread out before her on the desk. If she was aware of my presence, she did not for one minute show it.

As I neared her desk, I focused on what she was doing, tapping on the keyboard, and stroking the surface of the tablet and picking up a Mont Blanc fountain pen to annotate the diary. The closer I got, the less I focused on her work and the more I focused on her.

She was the most beautiful brunette that I had ever seen. Her hair was long and thick and wild, tamed by a thin green velvet hair band and a sharpened pencil protruding through the bun at the back. Her neck was long and thin, the hair cascaded over her right eye as she looked at her work, but I could make out high cheekbones and full lips. Her silk cream blouse and her red waistcoat hugged her body.

I was sure she had on a Britannia blue skirt or trousers hidden by the vast desk, the brown expanse of which dwarfed all her tech and office kit. I guessed that she would be wearing a skirt; she was the type who enjoyed her femininity.

'Good morning,' I said, trying to sound casual and trying to hide the fact I was a little out of breath having scampered to her desk. I was worried she might interpret my shallow breathing as lust.

She looked up and that was when I saw it. She had one blue eye, which was the colour of the most beautiful sapphire; it was obviously false, made of glass, but it still seemed to be staring at me. Her other eye was hazel, and it was watching me looking at her false eye.

There was warmth and amusement in her gaze.

'Good morning, a fetching colour, don't you think?' She asked, smiling so naturally and warmly that my heart melted instantly. I immediately closed my gaping mouth and smiled back, locking my eyes on her good eye, knowing the importance of eye contact.

'Yes, indeed,' I agreed. This was the woman I had been charming for a whole month to get this appointment. I was not going to argue. In truth, the eye did look good and she looked good, too, a real eyeful.

'I lost the real one in a food riot, trying to get food for my daughter. Silly really but I couldn't see her die, could I?'

'No, not all,' I whispered encouragingly.

'Mr. Lawless paid for the operation and replaced the eye that had been gouged out. He'll see you presently.'

'Your daughter?'

'Safe with her grandmother in Gdansk.'

'I'm relieved.'

'Yes, I suppose I am, too. Still, I must be the only Polish clerical worker in the whole of England.'

'I thought all Europeans had been expelled; my mother was sent back to Ireland.'

'We were expelled but Mr. lawless had a small cartel of friends that he looked after.'

'He said you were fundamental to his business.'

'Of course, and the guards, too.'

'They looked very fierce when I came through security but I'm sure they are like pussy-cats.'

'Oh, no, they are tigers! Do not put a foot wrong, many of his security guards speak no English at all. On the whole, they merely react to stimulus. Please do not stimulate them in any way if you want to live.'

'Thank you so much for the advice.'

'It's my job to ensure everyone is happy.'

'Well, I'm very pleased that we have finally met, you have been so helpful to me in setting up this meeting. I know how difficult it is to see Mr. Lawless. You've steered me through and given me great advice in the past, thank you,' I gushed.

I was genuinely impressed with her in so many ways. She was efficient, intelligent and charming. She was also drop-dead gorgeous. Despite everything, I could feel myself becoming mesmerised by her. Realising that she most probably had to deal with such adulation all the time, I looked down at my shoes.

'It's been an absolute pleasure. Mr. Lawless is ready for you, his call finished earlier than expected, would you like to walk through the door behind me?'

I heard a hiss behind her head and watched as a narrow sliding door automatically opened. The light that spilled from it lit up part of the carpet. Looking into Lawless's office was like looking at the opening to a well-lit operating room or like moving from a dark vestibule to visit the Sun King at the Palace of Versailles.

Normally, I would have chatted more, but I recognised a dismissal when I heard one. I also understood that she was so badly out of my league that extended exposure would only cause misery for me.

Obediently, I sauntered as confidently as I could into the office of the most powerful and richest man in the whole of England and that included the king.

Poor blighter, the king, that is, holed up in Buckingham Palace for months now surrounded by guards for his own protection and all his lands in Cornwall squatted on by starving subjects. The Duchy of Cornwall lands belonged to the smugglers. I was part of an elite clique; very few people had seen Terence Lawless. Being on twenty of the eighty-three counties most-wanted lists made him camera shy, media shy and generally slightly authority shy.

A quarter of the police forces in this disparate land we called the United Kingdom wanted a mug shot of this man; half had a warrant for his arrest, but Poseidon Bay was a safe haven.

Sitting behind his desk was a fit-looking man, a grey-haired and good-looking fifty-five-year-old man; he was a silver fox whose hair had not fallen out, merely lost its colour.

He wore a navy tailor-made suit and he rose to meet me; he was as tall as I but a bit broader and carried himself like a solder.

'Good morning, young man, how delightful to finally meet you after chatting so much on the phone,' Terence chortled.

'Good morning, Mr. Lawless,' I replied stiffly, I was not feeling at ease.

He clenched my hand in a firm grip and smiled at me. I clasped his hand in return. We were men with dry hands.

'Aubrey, you young cove, bet you don't have any trouble getting the girls, take a seat,' Terence exclaimed, full of bonhomie and charm.

A perfectly manicured hand indicated a high-backed dining room chair in English oak of course, its plump cushions covered in thick brown Connolly hide, the best leather money could buy, naturally.

I noticed a silver cufflink on the end of a white cotton poplin Hilditch & Key shirt. I hitched up the legs of my trousers, a habit I had adopted during my time with my boss, sat down and fished out my mobile phone, switched it to meeting mode and opened my 'Lawless Folder'.

Even his favourite brand of shirt was detailed in the dossier that I had read countless times since Mr. Campbell-Lamerton had given it to me two months previous to the meeting.

'Good morning, Mr. Lawless, it's a pleasure to meet you and I'm grateful that you could take the time to see me, I know how very busy you are,' I replied, full of confidence. He smiled the smile of a busy man who could spare enough time for a Young Turk trying to earn a crust.

We were going through the motions; it was the dance of the business negotiations where I pretended that I was selling something. I knew full well that by agreeing to meet me, he was interested in doing a deal.

We merely had to fix the price.

'Well, I remember your boss from the old days. Tim, Tim, we used to call him, like the Belgian detective, Tin, Tin – do you know him?'

'I think we had one of the picture books, *Rocket to the Moon*, or something.'

'Yes, a classic, can I offer you a drink, a beer perhaps?'

'So, you know about last night, then?'

'Well, I do own the pub; the manager works for me and you did humiliate my son.'

I was going to protest but Terence put his hand up. My embarrassment made my face flush. Of all people to pick.

I had heard nothing, but I smelt the exotic bouquet of heady jasmine, intoxicating ylang-ylang, spring-fresh Lily of the Valley and white gardenia.

I breathed in, stopping myself from gasping at the delicious aroma of that heady perfume. Adel looked great, Adel sounded great and Adel smelt great.

'Can I get you anything, Mr. Lawless?' she asked, her clipped English accent belying her Polish origins.

'Mr. East?'

'Nothing for me, thank you,' I replied.

I desperately wanted a coffee to get rid of the taste of tinned pilchards that remained in my mouth despite brushing my teeth three times with two different toothpastes on the end of an electric toothbrush.

I could feel the tomato sauce hanging at the back of my throat reeking of tinned fish. However, my nerves would not allow me to hold a coffee cup without shaking.

Lawless filled the pregnant pause with his mellifluous voice.

'No thank you, Adelajda. I'm glad to know that you are wearing the perfume I bought you: Illuminum White Gardenia Petals, if I remember correctly, you wear it well.'

She nodded her head in recognition and thanks.

'Thank you, sir. If that will be all, I have some shipping manifests to type up for the evening tide. Will you both excuse me?'

Neither of us wanted that stunning woman who smelled as good as she looked to ever leave our side but to admit it would have been embarrassing for all of us.

'Of course,' Terence responded. He smiled charmingly, then grimaced as if he knew what a wretched task filling in paperwork could be.

I suddenly remembered there was something I wanted. I wanted to marry Adelajda and live happily ever after.

Was I allowed to fall in love that quickly with a stranger?

Is there such a thing as love at first sight?

Did I love her because of her one eye or despite that? I had to see her again, breathe in that exotic perfume, gaze on that wonderful face. I had never been in love before.

'Am I in love, now?' I wondered.

It was as if Lawless could read my mind; his next question threw me.

'What do you think of my secretary?' my mate Terence asked.

He was keeping an eye on me as I turned my head to follow her out of the room. She was wearing a skirt to the knees; her bare legs were brown; she had a good turn of ankle. My Love had lovely legs.

I pulled myself together, blushing at my crass behaviour; I was meant to be focusing on making a deal.

'She is strikingly beautiful and very efficient, I have dealt with her on the phone for many weeks, she is charming,' I replied, no word of a lie.

'Indeed, she is a treasure, I would be lost without her,' he conceded gallantly but I noticed him looking lustfully at her.

'I'm sure that's not true,' I argued.

I wondered if he could notice my flared nostrils, detect my beating heart, feel the pain in my chest that ached so badly. Would he be able to see the love in my eyes?

'Everyone thinks so. I rescued her from the gutter after a food riot, her and her daughter – she must be six by now. She came to work for me. The last Polish person in England, well, certainly in these parts, Adelajda Onawiewszystko, is a great asset to my organisation.'

'I totally agree,' I opined confidently, trying to sound like a big shot but the squeak in my voice undermined that intention.

'She looks great, too. That is always an advantage; even though I am old enough to be her father, I admire her beauty from afar. Still, you two have something in common.'

Did he know?

Had he guessed, could you give away the fact you were in love with someone? I wondered.

'Really, what's that?' I stammered.

I could feel beads of sweat collecting around my hairline; the collar of my shirt was suddenly too tight. I willed myself to be calm, but my reflexes refused to obey.

A trickle of cold sweat escaped from under my arm, trailing down my flank but luckily my shirt was loose there so only I knew about the rivulet of fear rolling to my waistband.

All thoughts of my 'Love' disappeared under the flight or fight hormones. I just hoped dear Terry could not interpret the tell-tale signs as more than deal-making nerves.

'You're Irish but you hide behind a British name; she's Polish and she hides behind an English accent.'

I laughed, it sounded hollow; it was. He thought he was funny; he was the opposite, but he was the client so if he laughed,

I laughed, if he made a tasteless joke, I took it as a proper joke. These were troubled times, the times before the French Invasion.

I spoke confidently, again, relieved: 'Yes, of course, I had no idea what you meant.'

'Don't look so worried, I'm not going to deport you, well not today, anyhow,' he assured me smoothly, laughing out loud at his own pathetic joke. I smiled back at him, dumbfounded.

He finished laughing, then straightened his red, white and blue tie, adjusted his sombre suit on his shoulders and put on a serious expression before continuing, 'To business, my young friend, time and tide wait for no man and time is money.'

'Of course, Mr. Lawless, I understand,' I agreed, relieved the small talk was over and the big deal had begun.

'Please, call me Terry,' he insisted.

'Certainly, Terry it is. One main concern Mr. Campbell-Lamerton has, sorry, Tim, yes, the main worry he has is transporting the silver ingots from Blackpool to you.'

I paused, I had been told to let Lawless sort out the transport, but I had to offer delivery; that was good business practice.

'Why worry, he still runs all the casinos, all the bars, except Wetherspoon; the other Tim has those as far as I know.'

'Tim Martin, Brexit Man,' I chuckled, trying to connect with Terry.

'The town's sewn up; just like here, the police daren't encroach, they've got enough on their hands with burglary and theft.'

'True, but the military are mounting patrols.'

'Spasmodic patrols, you mustn't listen to reports on the radio, you should be tuning in to Poseidon Radio on your laptop.'

'I'm sure they have the inside story.'

'Too right and you get instant news as it happens, and we filter out all the government propaganda. I spend a lot of money on research and reconnaissance.'

'Time in reconnaissance is seldom wasted,' I repeated my boss's maxim. It was the only other time I had heard the word.

'Precisely, my intelligence tells me that the military is pared back to the bone by spending cuts and they're far too busy keeping order in the north.'

'That's sounds feasible.'

'Newcastle and Carlisle are like Northern Ireland in the twentieth century, the Scots are always stirring up trouble there. Sour grapes.'

'I see,' I replied.

I wanted to say something that made me erudite or worldly, but nothing came.

'The elite troops – Parachute Regiment, Royal Marines, SAS and SBS – are attached to our allies in the Middle East, the really good regiments. The Household Cavalry are protecting parliament and the king. What's the problem? We can operate with impunity. The authorities actually enjoy the fact that we keep order for them.'

'I suppose so.'

'Too right, they save a fortune on policing this area.'

'True.'

'My businesses help the black economy and help keep the nation from slipping out of recession and into depression. You've read the papers.'

When he said papers, he meant the newsletters produced by disparate groups in different areas. These desktop publications were disseminated through the smugglers' networks, either through email or in pamphlets printed by groups, exposing weaknesses in The Administration's network and reach. Combined intelligence was gathered from around the country.

'It's not getting caught by the authorities – dealing in silver is illegal but transporting isn't; we do deals all over. It's the mode of transport. Mr. Campbell-Lamerton would like to send the merchandise down by sea.'

'Really?'

'He's got a beautiful speedboat that can do the job nicely. He just wants your agreement to this mode of transport,' I explained, surprised at how easily I had lied to this man who literally could have me deported.

Mr. Campbell-Lamerton did not want the expense of paying for all that fuel. Diesel was exorbitantly expensive, and he would have to bring the boat back empty.

It would have wiped out my commission and most of the profit on the deal. It was not a genuine offer; it was designed to show willing.

I had been instructed to let Lawless come up with the solution. The vanity of the man would help make this silver deal earn me the commission that six months' work deserved and help Campbell-Lamerton make a profit; he would sort it. Campbell-Lamerton had kept me on only because of the potential of this deal.

Adel had opened the door for me, I had her to thank for getting the negotiations thus far. It was because of her that I still had a job. Gold was stratospherically expensive, but silver provided a stable and transportable alternative; the ingots we made were smaller and therefore lighter.

'Too risky. You're forgetting the Welsh Privateers in Cardiff Bay and those Bristol Buccaneers have the Irish Channel covered. I can send some high-speed cars and several support vehicles to refuel them.'

'Sounds like you know what you are doing,' I said, giving him my most charming smile, relieved that he would be taking all the responsibility.

'We'll have the goods down here in less than five hours, the roads are pretty much clear. It's only three hundred and fifty miles warehouse to warehouse. I've got some fresh petrol just delivered and I want to see how well my snatch squad operates.'

I reckoned it would take at least fourteen hours in total: seven hundred miles at an average of fifty miles per hour. Seven hours, each way, minimum. Terence's claim of five hours from our works seemed pure hyperbole but I had not driven the roads recently and his men had. His tentacles extended into every corner of England. I was convinced it was bluster but the roads were clear in those days, the army maintained them to move troops up and down, but they were practically deserted.

'Very well, we'll have to give you a good price if you're taking responsibility for moving the goods. I was going to quote Freight on Board.'

'Come up with an Ex-works price and I know we can do business.'

He smiled charmingly.

We both knew where we stood, I had a minimum price I could let the goods go at; he had an idea of how much he would have to pay to get between ten and twelve per cent profit on the silver ingots.

I started off at the highest amount my boss Tim Campbell-Lamerton had judged that he could ask a tough negotiator like Lawless to pay. Lawless beat me down to about halfway between the lowest and highest figure. He seemed happy.

I was bursting with pride at pulling off my first really important and properly lucrative deal. We smiled at each other, we rose from our chairs and we grasped hands in a firm shake across the green leather of Lawless's Victorian partners desk.

As if by magic Adelajda reappeared. I did not hear her soft doeskin moccasins on the red Wilton carpet, but I smelt the aroma of her intoxicating perfume.

'Ah Adel, do please show our young guest out. It was a pleasure to meet you, young Aubrey, I take it you are leaving tonight?'

'I have transportation organised, thank you, I will be leaving at six.'

'Good, I have no idea how my son Freddie will react to your behaviour last night. He has a gang of friends. I would not like to see you get hurt.'

'I'm not keen to get hurt either,' I assured him.

'No one would want that; you are now officially a friend of the Lawless family.'

'Thank you.'

'A word to the wise, try not to make so much of an impression on your next visit. I hope your exit will be slightly less dramatic than your arrival.'

He was smiling at me; he thought the whole incident was amusing.

I felt another trickle of cold sweat glide down from my armpit and trickle down my flank.

'Thank you for all your hospitality and I will definitely take your advice. Do apologise to Freddie for me,' I grovelled, not caring how feeble it made me seem, too busy concentrating on sounding as obsequious as I could.

I did not want to sour relations after cementing our deal. I was relieved that my shirt was loose where the rivulet of fear snaked down to my waistband. He would never know how terrified I was because my hands were miraculously dry. Surprisingly, there was no clamminess there. Annoyingly, the antiperspirant had failed in just one spot, damn it.

'The pleasure was all mine, and you seem like a sensible lad; I am sure no harm was intended, you just wanted to make an impression here; you succeeded by the way. I'll pass on your apology to Freddie.'

He could say what he wanted, the deal was done, and I could not care less about him and his freckly Freddie who I reckoned loved himself more than anyone else on the planet.

I smiled and bowed. We had sealed the deal; shaking hands again would have been superfluous and suggested a burgeoning friendship. He was my father's age and a snake; I was young, good-looking and about to get married to a lovely Polish girl. My 'Love' led me next door. I breathed in her heady aroma, took in her face, admired her hair and watched her lovely derriere as she led me from the room.

Lawless and I had nothing at all in common except the euros that I would make by selling him silver ingots and he would make by selling them on to people who had no trust in their own currency, gold, or Bitcoin. Euros would buy him more contraband to sell.

The domestic currency was useless, gold was exorbitantly expensive and with a yo-yoing currency it was hard for anyone to value sterling against any currency, government or internet based. The dollar was no longer king; their economy had tanked, too. Euros bought contraband from our nearest neighbours, Eire and France; shipping costs from elsewhere were too exorbitant.

Within seconds, I found myself standing next to Adelajda, in her huge office. I had been right about the skirt and I was hoping that I would be right about the way she felt about me; our relationship had blossomed over the phone during the previous months.

We were like old friends; it was time to take our relationship on to another level. So, I thought. I was shocked by what she said next; she was so cold and so business-like.

'So, Mr. East, I trust the business was concluded to your satisfaction, the order has already been placed and confirmed on your system.'

I wanted to ignore the fact that she addressed me so formally, but I cannot claim it did not wound me slightly.

'That's very efficient, thank you, but please, the name's Aubrey. Please, call me Aubs, all my friends do.'

'Very well, Aubs, I like the name, it's cool' she said smiling at me; it was then that I knew she liked me too. Her eye looked into mine, she bit her lip before she continued, 'It would be great to see you again, I've very much enjoyed getting to know you over the phone calls we've had. I work so very hard and seldom get the chance to meet people. I feel we have forged a friendship.'

My heart stopped.

I wondered if I was hearing right; she was interested in me. I could not believe it, a spotty-near-teenager like me, barely twenty-two years old. It was unbelievable.

'I would like that very much,' I breathed, wondering how I could engineer that from Blackpool.

'So would I.'

'I'm sure we can manage it,' I replied; it sounded like a plea.

I suspected her accommodation, salary and lifestyle as a personal assistant to one of the world's wealthiest individuals would not predispose her to running away with me to a bedsit in a Lancashire village twenty miles outside Blackpool.

'Well,' she began, and then looked down.

'What?' I whispered.

She tossed her hair as she looked away briefly; it moved like a wave and exposed the soft skin at the nape of her neck. Her neck was slender and eminently kissable. Everything about her was great. Then she turned her head back towards me and looked me in the eye with such a look of love that I thought I was going to burst with joy.

'I'm swimming with Freddie this afternoon; we often go swimming together, perhaps you could join us?' she asked.

'Freddie and his friends?'

'Just Freddie.'

'Where?'

'Near Polperro, I'll take you there; it will take no time. Have you ever been for a ride in a Maserati Quattroporte?'

'I've never been in a sports car. That would be great, but I don't have any swim shorts.'

'There's a uniform shop in the lower high street, it's near the pub you had the row in last night. I'll smooth things over with Freddie. We have an account at the shop, charge the swimwear to Lawless Enterprises; tell them Adel sent you. I'll ring them and forewarn them.'

'Thanks, where will I meet you?'

'The Captain Benbow, of course. I'm meeting Freddie there at one thirty, you come at two.'

'Can you just walk out of work like that?'

'Of course, Mr. Lawless goes for lunch and a siesta until six and we do a few hours after that.'

'Sounds great.'

'Besides, if I'm with Freddie, I can do what I like.'

'Mr. Lawless doesn't mind?'

'On the contrary, he encourages it.'

'Really?'

'Of course.'

'Why?'

'Because he wants me to marry Freddie.'

I was so stunned that I almost fainted.

Chapter Two

Some Simple Shopping and Traffic Blocking

Before leaving the office the way that I came in, through the Portakabin, I promised profusely to be at the bar on time. It took all my acting ability to pretend to be enthusiastic about our meeting later on in the day. My good mood had evaporated quicker than dew in the desert.

Inside, as I plodded through the town, I was crying. My shallow breathing told me I was dying. I no longer wanted to breathe, let alone swim, after the discovery that Freddie was going to marry my new girlfriend, Adel. I did not stand a chance; she liked her cars fast, her champagne chilled and her boyfriends as rich as a Croesus.

By the time I had reached the hotel, I had decided to make the most of the afternoon. There was a warm breeze coming off the land; I knew the water would be ice cold but at least I would not freeze once I got out of the water and if I had to share Adel with feckless Freddie, then it was better than not seeing her at all. I had to see her one more time so I could convince my heart that it should not break over her.

In my room I folded and packed my work suit in a special suit bag; from my gorse yellow Millican Smith waterproof roll pack, I took out a pair of white tennis shorts, a Britannia blue polo shirt, a pair of navy tennis shoes and a change of underwear.

I always packed these extra items; you never knew when you might have to play a game of tennis or round of golf to cement an important deal.

Luckily, Lawless did not play sport; he was a sailor who enjoyed Pilates and hot yoga or working out under the auspices of a personal trainer.

My work shirt and the underwear I had worn for the meeting went into a beige linen laundry bag that I had hung on the bathroom peg and I showered for the second time that day.

I washed away the tension of the security shield around Lawless, the elation of being in love with Adel, the stress of meeting with the richest and most dangerous man in Europe and I scrubbed away the disappointment of unrequited love. The shower was cold.

Packing up and dressing in the clothes I had laid out on my bed, I checked out before midday, paid for a locker to keep my suitcase in, made sure I had my mobile in one pocket of my shorts and my wallet in the other. I had spotted the shop on the way up. I could hardly miss it; the double sliding doors were open, and a security guard was holding an old lady's arm behind her back with one hand while pulling a pair of white sports socks from her raincoat with the other.

I suppose he was suspicious of a woman wearing a raincoat in a heat wave. She could have been anyone's granny. It had not improved my mood; I was suffering from the ennui of a jilted lover – I had forgotten to wash that incident from my mind. I suppose that I must have been so depressed about Adel that I was numb to the pain of others.

Distractedly, I walked in. The security guard was still there; the granny had gone. Every single person in the shop, including the person on the till and the security guard, looked like a villain. It would have been comical if I was in a better mood; everyone shuffled along the aisles, looked around, met someone else's eyes, then moved along another few feet and repeated the process. Six people performed the pantomime: click clack went the hangars on the rail, as items were examined, head bowed, then the heads rose in unison, followed by a quick look around like a startled meerkat spotting a mongoose and looking for an escape route. Immediately, they bowed again, shifted along the row like swans drifting down a river; then, the click clack was repeated.

Another security man stood at a screen built into a podium and watched an array of screens that tracked the people in the aisle. He was too busy scanning the screens to notice me swanning in.

I went straight up to the cashier's desk.

I like the personal touch; internet shopping is great for suits and shoes. I'm 34 waist, 34 inside leg, 42-inch chest, so a 42-long suit off the peg fits me like a glove. I wear size twelve shoes and my shirt collar is sixteen and a half. I can get everything I need delivered to my door within twenty-four hours if I have the money for it. Cycle couriers can make a fortune delivering clothes.

When it comes to swimming trunks, I had to try them on; I bought a pair of speedos once and it looked like I was smuggling a pigeon in my swimming briefs – not a good look. I bought a pair of swimming shorts next and the waist came up to my nipples and the hem at the bottom reached my knees.

'Hi there,' I breathed, all cool and confident, sounding like an experienced shopper who buys something new every week. 'I'm new in town.'

'I know, otherwise I would have seen you in here before, wouldn't I?' said the 'Surly Sue' behind the counter.

She wore black jeans and a black T-shirt, but the shop had made her put on a pale pink pinafore. She had left it undone so her own clothes could be seen from the side. She was about my age; I might have flirted with her if I was not feeling so morose. Besides, she was giving me a look to match her clothes, dark and cool, which did not help.

We were both low; I did not have the strength to bring us both back to normal with a bit of banter and a few jokes, but I never give up.

'Why are pirates called pirates?' I ventured.

'Because they argh!' she spat, looking at me like I was the lamest of lame dogs and she wanted me put out of my misery.

'Where are the swimming trunks, please?' I asked not disguising my defeat. I felt like a helium balloon that had lost half its gas.

'See the sign that says swimwear, over your shoulder?'

'Yes.'

'Well, Einstein; what do you reckon you might find there, a ball gown?' she asked incredulously. Her attitude and response did not deserve a reply; besides I could not think of a comeback quickly enough.

Wandering off, I decided I hated all women.

Normally, I would not countenance such rudeness and would have responded in kind but the new broken-hearted me would take any shoddy treatment from anyone.

The security guard looked up from the screen as I passed wondering how I was going to shoplift, dressed in what I was wearing. There was nowhere I could stash the items unless I slipped a pair of socks into my trousers. Click clack like a train on a track, I decided I would not look back.

Selecting a fetching pair of swim shorts made from navy sailcloth and lined with natural canvas, I looked at the price tag. I hated the fact that I could buy a pair of trousers for a fifth of the price, a pair of shorts for a third of the price.

Supply and demand had pushed up prices for items in demand and depressed prices for those everyday items no one needed or wanted. I took the most expensive item of clothing that I had ever bought in my life to the counter where the 'Surly Sue' sat and stared at me.

'Is that all?' she asked.

'Are you kidding; I've never bought such an expensive item; the price is exorbitant. It might as well have a gold-plated gusset,' I complained.

'Gusset? You mean crotch, you Wally!' she guffawed, her face creased up into a sweet smile, she was quite pretty when she smiled.

'I used to work in fashion, we used to always say gusset; besides I bet you don't know what a Wally is you great sissy.'

'Yes, I do!'

'Really?'

'Not really.'

'Wally is a pickled cucumber, a gherkin. People in the East End of London used to order salt beef sandwiches with a Wally on the side. Take a bite of beef sandwich, take a bite of gherkin and you have an explosion of taste in your mouth.'

'You're a bit of a blooming know-it-all, aren't you?'

'If you say so,' I protested, feeling crushed, again.

I was not warming to the female sex that day, after all.

'Aren't you the one who Adel rang me about, the one who's going to put his swimsuit on Mr. Lawless's account?'

'I pay my own bills, thank you,' I huffed, 'and make up my own jokes, too.'

I fully expected her to say how awful they were but instead she offered to tell me a joke. Did everyone in this town use push–pull psychology to win friends, play unfriendly and cold; play warm and friendly, switching from one to another like the wink of a lighthouse beam?

'Bet you haven't heard the one about the baby balloon?' she bragged, spitting out the last two words with venom.

'No, but I'm not sure I want to,' I assured her.

'Well baby balloon is used to sleeping with his mum and dad – some people do that with a newborn baby. Anyhow, after a few months he's getting too big, so daddy balloon builds him a cot and insist he sleep there.'

'Is this a long joke?' I interrupted, 'I've got an appointment at two.'

She smiled patiently at me, which won me over, immediately.

'Bear with me, it's worth it; so, after a bedtime story, baby balloon sleeps but during the night he get lonely, he bounces out of the cot and into his parents' bed but there's no room for him, he's too big.'

'A big baby balloon?'

'So, he decides to let air out of his mum, but still, there's no room.'

I did not know if I should laugh; was it the punch line? I wondered.

'Do you have this in extra-large,' asked a stranger, not part of the original six; that made a magnificent seven customers in one shop, a record for post-Brexit Britain.

'Anne, you know we don't keep stock, if it's not out on the rack, we don't have it. You're interrupting my joke.'

'And your traffic-blocking the till,' Anne spat back, staring pointedly at me and wandering off to the rail, watched like a hawk by the security guard.

'So, baby balloon lets the air out of daddy balloon. Still no good, but then he lets some air out of himself and he can fit in nicely and sleeps like a baby for the rest of the night.'

'Ha, ha,' I said sarcastically, 'Slept like a baby, that's a killer joke, hilarious, you should be on the telly. You remind me of Jack Dee – remember him from the old days, dry but funny?'

'I 'in't finished yet,' she protested. 'The next day, daddy balloon was furious; he was so angry he bounced off the ceiling, he sent baby balloon to the naughty step. Then he bounced to see him: "Right," says he, "you were meant to sleep in your own bed, but you crept into ours, you're a big balloon, now, far too big to share the bed with us. I am disappointed in you."'

'I'm not surprised,' I said.

'The price has come off this one,' announced a man wearing overalls, holding a pair of jeans

'Was it on the rail marked everything for twenty pounds?'

'Oh, right, I didn't see that, sorry. I've got so much on my mind.'

'I know, Theo, it's a big job you're doing; don't go around buying clothes for your painters, they'll take advantage.'

'You're right, Kate, I'll get back to the job.'

When he went, she continued.

'Poor Theo, he's a shopaholic, I have to set him straight every time, plays havoc with my commission.'

I raised my eyebrow to signify that I could not care less.

'So, we were at the point where daddy balloon tells off baby balloon,' I exclaimed pointedly, I had already had enough waffle that day; I did not need more. 'He's sitting on the naughty balloon step, no doubt.'

'So, the baby balloon says sorry. Daddy balloon says that he's still cross and baby balloon asks why. Daddy balloon says, I'm angry because you were meant to sleep on your own and you didn't; you let your mum down, you let me down but worst of all you let yourself down.'

I laughed, relieved that her story was over; it was a rubbish joke and I laughed and laughed, so much so that I hardly noticed another customer actually buy something.

Theo sidled back into the shop and told Kate that he needed a pair of swimming shorts and started eyeing up the pair in my hand. That wiped the smile of my face and focused my mind on completing the transaction.

'Kate, you've cheered me up; thank you,' I assured her, desperate to get out of there.

'And you wanted to cheer me up when you came in,' she observed.

'How did you know?'

'You trotted over to me like a happy puppy.'

'I can be a bit obvious,' I admitted, smiling at her to know I appreciated her foresight and forthright psychological profiling. I am like a puppy, I suppose. 'What are you doing for lunch?'

'Eating my cheese and pickle sandwich in an empty storeroom while the manager covers the till for half an hour, why?'

'Come and have lunch with me at The Captain Benbow; it might be a laugh.'

'I doubt that but I've nothing else on, so I'll see you at one.'

I smiled broadly, looked into her pale blue eyes and thought briefly about falling in love for the second time that day. Deciding against further heartache, I paid with cash: eighty-four pounds. I'm sure the manufacturers had no idea their goods were being sold at seven times the recommended retail price. I hoped that they would be suitably horrified if they ever found out.

Chapter Three

The Sea, the Sea, the Ever Free

By the time Adel arrived, Kate had gone back to work; she enjoyed lunch, so she said, but had to leave to walk back to the shop.

Pie was the only food on the menu; my beef pie had mushrooms, broccoli, carrot and cauliflower, in it, and a forkful of beef somewhere mixed in. Her fish pie had leeks, carrots, diced cabbage and shavings of a quarter of a grated fish finger swimming in a white sauce, which was so peppery it tasted like grit.

Eating out, since BA-Day had been interesting to say the least. You must remember the celebrations of Break Away Day, 4th July 2020. Nine years later, people were talking about another Wall Street Crash. The Crash was in 1929 and we were heading for the one hundredth anniversary and as far as the markets in America and the Far East were concerned, we were heading for the worst stock market crash in the history of the world.

We caught up on our life stories: her parents were together still, both working all hours to put bread on the table. She reckoned that she would meet a local boy and settle down. Her parents lived in a cottage called Rover's Rest; she shared the irony – her parents never rested, her mother and father were not ones to rove around anywhere except the local pub and Kate had no desire to travel, she knew and liked the area. I had seen in the shop how she knew everyone.

I was sad to say goodbye to her, but I clutched the swimming trunks in my lap as I waited for the minute hand to click on to two o'clock. My heart started to thump and ache as I thought of Adel, again. Kate had helped me to forget my broken heart.

At the precise moment the clock moved to one-minute past, she entered. I stood up and noticed freckly Freddie following her like an obedient puppy dog.

I had sat at a table that had a bench seat built into a nook and faced the door. I struggled up and around the table almost tripping over one of the two stools on the other side. I was not sure what to do so I held out my hand and she clasped it, her hand felt cold and wet, she had obviously just put on some hand lotion. I had dived forward at the same time and kissed her quickly on both cheeks and then planted a third kiss on her right cheek.

'A Polish greeting, the third kiss; we do not know each other that well, yet, Aubrey, but a charming gesture, nonetheless,' she gently chastised me, smiling and meeting my eyes.

I had always greeted my Polish friends that way before they were all deported. I was aware that I had overstepped the mark but giving one kiss to Adel was just not enough. My eyes stared into hers, one glass and one brown. I felt, or perhaps I wanted there to be love in her eyes.

'Cold hands and a warm heart, I hope,' I responded, summoning up my most suave voice.

She smiled in approval. I had been observant, noticing that her hands were cold, she appreciated intelligence.

'I've just loaded the Masser with champers for our tea; I have cucumber sandwiches, tongue pate on toast and Madeira cake. I see you have your swim shorts,' she gushed, looking at the mass of sailcloth and canvas bunched up in my left hand, 'don't worry about a towel, we have loads – thick Egyptian cotton, not flimsy beach towels. I wanted to introduce you to my boyfriend, soon to be fiancé, Freddie Lawless. I believe you have already met.'

That explained the cold wet hands, handling the champagne I thought as I took in the sight of my richer and better-looking rival. He was young, rich, good-looking – did he need to be charming and disarming If I were a girl, I would think he was a catch.

'Pleased to meet you,' he blurted out just as I spoke.

'Indeed,' I said, meaning, indeed we had met before, but it sounded as if I was saying indeed it was a pleasure for him to meet me.

'I see,' he sighed, not sure how to take my remark and frowning in confusion. I had to recover quickly.

'The pleasure, I assure you, is all mine,' I insisted charmingly. 'I had no idea who you were last night, and it was my way of letting your dad know I was in town. I hope it won't have an effect on this afternoon.'

'I know how it works,' Freddie soothed, smiling at me with the same disarming and charming smile that was his father's trademark. Our eyes locked; our smiles were locked; we looked like rigor mortis had set in our faces. 'The incident is forgotten about, don't worry.'

He struck out his hand, watched by Adel. I took it and immediately regretted my foolishness; he gripped my hand like a viper swallowing an egg. I guessed he was investing all his hatred into his vice-like clasp.

'Pleased to meet you; I'm glad there's no hard feelings,' I managed to breathe as I felt my hand being crushed. I had intended to give him a firm grip, the sign of a strong person but his grip was far superior, and I had not noticed the big boy's bulk when I had humiliated him last night.

This guy had the body of a protein-drinking gym bunny who spends four hours in the gym seven days a week. His well-tailored jacket and grey flannel trousers hid his bulging muscles. The pain he was inflicting made me wince and fortunately Adel noticed.

'You can let go of poor Aubs; swimming is such a bore with one arm in a sling,' purred Adel, smiling first at Freddie, then more broadly at me; maybe she did like me more than Freddie.

Like an obedient gundog dropping a dead pheasant at its master's command, he let go his vice-like grip. It was the most frightening thing I could imagine; a woman who could control a killing machine with one command. Far from enjoying the afternoon, I would have to watch how I behaved with both of them.

He was her Rottweiler. I shivered before deciding that going for a swim was a bad idea, all that expanse of water to drown in. If Adel did me in, she would pocket my commission because the payment for the goods and my commission for doing the deal were two separate transactions.

I had only seen the transaction for the silver ingots, not my cut of the deal. I had been working too hard and too long with crooks. It was beginning to rub off on me. I used to boast: 'I know every crook and nanny in town; I mean every nook and cranny in town.'

It had all got too much for me; I was suspicious of even this beautiful girl who had struggled to save her daughter and lost her eye for her trouble.

'You've gone pale; are you okay?' Adel asked with such concern and conviction that all my suspicions disappeared.

'It might be the beef in the pie,' I offered just as the landlord arrived with a tray with three glasses half filled with champagne; his tense expression showed that he had heard the remark. He was not happy, but he hid it for Adel's sake.

I was beginning to see a pattern. Everyone seemed obsessed with Adel, but it was not clear which of us she was most fond of out of all the men she knew. I willed it to be me, but she seemed equally happy talking to anyone.

'A flute of champagne for Adel and her guests,' the landlord cheerily announced, smiling at her, 'compliments of the management and on the insistence of Mister Lawless, himself.'

'Thank you, we chorused.

Freddie and I were clearly not the only people in town who were in love with this one-eyed Polish beauty; he almost devoured poor Adel with his eyes, the dirty dog. There was a lot of competition for her attention but the more I learnt about Terence Lawless and his generosity, the more I liked him.

'Thank you, Sam,' Adel purred for the third time, taking hold of the glass and holding it up to the window, the only source of light in that dingy snug bar, 'twoje zdrowie.'

We all raised our glasses and clinked them together. She was purring so much that day, at all of us. I could not help but think of Edward Lear's poem, 'The Owl and the Pussycat': 'Oh lovely Pussy! O Pussy, my love, what a beautiful Pussy you are, you are, you are! What a beautiful Pussy you are.'

I was thinking about Lear while trying not to leer.

'Good health,' Freddie echoed, unintentionally translating for me.

'Slante,' I countered.

'Cheers,' the publican added though he had nothing to drink.

All thoughts now centred on the afternoon to come; it was going to be the best one of my life! I was going to be spending time with the first woman I have ever loved, and Freddie would be too busy showing off his swimming skills to stop me putting my arms around Adel and kissing her, not on the cheek but on the lips.

'Down the hatch!' cried Freddie boorishly loudly before knocking the glass back; did he not realise champagne needs to be sipped and savoured, especially a Grand Cru champagne like Barnaut Grande Réserve Brut, Grand Cru Bouzy? Surely? I knew what it was; I had seen the bottle on the bar counter. I was an observant and vigilant salesman. This was the high life. I was taking it all in. Such a situation might not be repeated.

We sipped our champagne, Adel and I, our eyes meeting over the rim of our champagne flutes; it was as if Freddie was not there. It only lasted for a moment, a glance between two star-crossed lovers. No one noticed our furtive flirting. It was our secret coup de foudre.

That might have been due to the fact that the landlord, Sam Taylor, was talking about his band and trying to convince

Freddie to play bass guitar at his next gig. Freddie knocked back his glass and Adel, showing him favour, topped up his glass.

I secretly filled my glass as she listened to the two of them chatting away. I needed the alcohol for Dutch courage; I was going to have to tell Adel how I felt about her.

There was just no alternative.

I was convinced, more than ever that I was in love with Adel; my heart ached and the way she looked at me convinced me she had feelings for me.

I had been told that love conquers all; I had been told Santa Claus brought my bike and delivered it down the chimney.

'I'm playing at the West Looe barn dance,' bragged Freddie as Sam slipped away, pleased now that he had a guitarist.

'That's wonderful Freddie,' crooned Adel, she sounded like a mother telling everyone her daughter had taken her first steps. Sometimes I hated the way she spoke to Freddie like he was the only one. I think he felt exactly the same way about me.

I loved her so I did not care what he thought about me.

'Well done, Freddie,' I added, sounding as genuine as I could; it was a miracle he had the discipline to play, let alone be part of a headline band.

I quickly reminded myself that bitterness was colouring my judgement of him. Anyone who got as fit as he had, definitely needed serious discipline; his arm muscles were as thick as bull's thighs.

Luckily for me he was so busy basking in his own success, he let down his guard, allowing me to move closer to the girl I loved.

'We'd better get going,' Adel decided draining her glass.

Freddie was too slow; he was walking towards the bar to ask Sam about the gig. He'd obviously just thought of something, so I slipped in right behind her and headed for the door, making poor Freddie follow on behind like the obedient hound dog he was.

Outside the sunshine was almost blinding. The Benbow had the type of dark and dingy snug bar designed for a cold winter's night. I took a while to adjust my eyesight to the bright light, but before me were two beautiful sights: Adel who shrugged herself out of her linen blazer revealing a red T-shirt and a superb dark green Maserati Quattroporte glinting in the sun. It was not a Jaguar as all the factories making English cars had closed and the surplus snapped up by Administration Ministers.

She had not locked the car; Lawless would not have tolerated theft. The number plate was TL 27 TLE; only two years old. How they had smuggled it into England, I could not guess. Lawless made things happen.

Even though I was smarting at the sun, I had the presence of mind to jump into the passenger seat so I would be next to the gorgeous driver and could admire her by glancing across and taking in her profile. Feeling smug, I settled into the leather seat; the car smelt of luxury and Adel's perfume. Adel opened the driver's door as I pushed the button to open my window.

'You can drive, Freddie,' she said, waiting for Freddie to walk around the back of the car and sit in the driver's seat. She shut his door for him.

What was this guy, I wondered, a prince, for goodness sake? He smiled over at me, pressing the button to start the motor.

I suddenly realised how rude I had been, I should have been gallant and opened the pub door for her or the car door for her, one or the other. Then I had plonked myself in the passenger seat without offering her the seat in the front. I wanted to leap out and open the door for Adel, but I heard the clunk of her door closing before I could move. I hoped that she always travelled in the back when someone else was driving but I somehow doubted it. She was a magnanimous hostess and would not have embarrassed me by making a fuss.

Infuriating Freddie was handsome, hunky and an extremely competent driver; I would say expert. ,He turned the car around in the narrow street in only four movements and guided the car through the town using just the right amount of assertion and respect for other drivers and pedestrians. Okay, post-Brexit few people come to Poseidon Bay and we only came across a farmer in an old Land Rover Discovery converted to run on biodiesel, but you get my drift.

Despite myself, I was beginning to like him, which only served to make me love Adel more. I knew it did not make sense but the fact that he found Adel desirable made me desire her even more. It was a strange state of affairs, you might say.

My optimistic spirit told me I had a chance against Freddie; love is blind, deaf and dumb, it sees no evil, hears no evil and speaks no evil.

The warm breeze ruffled my hair, so I closed my window just as Freddie opened up the throttle and gunned the car into the first bend on the road. He had drunk two flutes of champagne; I think he was just on the limit, but I am no expert, no one I know drinks and drives. It was like being in a rally car.

I had to admit he was a superb driver. Despite my hatred of his type, hatred of his grip on Adel and hatred of his charm, I had to give him credit where credit was due.

'I love it when Freddie drives,' announced Adel; every positive comment about him was another arrow in my heart. However, I was determined to have the best afternoon ever, and it would be – barbs and all.

'Where did you learn to drive?' I asked, surprised at my own admiration for Freddie as we powered out of a bend and he set the car up for the next.

'Italy, my mother is from Lugano in the mountains near Monza, she had me coached by a few racing drivers; I picked up a few tips on technique.'

'Faster, Freddie, faster,' cried Adel.

They had a conversation in Polish for the next few bends; Freddie kept to a swift but sure pace. It ended with Freddie insisting that he would not give in.

I knew that, not because I speak Polish – I don't – but because Adel called him a 'spoilsport' in English and laughed.

'So, you're half Irish and I'm half Italian,' Freddie confirmed.

'Actually, both my parents are Irish; my father went out to Hong Kong and was never heard of again.'

'So, you're an orphan, then?'

'My mother's in Ireland but I guess you're right, technically here, I am an orphan,' I admitted, I had never really thought about that. 'What about you?'

'My mother was deported in the second wave. I guess your mother was in the third wave with the Commonwealth; they should have deported my dad.'

He paused to allow me to be suitably impressed. The silence weighed heavily on the conversation; I felt obliged to fill the void by speaking.

'Really, how so?' I asked.

'He's actually originally Swedish. He should have gone in the second, but he had bought his British passport. Not that he needed to as entrepreneurs worth more than five million were exempt.'

The first wave had been the Muslims; the second wave had been the Europeans and the third wave had been Commonwealth and Irish from either the Republic or the North.

So, Terence Lawless was Swedish. That stunned me. I had them both pegged as two racist moneygrubbers who supported the repatriation of nationals. The opposite was true. Here were two Europeans who had used the opportunities provided by Brexit to build a big business.

I had the family pegged as exploitative tyrants who hated all foreigners and bled dry the smugglers who worked for them. They were not the Fascistic, jingoistic thieves that I had been brainwashed by the tabloid newspapers to believe. It riled me that they were not who I assumed they were. I had been happy with my preconceptions. I was learning on this job. Do not believe what you read in the papers, don't leave your pint unattended and never judge a book by its cover.

'I'm the only other deviant that Terence could manage to save. He insisted I was vital to his business,' piped up Adel from the back.

All my preconceived ideas about the family and the firm were rapidly unravelling. How many times had my boss said: 'never make assumptions'? Old Campbell-Lamerton was certainly a canny Scotsman that was for sure.

'So, you haven't seen you mum for years?' I continued, wanting to know more about Freddie all of a sudden.

I was intrigued. Maybe he wasn't the boorish moron after all. I felt a bit sorry for him, he had no mother while he was growing up; she was an outcast who he saw once a year. Poor Freddie: he was also having to fill his father's shoes. His life was not easy.

'I know you cannot get to see anyone in Ireland, and I know how you feel,' he said as we climbed a steep hill, the engine roaring as it complained about having to work harder.

'Well, at least I grew up with her in the house.'

'True, I hate mum being in Italy but I'm very lucky as I get to see my mother for two weeks at Christmas. My father puts me on a freighter to Gibraltar. The journey to Gib can be rough especially in the Bay of Biscay.'

'Really?'

'Absolutely, it can be horrendous, and it takes forever!'

'Why?' I asked, not knowing why I was so suddenly interested in Freddie's journey to reunite with his mother.

'The waves throw the boat about like it's a toy even on the calmest days and I'm talking about a Panamax with a dead weight of 52,000 tonnes. I can fly to Italy from Malaga via the Toulouse hub – the latest Airbus is amazing, small quiet and comfortable. The Europeans have made real efforts to improve air travel, especially connecting European small cities using light and economical planes.'

'Freddie bought me back a delicious Cassoulet from Toulouse after Christmas,' Adel simpered from her seat in the back.

The owl and the pussycat, I was the five-pound note!

I looked in the rear-view mirror but all I could see was the back window. Naturally, Freddie had the rear-view mirror angled to see her for his pleasure. I noticed he looked in the mirror in rotation every two minutes: rear view, passenger door, driver door – only professional drivers do that.

'I haven't been in a plane since I was a toddler,' I sighed.

Most of the passenger airports in England had closed. Even Gatwick and Heathrow ran a skeleton service. They needed the runways to transport humanitarian aid to the north, and other commercial and military flights.

The majority of the airports in the United Kingdom had been partially turned over to freight companies like DHL and FedEx who made a fortune by importing food to the island; and partially turned over to the military aid helicopters that provided succour to the poor. Of course, there were also helicopter gunships and fighter jets belonging to the Royal Air Force that kept order and protected the rich people's flights.

Food was either sold to the rich at inflated prices by unscrupulous merchants or distributed to the poor depending on the type, quality and use by date of the food. Bags of American and Vietnamese rice went north – food aid – while tins of caviar and boxes of smoked salmon went south; they were delivered on to the merchants who stocked high-value foods for their very rich clients.

Due to pollution scares and the cost of aviation fuel, all air travel had been discouraged by all governments around the world hiking up the cost of airport tax. Only the richest one per cent of the population could afford flights. It had returned to an exclusive club just like the start of air travel all those years ago. That was post-Brexit progress.

I was feeling more and more depressed. I had once seen a picture of Saint Sebastian in a church; the expression on his face and the pain he felt after being hit by all those arrows must have been etched on to my face. My heart looked like a porcupine with all the barbs shot into it from Adel and Freddie every time they said something nice about each other.

Coming to my senses, I realised we had stopped.

It was not the only thing I realised; Adel was actually properly betrothed to Freddie as surely as a medieval princess. He was the prince, a knight in a shining motor; I was somewhere between a stable boy and a servant at the king's dinner table.

This whole charade was a charm offensive by the royal family in order for me to feel even worse about my behaviour on my arrival. It was, then, clear to me that they wanted to do business with me again; silver ingots were the only secure and portable trading item.

It was necessary to build up a relationship with me. That was the only reason that they had included me in this little 'ménage trois'. Those two lovebirds besotted and betrothed were bringing along the third wheel to make me feel wanted. I felt like a spare tyre at a car parts convention. I was being oversensitive, I knew that, but I was beginning to realise that people in love do not act rationally. I did not feel like swimming, but it would have been rude not to accept their hospitality.

Despite myself, I was growing fonder and fonder of both of them. What is it about wealth and power? My mind said these were people who made money out of people's misery and penury. They bought cheap and sold dear. They exploited people. They worked for a ruthless organisation.

I should have despised them for making all our lives poorer, but they were putting bread on the table for all those who worked for them. The Lawless family, through their magnificence in pushing the deal through were, to all intents and purposes, allowing me to send money to my poor mother. She would have said: 'Curiouser and curiouser.' She loved Lewis Carroll as much as she loved Molière, Proust, Shakespeare and Voltaire. The Lawless people were producing wealth in a poor community and I was part of that community. We all needed the money, and they provided the means to get it.

Freddie Lawless was not flawless but I liked him.

With a heavy heart, I undid my seat belt. Freddie would steal the love of my life from under my nose and I would be best man, in love with the bride for the rest of my life. I could see it all coming.

'You boys go ahead and bond in the water, I'll set up the picnic. The towels are in the boot, Aubs,' Adel said.

She was heading towards the boot. This time, I was beside her in a flash. I managed to open the boot for her, and she thanked me for it. There was a wicker hamper in the back, a light blue woman's swimsuit lying on top of three fluffy white towels and a spare wheel. Freddie joined us and palmed the keys into Adel's hand.

'Thanks for letting me drive,' he breathed. He was indecently close to her and I hated it.

He stood behind her, his body almost brushing hers; his breath was on her neck. My heart thumped as I realised that he was about to kiss her.

'A pleasure, but I'm driving back,' Adel insisted firmly.

She spun away from him, turning towards me, smiling shyly, looking at me lovingly, and whisking the swimsuit off the pile of towels. A wave of relief swept over my body. She still loved me. It was as if she was telling me that had circumstances been different, I would have stood chance. She was letting me know that although we were like ships that pass in the night, she would love me and remember me forever.

Suddenly, I was incredibly happy.

'I'm going to change in the back of the car, are you coming, or do you want to wait until I'm out?' Freddie announced, jumping in the back and closing the door.

'I'll wait,' I replied grabbing one of the towels.

I had a good body, but it was not as toned and muscular as his and I did not fancy getting naked next to him. He had huge hands and feet and that was all I needed to know.

'He was talking to me! I'm just coming,' she said, swinging her swimsuit over her shoulder before opening the door and joining him in the back.

The boot lid hid them both, but I supposed they would not be shy when becoming naked; people with good bodies seldom are and the other two towels that would have hidden them were still in the boot.

Idly, I opened the hamper. Two bottles of the same champagne from the pub lay on either side of the food; there were proper plates made of china strapped to the roof; silver cutlery was similarly suspended from the lid. This was a posh picnic.

Nestled in blue gingham napkins were four wooden boxes and three different types of bread rolls were packed in paper bags as if they had just come from the baker. I wondered what delicacies awaited us in the boxes.

My stomach was begging for good food. I should not have been hungry, but it was difficult to feel full after my meagre pub lunch.

As I closed the lid, I heard the two back doors clunk shut; they were ready for the waves.

I threw the towel over my shoulder and returned to the car to fetch my swimsuit from the side pocket in the front passenger door. I changed while they raced down to the water. By the time I had caught up with them, they were splashing around in the water like a couple of kids on holiday. I could never do anything like that on a normal workday. These two lived in a different world; an afternoon off during the week, I was jealous, especially, as I should have been walking back to the station to get a train back to the north-west and my boss would want to know why I was delayed. The deal would mollify him somewhat. The breeze was warm but the tarmac on the ground was still cold. There was a stone apron, and it was painful to walk across. Perhaps you were meant to jump. Anyway, the path was sandy and not too gravelly. The sand was moist and cold too, a foretaste of the water; I knew it would be freezing.

I had been dragged into the water enough times by my friends on holiday in Ireland to know two things: one, the water surrounding the British Isles is freezing, no matter whether it's in Dublin Bay, Camber Sands or the Bristol Channel; and two, people who live near the sea never feel the cold. There they were swimming around as if they were in a heated pre-Brexit leisure centre, where the water legally had to be twenty-nine degrees. Leisure pools have since closed, cutbacks of course, not that we could afford to heat the water nowadays with the energy crisis. Many pools had simply closed; no one could afford the prices.

'Come on in!' cried Adel, encouragingly.

My heart melted at her voice; I could refuse this woman nothing; I was her slave. I had not yet seen her in her swimsuit. All I could see were her tanned arms waving. At least the mystery of her tan had been solved; if she spent her time out here all summer, she would go brown. I was reminded that Saint Sebastian was the Patron Saint of Athletes, martyred by arrows, but fit and handsome and these two were clearly good-looking and athletic. They were like brother and sister, old friends. I was searching for a soul mate; unfortunately, they had found theirs.

'What's it like?' I asked as if I did not know.

The soles of my flat feet were traipsing over the wet sand and they did not like the icy feel of it at all.

'Great, at first it's a bit cold,' called Freddie.

I knew what he meant by a bit cold. Icebergs were a bit cold in his book. Why is it that the British are famed for their understatements? Freddie was the master; maybe being educated at an exclusive public school in England counted for being British or imbued you with a sardonic sense of humour and a love of the cold.

I walked over the cold, wet sand towards the water, which I reckoned would be both those things. When I crossed the line where the sea was lapping on the brown sand, my toes curled as the water rushed between them. It felt like someone had inserted ice cubes between them as some sort of sick practical joke.

However, not to lose face, I kept on walking. The next wave washed over my feet and I felt them go numb, but still I walked on; the third wave engulfed my calves and splashed my kneecaps but still I walked on.

Each new wave shocked a new part of my body. I gasped but still I walked on. Maybe I should have run in, but I was not brave enough for that and my heart that kept stopping at each outrageous freezing drenching would not have thanked me for it. Arrows, melting and ice, my heart was already thumping in my chest at the shoddy treatment it had received thus far.

There was no alternative but to take the plunge; my crown jewels were next to be cryogenically assaulted and I wanted to get that pain over and done with as soon as possible. I had never learnt to dive so I performed a pastiche of a swan dive; arms outstretched I launched myself into the English Channel's icy grip.

I sank like a stone, my body enveloped in fluid so cold that it should have carried a health warning. Had I spotted red flags up as I entered the water? I wondered. I did not even know where the nearest lifeguard station was. We had the beach to ourselves. The car park was empty. All these thoughts flooded my head as it came to terms with being doused.

'Now, I can see why the beach is deserted,' I noted, surfacing.

Salt stung my eyes as I shook the sea from my hair, treading water to enable me to keep my head above the surface. I was still six foot away from my favourite couple, which necessitated raising my voice; I was still feeling the cold and my voice went up an octave, I must have sounded like a schoolgirl.

'Don't worry, in half an hour this place will be packed. It's Poets Day today,' Adel assured me as she swam towards me.

Freddie was matching her stroke for stroke like her bodyguard, which I guess he was in many ways. He was certainly guarding her from me.

'Fifteen minutes and I'll be as frozen as a fish finger,' I joked and joy of joys, they both laughed, my new best friends. 'What's Poet's Day?'

'Pop off early tomorrow's Saturday,' Freddie explained. 'You've never heard that expression?'

'My boss has "Waalt Days", which is work at all times.'

They laughed again. I was their clown.

Momentarily, I was the happiest person on the planet; I even joined in their splashing of each other and swam around a bit. Their bay etiquette was spasmodic splashing followed by swimming around in circles and starting the splashing again; mine was flicking water and floundering around in a circle.

They swam like professionals, performing the Australian crawl in slow languid movements, I could only do breaststroke. When particularly high waves lifted me up, I resorted to the safety of doggy paddle but only if I was sure they were too immersed in their swimming to notice me.

When I finally thought about clowns, I remembered my mother's music. One song's lyrics said: 'the tears of a clown when no one's around'.

My emotions were up and down like a yoyo. If this was love, I did not think much of it. I was ecstatic one minute, morose the next. I shook off all negative thoughts, determined to spend the last few hours in Cornwall enjoying myself with my new friends. I would deal with my heart another time.

Thankfully, splashing each other lasted only a few minutes. Adel was the first to leave the water. I tried to watch as she emerged from the sea, but Freddie was talking to me and it would have been rude to turn my head around.

'Are you having fun?' he asked, swimming towards me.

'Yeah, but the water is so very cold,' I replied, treading water.

'I'll do a few more minutes, you go in.'

'I'll do a few strokes with you if you like.'

'I think I might go in myself; I'm feeling a bit woozy all of a sudden.'

'So am I. I thought it was the cold.'

'You make me laugh.'

'That's good.'

'Have your legs gone numb?'

'No, I just feel a bit sleepy.'

'Let's go back, I feel like I've been drugged.'

'Ha, your body's closing down with hypothermia. I told you it was cold.'

'No, I've been drugged before.'

'You're kidding.'

'No, I'm not, help me get to shore.'

'How?'

'Please, just do it. My arms are going numb, now!'

'Okay.'

'Help me, I'm going under.'

I swam towards him, confused.

It was incredible.

A strong athletic youth was losing consciousness. He was not fighting to stay on the surface. He was letting the water swallow him up. I snapped out of my daze.

His head had slipped under the water.

I had to do something. I grabbed for him – his arms were slippery. I tried to get a grip on his shoulders, but he sank further; I had dived under the water and grabbed his biceps, lifting him up as best I could. Kicking wildly, we broke the surface.

'Help me,' he whispered.

I had a chance; he had not swallowed any water.

He was so heavy, and I was feeling weaker and weaker.

'Help me, Freddie!' I begged, 'Kick your legs.'

'I can't,' he sighed, 'Adel?'

'She's on shore!'

He was lucid for the time being, but he was falling in and out of consciousness.

'Adel,' I shouted, turning around, I could not see her on the beach.

Freddie's head lolled forward into the water.

I pulled his face out of the water pulling his head up by his hair. He did not so much as wince.

'Freddie, you're too heavy, wake up, I need you to help me!' I screamed in his ear.

No response.

I pushed my nails into his arms.

No response.

I kneed his leg.

No response.

Willing myself to be stronger, I pulled Freddie towards the beach; we were too far out for me to touch the bottom.

He was under the water. I had to get his head above the surface.

Why had we followed Adel so far out?

I was not a strong swimmer at the best of times, I should have told her; I thought I had in conversations before the meeting.

'Come on, Freddie,' I hissed, impatiently, as I brought his head above water again. I supported the back of his head, keeping his nose and mouth above the surface.

A huge wave lifted us up, I lost my grip and water gushed over Freddie's head. He choked and came around. Shaking his head slightly, trying to get the sea out of his ears.

I thought we could make it, but his eyes were still closed. It was like he was asleep. I held his head and kicked for shore. Now I was feeling weak. His head was heavy, and kicking was exhausting. I turned my face to shore; no sign of Adel but there were people on the shore.

'Help, help!' I shouted as loudly as I could.

No response.

Luckily a wave came and pushed us towards the shore.

I let go of Freddie's head and started waving both arms while I was treading water.

No response.

I grabbed Freddie's head. Another wave came and pushed us towards the shore.

'Hey,' I screamed at the top of my lungs reaching out for Freddie's head as the third wave came.

No response.

No Freddie.

He was gone.

The undercurrent in the last wave must have taken him under. I swam around in a circle, dived under the water and searched around.

Nothing: no head, no body, no arms and no legs. I was feeling weaker and weaker; I had to get myself to shore; I had to get help.

Swimming as fast as my breaststroke allowed, I saw a crowd gathered on the shore.

As I neared them, I heard raised voices.

'I heard cries for help, are you okay?' asked a man dressed in a wet suit, standing next to a surfboard.

'It's not Freddie,' the woman announced.

She was similarly dressed and similarly equipped.

'Where's Freddie?' Adel asked, her voice slipping between the shoulders of the surfers as she arrived.

They parted to allow her to slide between them so that I was facing her; she was searching my face for answers.

'I lost him.'

'No,' she cried, stepping around me, she ran into the water; she had dressed, and the water lapped over her fresh pair of beige tailored trousers, but she pushed on through the waves.

As she waded in her white shirt became transparent, clinging to her back and then she was under the water and swimming out to sea. The surfers followed her. When they had reached a suitable depth, they crawled onto their surfboards and paddled out behind Adel.

Adel duck-dived twice, and then swam on.

She arrived at the exact position where I lost Freddie; it was uncanny that she had the sense to go to that spot. Was it female intuition? Diving down again, she surfaced and spoke to the surfers. I distinctly heard her asking for help. Yet, they seemed not to have had heard me. Like a magician, she pulled Freddie's head from the water, her hand resting under his chin.

In a flurry of activity, the surfers slipped Freddie's body on to the nearest surfboard, kicking for shore. Adel took the far surfboard and slipped on to it, paddling behind. I was standing in the warm breeze, still frozen like an ice cube, helpless but relieved. I loved Adel even more at that moment; she was a heroine. I had missed the first aid course at school, but I felt sure she could perform mouth to mouth or CPR.

She could bring Freddie back to life. As they neared the beach, I braved the frozen water again and tried to help but they ignored me all three of them; they had gone into rescue mode.

The three of them manhandled him off the board and on to the soft sand of the beach above the waterline. Freddie looked white like marble; his eyes were closed he looked like he was asleep. Adel knelt down next to him and felt for a pulse, she bent down and put her ear to his chest. Then, she shook her head.

That was that.

'You killed him,' the woman said.

'No, I was trying to save him,' I argued.

'I heard him crying for help,' she protested.

'That was me,' I explained.

'You deliberately drowned him, we saw you,' she insisted.

'Adel, you don't believe, that do you?' I appealed to Adel.

'Freddie's dead,' she sighed.

Those were the last words I heard from her that day; the day Freddie died.

'Murderer,' cried the man, taking up his girlfriend's chant.

He lunged at me but even in my drowsy state, I was able to step back and out of his grasp. Adel was on her haunches hunched over the body; the woman was trying to comfort her while looking at me with daggers. The man was floundering in the sand. He would be on his feet beating me to a pulp in a few seconds.

Adrenaline kicked in and I was off.

I have never run so fast in my life. I could feel the man running after me, hearing his panting as he gained on me.

Everyone was so damn fit; it was sickening. I pumped my arms and kicked my heels up, heading for the car. I was going to be accused of murder and, running around the country in swimming shorts I was going to alert the police to my presence in any area. The boot was still open, the man was still gaining, he wasn't as tall as me and I had longer legs, but he was far fitter.

Just as I reached the car, he put his hand on my shoulder. I slipped from his grasp, but he came at me again, gripping my shoulder so that I almost passed out with the pain. I looked down into the boot, grabbed the bottle of champagne and twisted my body.

The swine did not let go but I biffed him on the head with the bottle, which sent him flying and magically made him release his grip. He was lying right in my path, if I was going to reverse the Maserati out, I would have to run him over. So, as he staggered to his feet, I lured him away from the car.

As I fully expected, he grabbed for the bottle. He did not want to get another bruise on his noggin. I could see the bump already forming on his temple. He had expected me to struggle but I just let him take and as he did so, I planted my knee in his crotch.

I felt a squidgy contact, heard a groan and watched as the poor man dropped to the ground and curled into a ball. The pain was obviously agonising; he wriggled like a worm that had salt poured on it.

I raced to the car, threw open the door, jumped in and pushed the starter button. Nothing, the fob was missing. I had no idea how the man broke through the pain barrier, but he was at my shoulder again and he grabbed the sore flesh and bruised muscle once more. I winced in pain and roared in frustration. I threw the door open, knocking him off balance, and stepped on his toes, jabbing down hard.

As he hopped on one leg, I opened the door fully, knocking him to the ground. If he could worry my shoulder, I could worry his crotch.

As he tried to clamber to his feet, I planted another kick between his legs with the arch of my bare foot this time. I think it had more power this time and was more effective because I felt a spherical mass on the end of my foot. My assailant went down again, curled into a foetal ball, moaning in pain.

At the back of the car, I scoured the boot; the fob was lying in the hamper. Why, I could not tell. Returning to the driver's door, I checked that my assailant was still down; he had got to his knees but was still doubled in pain. I had time.

I slipped into the driver's seat, started the car; reversed out of the parking space, avoiding their black car-club rental Jaguar F-Pace and headed for the border.

I was leaving Poseidon Bay forever.

As I turned on to the main road, I saw a Toyota Hi-Lux pick-up in the distance. I knew it was packed with Lawless's security men, armed to the teeth, speeding up the hill towards the point.

They were coming for me.

Chapter Four

Run, Run as Fast as You Can

I collected my thoughts. All I had to do was steer. Driving barefoot was a little strange at first. I soon got used to it; there were only two pedals, but the acceleration was so brisk, and the brakes were so sharp that I was paranoid that I would take a bend too fast or brake too hard and spin her into a skid.

It was clear that heading for the border would be my safest bet in my bid for survival. Whoever had drugged us, had failed in my case, just. Adrenaline was fuelling my recovery; the drug was wearing off, I could tell. I felt less helpless. I could feel that my mouth was dry; I was becoming more aware. That had to be a positive sign.

However, heading for the border would also drive me straight into Lawless's security guards. They patrolled all the entrances and exits into Poseidon Bay. I was being blamed for drowning Trevor's son and I think my explanation would have received the same response as I got from everyone on the beach. I had managed to survive the sea; I needed to survive Poseidon Bay.

Was there no one who could help me?

Suddenly, I remembered the girl in the shop. Where did she say she lived? 'The Rover's Rest', that was it.

I pulled over into the gateway of a field, and punched the name into the satellite navigation system. I cannot multitask.

There were hundreds of cottages with that name but only one in Poseidon Bay. It was ten minutes away, back into enemy territory. Admittedly, I risked bumping into one of Lawless's patrols but ten minutes to relative safety seemed like a reasonable risk. I had very few other choices and bursting through a checkpoint and being riddled with bullets did not seem a sensible one.

Driving a little further down the road, I came to a junction and performed the most perfect three-point-turn I ever have. The car was a dream to drive. No traffic coming, I pulled off and headed for the refuge singing the 'Wild Rover': 'And it's no nay, never, no nay never no more, will I play the Wild Rover, no never no more!'

The car roared as I powered it down the narrow lane towards safety. I screeched to a halt outside a nondescript Cornish bungalow built in the nineteen seventies. Scrambling out of the car, I grabbed my clothes from the back seat.

Kate came out immediately. She was wearing white shorts and a navy polo shirt. She looked far prettier than she did in the shop, her hair was down, and it reached her shoulders.

Kate did not comment on how well the swim shorts she had sold me fitted. She shut the car door and pinned me against the door as if she was going to punch me, her face was in mine as she hissed angrily at me.

'What are you doing here in one of Lawless's cars?'

'I'm in trouble.'

'I heard. It's all over the five o'clock news. I heard it on the bus on the way over; people are tweeting and messaging about it.'

'Will you help me?

'Well, you haven't helped yourself, have you? Why didn't you dump the car? They'll track that car in no time; you're as good as dead.'

'The transponder – of course! What was I meant to do?'

'I would have dumped the car at the nearest Car Club point and picked up a car there. That would have got you here and with a lot more time to figure out what to do, next.'

'Well, what, can I do?'

'If they catch you, you're dead. Get changed, my dad's clothes are drying in the kitchen; there's a boat you can use. Thank my giddy aunt, my parents aren't back from work but they're due soon, so for flip's sake hurry up. The boat's down there.'

Kate pointed down the path before she set off down it herself. Looking over her shoulder, I could see the path snaking down to the sea. Turning on my heels, I rushed into the house. Inside, there was one of those floral sofas and a matching armchair in the lounge – nineteen-fifties furniture in a nineteen-seventies house. There was a wall of glass that looked out on to the sea.

The sliding doors were open fractionally; fresh air blew in; the country people loved that purity. There was no one there so I striped as if I were leaving a burning oilrig.

Passing by the fridge, I helped myself to a small bottle of water. Kate had left a pair of Levi jeans and a thick corduroy shirt folded on the breakfast bar, there was no underwear, so I had to go commando.

Dressed in her father's clothes and barefoot, I walked to the back door and put on a pair of pristine men's boots. They looked new. Kate's dad obviously looked after his clothes.

I should have grabbed a jumper from Kate's parents' bedroom, but I did not think of it at the time, fool that I was. I was outside and following Kate down the path before you could say: 'They're coming to get you'.

In a small cove on a shale beach stood my saviour. Kate had already wheeled the trailer into sea and was knee deep in the water. She was shivering and there were goose pimples on her arms, the fine hair standing up.

Someone else felt the cold. It was a relief.

The boat floated off its cradle and she held it for me.

'I didn't do it,' I announced as she stared truculently at me.

'Just get in. There's no time for explanations.'

I did as I was told; I did not even bother to complain about the temperature of the water.

'We were both drugged,' I protested.

'You don't look drugged to me.'

'Don't I sound it?'

'Do you want to get caught? I'm helping you all right, get in.'

'I grabbed a small mineral bottle from the fridge on my way down,' I explained, holding up the bottle for her to see.

'Get going or you might not live to enjoy it.'

She held the boat as I climbed in at the back. The propeller scraped on the shale shore as I stepped in.

'Thanks, Kate.'

She pulled the gunwales along in the water, feeding them through her fingers like a rope; then she pushed me off.

'Pull, the cord, it's like a mower.'

'I've never had a garden.'

The boat bobbed on the water, drifting very slowly out to sea. It was hardly going to get me beyond the bay.

'Just pull the chord hard, you plonker! No, don't stand up and do it, lean forwards and pull with your left hand. That's it.'

The engine spluttered. She encouraged me to try again and the motor grumbled into life. She told me to twist the throttle and the boat lurched forward. It was still light, but it was getting cold and all I had was Kate's corduroy shirt, well her dad's anyway. I shuddered.

'Thanks.'

Turning around, I waved. She waved back, a solitary movement of the hand mirroring mine.

That was when I noticed the lights on the hill above the cottage. They were headlights and as I made it to the headland, I saw the security men running down to join Kate on the beach. I stopped waving and pointed to the armed men behind her.

She started frantically waving me off to the left; her palm of her left hand seemed to be trying to push the boat around the cove. I immediately steered off at an angle and looked back, she was waving even more urgently. I figured out that she wanted me to get into the shadow of the point and turned sharply to the left, not forty-five degrees, but ninety.

The cove exploded around me, it was like a bomb had gone off, and I literally felt the bullet whizz past me. I could not believe it; it was like a wasp passing my ear.

I tried to open up the throttle even more, but I was at full power; another wasp whizzed past, silenced weapons. I slipped down into the bottom of the boat. I was fast approaching the rocks that surrounded the point.

I dared not look back. I just focused on staying in the shadow of the point and getting around it. A blinding light lit up the sky like a lightning bolt, followed by the sound of a giant sigh filling the air, then, a thump and an explosion.

The rocks ahead of me were obliterated sending a shower of rocks flying into the air.

My ears were ringing and the shock wave from the explosion pushed me against the bottom of the boat, winding me so badly that I could not move. My hand remained steadfastly on the tiller. I did not waver from the direction of my escape.

Only one or two pieces of cliff top made it into the small boat, striking my right arm and left leg. The pain was excruciating but I held on to the throttle. A shower of gravelly pieces rained down on me; it was like being stoned by gravel, but I guided the boat as a hail of bullets thudded into the rock above.

I heard a bullet hit the gunwale just above the waterline. It should have embedded in my kneecap but by some miracle it had missed – a ricochet.

The destruction of the rock at the end of the point actually allowed me to escape the cove more easily. Just as well because I heard the sound of a 'GPMG' firing; those 'general purpose machine guns' have seven point six two bullets and I have seen them slice someone in half during the riots against deportation in Manchester. The sound made my skin crawl and I shuddered.

Successfully rounding the cape, I sped off along the coast east, away from Poseidon Bay. The big black boats in the marina would be scrambling their crews and manning their searchlights, they would be hunting the coast for me.

I watched the wake behind me before looking for a suitable place to go ashore. I was conscious of the shore patrols but equally, I had no choice but to find somewhere to moor for the night, I had no idea how long the fuel would last in this little boat.

The engine coughed, spluttered and died. The tide was taking me out to sea and there was not a single thing I could do.

Chapter Five

All at Sea

I drifted further and further out to sea. The outboard motor was useless. The clothes I wore were not appropriate for a night sailing, let alone being adrift in a pathetically small boat. I knew what would happen,

I had come across people in doorways back home. They had frozen to death in the winter, having sold their warm clothes for food. It was considered a noble way to go. Too weak to work, too hungry to move, you let hypothermia put its icy grip around your throat and waited to die.

My teeth started chattering; I rubbed my bare forearms and shivered in the bottom of the boat. I could see nothing to the south, dim lights to the north: Dartmouth, Southampton, Torquay, Penzance, or Worthing, one of the south coast towns.

I could not tell you where I was, how long I had been drifting or in which direction I was headed. It had got dark suddenly and that added to my troubles. I was invisible to my pursuers but also to any traffic; I could be sliced in half by the bow of a freighter. One of Lawless's smuggling boats could run my small craft over and only feel a jolt like a bad wave.

I blew into my hands determined to keep alive, I rolled down the sleeves of the corduroy shirt and buttoned the cuff, flapped my arms to get the circulation flowing and made circular, windmill motions with my shoulders to get my fingers warm. The Administration, our government, had sent out podcasts during the first winter when the power failed. There was a long list of instructions you should follow if you wanted to avoid dying of hypothermia. I had also heard a few horror stories from my best friend, Paul O'Donaghue, who had left England and was working on the tuna fleet off Newfoundland.

He reckoned that if you fell in the water, you had four minutes to be saved before hypothermia took away your will to survive. I thought of Freddie and the way he went.

It must have been four minutes before I lost him. He could not struggle for long enough with the number of drugs in his system.

It was my fault, too. If only I had been stronger, I might have saved him. I had lost him and now I was lost, myself. I wondered whether I might last another four hours out in the open sea. The sky above me was a midnight blue though I was sure it was only nine or ten; the stars glinted like tiny sequins sewn into a dress that Adel might wear.

I was tired from my efforts to keep warm. I just wanted to sleep. The hairs on my arms and legs were standing to attention and I could almost feel the goose pimples popping out on my flesh all over my frozen limbs. I was not wet, so that was a relief, I had kicked off my wet, brand-new, boots that had filled with water as I scrambled into the boat and my feet had dried in the wind. I was chilled to the bone though.

The sky above me was clear; that meant there was no cloud cover to keep the heat in from the day. I knew my corduroy shirt and Levi jeans were almost the worst clothes to wear at night at sea off the coast of England. The cold water made the temperature plummet. I could not get warm. I knew confusion and violent shivering awaited me. For now, I was tired and just wanted to sleep. I no longer cared that a boat might crush my dinghy and throw me in the water. A long sleep was what I craved. Morpheus was my new best friend, forever, and I was waiting for him to embrace me. I did not care if I never woke from my sleep.

I would be joining Freddie fairly soon but my way of dying seemed infinitely less traumatic than his. Going to sleep and not waking up seemed preferable to having your lungs filled with water. I had not known him long, but I found myself missing him. He was not the boorish creep I had expected. He could have beaten me to a pulp on both occasions that we met, yet whether it was to protect family pride, by not reacting to provocation, or whether it was because Adel had interceded on my behalf I simply did not know. Now, I had no way of finding out.

Sleep swept over me like a wave and dragged me down into its depths. I awoke, shivering violently; my teeth chattered like fishermen loading oysters at the morning market. I had to bite on my index finger to stop them.

The pain woke me up.

Above, the midnight blue curtain twinkled with diamonds and around me was the black oily sea. I was freezing. I looked around me, kneeled up in the boat and could see no lights to the north and no lights to the south. My back ached, my legs throbbed with pain and my arms felt like they were coated in ice. Lifting myself up only exposed me to the biting wind that whipped off the waves, chilled by the sea. My stomach craved food, hot food.

I hugged myself, looked around one more time, then lay down in the dry bottom of the boat and curled into a foetal ball. It was warmest place to be but by no means warm. It was sheltered from the wind, which was a blessing. I had survived for a few measly hours; I could not envisage making it through the night. I was losing the warmth from my body.

Then I thought of something.

I knew that you lose most of the heat from the body through your head. I needed a hat; a woolly one would have been best.

Craving a First World War 'Flying Ace' helmet, I decided I should perform some warm-up activities. Lying on my back, I pedalled an invisible bicycle for a good ten minutes; my heart beat faster in my chest pumping blood around my body. That worked. I sat up when I was exhausted by cycling and stretched out my arms and rolled my shoulders; my hands rotated like the sails of a windmill, my heart beat even faster in my chest.

Those minute windmill movements warmed me up even more, but they were really tiring, utilising muscles that were hardly ever used. Finally, I flapped my arms like a demented crow, up and down as if I wanted to take off. When I grew weary of the vertical movement, I flapped my arms horizontally, clapping my hands with every forward stroke. Any hunger I had suffered was forgotten.

Eventually, I felt elated, exhausted and invigorated.

I began to think that I might just survive the night at sea after all. If I had regretted not taking a jumper from the Rover's Rest, I regretted not taking one of the boxes of food from the Maserati. My stomach rumbled noisily. I dreamed of pilchards in rich red tomato sauce and craved hard, brittle baguette. Thinking back to my lunch with Kate, I would have wolfed down either of the insipid dishes that we had been served; soggy pastry and peppery sauce seemed like a banquet seven miles out to sea.

In Alderney, the Braye Harbour Customs Chief had just called in one of his powerboats from a high-speed chase across the channel, I was later told by my rescuers; the radar showed that the boat had made harbour in Poseidon Bay.

The powerboat slowed and turned; it was a familiar story. I had read about it in one of the news feeds that were sent to my iPhone – the powerboats were just spread too thinly to be a threat. As a decoy boat was sent to lure the customs men away, the main shipment would slip past.

The pursuit boat would turn and give chase but just as they could pick up the boats on their radar, the smugglers could pick them up on theirs and made sure they saved their speed for when they were pursued while conserving their fuel by travelling at the speed of other traffic when they were undetected.

The shipping traffic in the Channel had reduced since Brexit but it was still impossible to police the narrow strip with so few boats and the cunning tactics of the smugglers.

Forgetting my hunger, I concentrated on the red and green lights heading towards my craft. I knelt upright in the boat and waved my arms frantically.

Needlessly, I started screaming for help even though I knew that they could not hear me with their helmets on, the noise of their engines and the vast distance between us.

Closer and closer it came, louder and louder the engines sounded, bubbling away, the helmeted pilots following the search light that was mounted on the deck, lighting up the water ahead. I waved even more desperately as the boat approached.

I tried shouting again convincing myself that nothing would drown the sound of my voice. In reality, I knew they had not seen me; the searchlight did not waver, cutting a swathe through the darkness, the wake streaming out from behind, in all its phosphorescence, as straight as an arrow.

If they had spotted me, they would have veered to my left, appearing on my port bow. If they had seen me, they would have altered their course, steering starboard, off course, and towards me. They stayed steadfastly on their trajectory.

I stopped waving. I became silent. My voice was gone.

I could see their white helmets like two tiny golf balls on the top of a sleek, streamlined hull, but they could not see me at all. I sat down in the boat, my energy was spent, hunger still gnawed at my stomach like a rat.

I had lost hope. I had lost the drive to survive.

There was no way I would be rescued and, therefore, I was destined to die of hypothermia. I was convinced that I was curling up for the last time as I lay down in the boat. I had lost the will to fight back. I had given up the struggle.

I cursed my luck, dying without ever having been truly in love. Dying because I was in love. I should never have gone down to the beach. I should never, ever, have had anything to do with Adel.

I should never have had anything to do with Lawless either; I suppose bad things happen to people who do bad things and dealing with Lawless was a bad thing. I was taking payment from his ill-gotten gains. I was being punished for my bad deeds. I decided I deserved what had happened to me and should take the consequences.

If only I had convinced Mr. Campbell-Lamerton not to deal with such a complete crook, none of this would have happened. Then, again, I would never have fallen in love with Adel. I might have escaped the pain of loving someone who had a fiancé and would never be interested in me. There might be plenty more fish in the sea, but I did not think they would be there for me any longer.

My time had come to join Freddie. I shivered and shook, lay down in the boat and hugged myself. A lump came into my throat. I would miss Adel, my love. As for Kate, I had not thanked her for saving me. I was feeling miserable. I think I started to cry because I felt frustrated by the whole situation.

Maybe I cried because I was in love with Adel and I would never see her again. Maybe I cried because I was too young to die. Maybe I was crying because I knew I would never see my family ever again. Thoughts raced through my mind: I would never see my mother again, and I loved her so much; she had been so good to me, even sending money to me when she was first deported. I cried because I would miss my twentieth-fifth birthday. I was not going to last a quarter-century.

My tears felt warm on my cold cheeks; the saltiness tickled my dry and chapped lips. I licked my lips and enjoyed the salty taste of my own misery. I was too young to die but too weak to fight it. What was my mother's expression? 'To dig I am unable, to beg I am too proud.'

I must have cried for half an hour. I had never cried that much in my life.

I could remember crying when I was five and went to school but could not remember crying since. I was still aching from sleeping in the bottom of the boat but that did not stop me curling up again, crusted teary rivulets on my cheeks.

I think I was enjoying the discomfort. The wooden ribs of the boat digging into my flank and thigh reminded me that I was still alive. Sleep, like a thief in the night, crept up on me and knocked me out cold.

I awoke a shivering wreck, still bobbing in the sea that seemed to have become rougher since I slept. I woke with a jolt and crawled to the stern. Waves were lifting the boat up before collapsing beneath it and leaving it in a trough. Up and down, we rose; up and down my empty stomach went. I could feel the sway, feel the cold gripping at my heart and squeezing the life out of it; up and down, up and down. The words of Puck.

It reminded me of my Puck, my lines: 'I'll put a girdle round about the earth in forty minutes, Up and down, up and down, I will lead them up and down.'

That was when I felt my whole-body wretch and I vomited violently over the side, my whole body heaving. If my misery needed to be more complete, voiding the acidic contents of an empty stomach provided the icing on the cake; cold, hungry, aching, the painful contractions in my stomach and the awful taste in my mouth provided me with even more reason to hasten my own demise.

'I just want to die,' I mumbled. 'Please, let me die.'

I collapsed back into the boat and rolled from side to side, groaning intermittently.

The urge to vomit again brought me to the gunwales and as the boat rose up and down like a lift, I emptied bile into the sea. I coughed and spluttered and watched as the yellow liquid was carried off by the spume.

'I just want to die in peace,' I moaned.

Shivering, I turned on my side and curled into a foetal ball.

I swear it was more of a mumbled gasp than a cry for help, but I heard a voice booming across the water.

'Rules of the Sea forbid that course of action; it is our duty to affect a rescue.'

Sleepily, I raised my head.

All I could see was a wall of water in front of me. Then, the boat bobbed on the top of the wave and briefly I saw the white and black hull with an orange cockpit on top before I was plunged into another trough. The boat was lit up by the deck spotlights and the navigation lights. I could not mistake the colours of that beacon of salvation.

It was a Royal National Lifeboat Institute rescue boat. It was the most recognisable symbol of hope in the whole of the British Isles. The RNLI was one of the few organisations that had not been affected by Brexit. The smugglers ensured it was never short of donations.

The seven-man crew of the *Tamar* had been scrambled from Alderney after the powerboat crew had spotted me; it had raced at twenty knots to find me and used its listening devices and thermal imaging to pick up the boat and me. A monster of a vessel at over sixteen metres long, it had a range of two hundred and fifty nautical miles.

Despite the swell, the coxswain managed to bring the huge boat close to mine; my boat was three metres long and bobbed about in the swell.

A member of the crew, dressed in RNLI orange and blue oilskins, spoke through a Bluetooth headset connected to two loudspeakers mounted on the foredeck. I recognised the sound as that first voice I had heard when I thought all hope was lost.

'We're going to fire a painter across your bow, keep low and wait for it to land, then grab it if you can.'

'What if I can't?' I asked, shouting across the swollen sea between us. Then, he disappeared.

'We'll think of something else, then. Stand by.'

'Okay!' I shouted back, revelling in the sound of my own voice. I was alive, I had survived; it was incredible.

He popped up again as I rose out of the wave trough and we both rose up on the swell. I still had the taste of vomit in my mouth but all thoughts of cold and hunger disappeared as I awaited rescue.

I had little choice; I lay down, waiting for the rope to be fired at me, wondering whether I would be sick again.

There was a phut. It was the sound of an airgun firing. I peered over the stern; they had fired as both our boats rode the crest of the wave.

An orange bullet-shaped float arced above my head in the sky, and I ducked. An orange nylon cord sailed over the boat, and then dropped on the gunwales.

The cord thudded on the wooden rim and whacked my arm. I winced in pain but had the sense to grab it and hold on tight to the rope.

'I've got it,' I cried triumphantly.

My tiredness, my seasickness and my pain evaporated. I was saved. I heard a voice issuing instructions through a loudspeaker mounted on the cabin roof.

'Wind the rope around the outboard motor, twist the lose end into a lasso and hoop it over the engine then pull the loose end tight, wrap it round the motor three times then hold on to your end, we'll winch you in.'

I did as I was instructed, looping the rope over the motor, pulling it tight, then gabbing my end and wrapping it four times around, one for luck – I reckoned I needed some more. Then, I waved to my oilskinned saviour and I heard, actually heard the electric motor of the winch whirring. It was a distant sound as thin as the wind on the waves, but it was the most wonderful sound that I had ever heard.

Chapter Six

Recovery Stage

I awoke attached to a drip, dry-mouthed and groggy. I looked down at the wires and the tubes inserted into my forearm, held in position by a rectangle of white tape, cut precisely.

The nurse who came in was a redhead, thin and gorgeous or maybe the morphine made her so. I closed my eyes, opened them again. Was I in limbo? No nurse ever looked so good. I was in love yet again, not so deeply of course but still in love: Adel, Kate and now, my angelic nurse.

Opening my eyes again, the pink-lipped lovely smiled at me revealing even white teeth. I smiled back at her, lips closed, keeping my halitosis at bay; my mouth tasted like the inside of a parrot cage that had not been cleaned for a month. She smelt of soap and fresh sheets.

If I thought my nurse was beautiful, then I was in for a further surprise. It seemed that only good-looking people got jobs working for The Administration post-Brexit.

Dressed in military uniform, disruptive pattern camouflage trousers, and khaki shirt, wearing a black beret, folded over precisely and sporting a silver regimental badge, was the most stunningly attractive woman I have ever seen.

She was African.

Her skin was a deep, rich Nubian brown and along with the most mesmerising eyes, the fullest lip and highest cheekbones that I had ever seen, she left me gaping with desire. Her beautiful black hair was tied at the back and cropped short around her oval face.

She was wearing Chanel perfume. I was not sure how she had managed to get it from Paris, but she wore it well, it suited her.

The fragrance wafted to my bedside.

I later learnt that she was in the Royal Green Jackets, she was from Jinja, in Uganda, her name was Thomasina Mutesa; she was a major in the army and had been seconded into Military Intelligence. I came to know her as Major Thom, or simply as Thom.

I also learnt, later, that after the mass deportations, The Administration had found it impossible to find people of the same calibre to help run essential services and the Ministry of Defence.

Having rid themselves of anyone with a litre of foreign blood, they found that the remaining indigenous population with a modicum of skills had emigrated or had taken over successful businesses that had been run by the immigrant population.

Super-bright people like Major Thom had been brought over not as immigrants but as consultants on long-term temporary contracts. People like her had to be housed and paid well, of course, but The Administration had no choice. They could not afford to be seen to be encouraging immigration, so temporary status was granted, and they could not afford to ignore the option of importing skilled staff if they wanted to avoid the country falling into anarchy or civil war. Governing the country seemed to involve consultants from around the world, producing policies at great expense, most of which were not implemented.

The Upper Administration, which was stuffed with rich landowners, landlords and developers, passed laws that protected their wealth, The Common Administration struggled to field many representatives, such was the despondency with politics.

The country was in a mess. I was in a mess. The only comfort was my nurse in her dress.

However, Major Thomasina was going to change all that with her almond eyes, her high cheekbones and voluptuous lips. I had been in love with Adel; I was in lust with Thom. I would have walked over hot coals or slept on a bed of nails just for a kiss, a taste of her sweet lips. It was like I had woken from a nightmare and had arrived in paradise.

'How are you feeling?' she asked, her smile disarming me as she leaned over and stroked my forehead.

Her hand was a comforting balm on my fevered brow.

'Fine.' I whispered the lie through lips, which were chapped with dehydration.

My body felt emaciated and I had no energy. I could smile and that's what I did, not thinking about the halitosis that must have built up after three days in intensive care. A whiff of Chanel Number 5 filled my nostrils. This woman was beautiful and sophisticated.

'Good, we're glad we got you out when we did,' she whispered back. I could feel her hot breath on my face.

If I had been pallid when I woke, I knew that the colour had returned to my cheeks. I was embarrassed and excited at the same time.

My mouth had become dry despite the fact I had just had a cup of tea. She made my pulse race. I was nervous. I did not want to say the wrong thing. The more I looked at her the more beautiful she became.

'Thank you for saving me,' I sighed falling from lust into love in the space of a few minutes.

'We'll talk later, but I have an idea that you may be able to return the favour.'

'Ask me anything,' I insisted.

'I may well take you up on that,' she murmured huskily. 'Get some rest, I'll come and see you soon.'

'Is that a promise?'

'It's a promise.'

I watched her walk down the ward, wondering how she could have got such a figure-hugging pair of trousers. The nurse appeared with a plastic beaker of water some pills on a tray and I still watched her leave.

'She has her clothes tailored.'

'What do you mean?' I asked innocently.

'Your eyes are out on stalks Mr. East. If I took your pulse now, it would be racing. I saw you staring. You were wondering how her trousers managed to be so figure-hugging and tight.'

'I was just watching her leave. I just wanted her to stay,' I protested pathetically.

I knew my voice sounded hollow.

'I bet you did, you're obviously on the mend.'

'My head feels sore,' I complained.

'I've brought some pain killers.'

'Can you kiss it better?' I begged flirtatiously.

'After you've been lusting after my boss?'

'It hurts,' I maintained.

'It will hurt when my Royal Marine Major fiancé finds out some patient has been flirting with his fiancée. It will hurt when I report your comments to my commanding officer.'

'Just ask him not to tell Thomasina!' I begged.

'Major Mutesa is my commanding officer.'

'What?'

I had just shot myself in the foot.

'I'm wearing a nurse's uniform but I'm RAMC,' she explained as I looked on blankly. 'Royal Army Medical Corps. Major Thom is in charge of this facility; I have been instructed to report all your comments to her.'

'Not everything,' I pleaded.

'The instruction was everything.'

I squirmed like a freshly salted slug.

'Come on, please, have mercy!' I beseeched her.

'I can safely report that you have fallen for her. Now, take your pills like a good boy,' she smirked.

'I'm not a boy.'

'You are until you wear a green beret.'

I snatched the tray off her.

'Thank you,' I spat sarcastically, sounding like an ungrateful teenager.

I would not have been surprised if she was not a nurse, just someone sent to torment me. Through scowling eyes, I watched the beautiful redheaded vision, who was engaged to a marine and who I had fallen in love with when I first awoke, disappear and with it all the wonderful thoughts I had for her. I never saw her in the hospital ward again, although she did turn up in the weapons section at A.D.D.7, Administration Defence, Department Seven, in London but I'm getting ahead of myself.

Chapter Seven

Reconnection and Reunion

Kate placed the cup of hot coffee on the breakfast bar; I sat on one of the stools. She was wearing a blue denim skirt and a pale blue Thomas Pink shirt, which complemented her pallid skin. She spent too much time in the shop.

'Start at the beginning,' she said warmly, pulling up a stool so she sat opposite me. She folded her arms and leant forward leaning her elbows on the counter; she looked into my eyes, her expression begged me to open up.

'So, thank you so much for helping me escape,' I began.

'I knew you weren't a murderer,' she assured me, her cobalt blue eyes looking into mine. I was so relieved she believed me that I almost cried.

My emotions had been up and down, the doctors warned me that the withdrawal from the morphine would create havoc with my mental well-being. I could understand why the opium dens of China and the East End of London were so popular. It was clear to me now. That magic potion could wipe out any pain. It was time to leave my dependence on drugs behind.

'I was in the boat and it ran out of fuel. I drifted for hours. The doctors reckoned that when I stepped aboard the lifeboat, I was an hour away from getting hypothermia and then I would have been in a catatonic state.'

'That sounds bad. How did they know?'

'I suppose they must have worked out how long I had been at sea; the lifeboat crew took my temperature and pulse.'

'How did the lifeboat crew know where you were? That's what I meant, Dumbo. You were drifting in the middle of the Channel.'

That hurt, I have very big ears like an elephant, and I am not that stupid. I've got five GCSEs. I wanted to go to sixth form college, but my mother was deported and the government, The Administration, suspended all tertiary education in the year that I was to take up a place.

They had deported all the lecturers and privatised the Russell Group universities making them only available to the super rich and oligarchs; all the remaining lecturers were absorbed into those institutions or made redundant, adding to the burgeoning masses of unemployed. Many of them emigrated to China or sold their expertise to American students over the internet through Facetime, Skype and Zoom.

The message was clear: the privileged few were back in business and the rest of us needed to work and forget about getting an education. That was how I had ended up working for Campbell-Lamerton as his Sales Manager. That was a joke as I was only managing myself. The title allowed him to give me a small salary; managers had not been put on zero-hour contracts at that point. The fact that he promised me commission was practically a miracle, it was unheard of back then.

I thought I had struck gold with my silver deal but, instead, I had ended up in hospital with nearly critical hypothermia and an accusation of murder hanging over my head like a sword of Damocles.

Worse still, I was sent back into dangerous territory and had to suffer the ignominious fate of being talked down to by Kate. I replied to her question despite myself and to show her rudeness did not bother me.

'As luck would have it, a powerboat patrol passed by and spotted me, giving the coordinates to the RNLI and dropping off a GPS beacon in my vicinity. They just had to get there and put their radar and thermal imagery to use and they found me within half an hour.'

'What happened, then?'

'I was in intensive care for three days. Remember the rocket in the rocks? The blast wave collapsed one of the pockets in my lungs, so I had to recover from that.'

'You poor love,' sighed Kate, sympathetically.

I felt a huge desire to grab Kate and hold her in my arms, tell her I loved her and offer to take her away from this madness.

'Then, it gets interesting; I get a visit from a mysterious man.'

'Sounds spooky, was he a spook?'

'A spy, yes.'

'Really? I don't believe it.'

'He took me to his headquarters.'

'Where are all your gadgets, then?'

'Not that sort of spook.'

'Go on, then, what's the name of this mysterious man?'

'I could tell you, but I would have to eliminate you.'

'You can be funny. Go on what's his name.'

'The name he gave me was Major Thom Thorneycroft.'

I did not want her to know he was she.

'Major Thom, very David Bowie.'

'Anyhow, I was taken to this amazing place somewhere in London.'

'I've never been to London.'

'So, the exciting bit is that they know all about Lawless.'

'Well, I never. How would they know?'

'They've been watching Lawless for months – can you believe it?'

'Why?'

'They need him to stay in power, you know, like Colonel Gaddafi or that President of Syria, Bashar al-Assad?'

'Lawless ain't that bad!'

'He keeps a lid on the smugglers; they reckon without him there'll be total anarchy leading to civil war.'

'Are you're a Roundhead or a Cavalier, my dear?'

'Be serious, there's more.'

'Not for me there's not! As long as I have my job in the shop, I'm happy. Your Major Thom and Lawless can do what they like when they like as long as they don't close the shop.'

'Really!'

'Really, what do I care? As long as I can pay my rent to my parents, go out on the odd Friday night and can afford some food, I'm made up.'

'Is that all you're interested in.'

'I don't know where you come from but round here that's called a massive achievement; most of my friends don't have a job.'

'I know,' I said peevishly.

'The food stamps they dole out wouldn't keep an anorexic satisfied. What world do you come from where you can come in here and judge us?'

'I wasn't judging. I'm sorry. I know what you mean. I got carried away. It's just that I haven't told you the best part.'

'What's that, then? It'd better be good.'

'They know who killed Freddie.'

'What? Never! Who is it?'

'You're not going to believe this, but it was Adel.'

'Adel? You're joking me. She was going to marry Freddie.'

'That's what I thought, but she was just pretending. Apparently, she'll go for Terry and he'll end up the same as Freddie.'

I took a sip of coffee, which had cooled a bit while I was talking. Kate was cute but she was a bit mean with the milk and the coffee tasted like dishwater with chicory thrown in. It was warm and wet, and I was thirsty, so I drank some more. I looked at her and she had gone pale, the shock was too much.

'Who's helping her, who else is involved?' she asked.

'That's it, just Adel, working alone.'

'Okay, Einstein, if it was Adel, which I sorely doubt, how did she do it?'

'We had a glass of champagne served by the landlord; I saw him open it. There was no way he could have put the drug in the glass. He handed us the flutes and I remember admiring the craftsmanship that had gone into them, I even turned my glass upside down to examine it. They weren't your standard thin pub glasses; they were for VIPs.'

'Quite the posh connoisseur!'

'Just observant.'

'And snooty.'

'Can I carry on?' I sighed archly.

'I can't stop you wittering on.'

'As we chatted, we put the glasses down. Adel must have slipped the Rohypnol into our glasses when we weren't looking. Maybe she didn't have time to put the full dose in my glass and that's why Freddie drowned, and I didn't.'

'Amazing. Adel did all that?'

'Yes.'

'That's ridiculous. I think Major Thom should stuff his mad theories where the sun don't shine, personally.'

'You have to believe me.'

'Well, this time I don't'

'You have to! It's true.'

'How are you going to prove it?'

'I'm going to kidnap Freddie.'

'That's grave robbing. You'll never get away with it.'

'It's the only way I'll prove Freddie was done in. The drug won't have passed out of his bloodstream. An autopsy will prove that Freddie had Rohypnol in his system when he died. it will prove I didn't do it. It's my only chance.'

'Why don't you go to Terry with your mad theory?'

'Do you think I'd make it within a metre of his place, now all his men have been ordered to shot to kill? I'm sure that won't work.'

'Oh well, drink your coffee and we'll figure a way to get Freddie back to your friend.'

'You'll help me? That's great. You're amazing Kate.'

'That's true, more than you will ever know.'

I took a sip of my coffee. In the silence that followed, I felt sure I could hear the popple of a Maserati and the crunch of tyres over gravel.

'Who could that be?' I asked, distractedly.

'Who indeed?' Kate asked, rhetorically,

I heard the door slam, and everything fell into place.

'You called, Adel. You're working with her, aren't you?'

'What are you on about?'

'Of course, the text you sent to your parents to see when they were home, that was to alert her. How stupid I've been. I was meant to come to you for help and you were meant to give me the boat, but it was meant to run out of fuel sooner.'

'Not such a Dumbo, after all. You took your time to work it out didn't you, Einstein. I don't think your friends are all that clever either. Major Thom didn't figure out I was in the equation, did he?'

'What are you going to do to me?'

'Well, I know what I'd like to do you, you patronising arse! I should think Adel is going to hand you over to Terry Lawless.'

'But I'll tell him everything.'

'Did I say anything about you being able to talk? Oh, I don't think so, Einstein, dead men tell no tales. Lawless won't be able to refuse Adel anything when she delivers the body of his son's assassin.'

'Why are you helping her?'

'Why do you think?'

'Money – you really are a classic Judas.'

'Well, I've no need for anything else! Love won't put food on the table and keep me warm in winter.'

'I could have done that,' I complained.

She ignored my remark. I was in love with her, but she was heartless.

'I don't know how much Major Thom is paying you to do this, but I do know that Adel pays me handsomely to be her spy.'

'You're just a stooge, a stool pigeon,' I protested, fighting back tears of frustration.

Major Thom had told me this would happen but when it actually did, I was distraught. The morphine, the death of Freddie, betrayal at every step, finding out the truth about Adel, it was all too much for me.

'Sticks and stones, my love. My pretty boy thought he had all the girls falling for him. Poor old Georgie Aubrey, wanted to kiss the girls and make them cry. Looks like you're the one whose about to start blubbing, dun't it.'

'You better let your friend in. I bolted the front door remember?'

She got up and walked past me to open the door. That was when I leapt up.

Fishing the hypodermic from my jacket pocket, I plunged it into the side of her neck. The needle pierced the nape of her neck with alarming ease and I depressed the syringe top as I had practised on many an orange.

She gasped in shock and pain, looked sideways at me, clawed at the hand that held the Epi-pen and opened her mouth to scream. I wrestled her to the ground knocking the wind out of her.

I covered her mouth and started counting to twenty. There was a knock at the door. I ignored it and got as far as ten. A second knock followed; Adel rapped twice this time, much louder and more frantic.

Kate's eyes rolled in her head. The winding and the serum stopped her from fighting back but she wriggled like a fish on deck, trying to slip from under me.

I leant more fully on top of her to stop her breaking free.

I had her arms pinned by her side, but she thrust up with her hips and rolled her shoulders trying to break free. She wheezed under the pressure of my body, but I could feel the strength ebbing out of her as I continued the countdown.

The knocking became more desperate, but I had reached twenty and Kate had passed out.

Feeling much weaker after our wrestling match, I was breathless and panting when I dragged Kate's limp body back behind the breakfast bar.

The knocking started to sound threatening. I wondered if she might kick the door down.

'Coming,' I shouted.

I opened the bag that I had propped against the breakfast bar; took out the second of my five Epi-pens and a Taser. I slipped the Epi-pen into my jacket pocket and held the Taser in my right hand. Using my left hand to undo the bolts, I opened the door.

'So sorry, Kate bolted the door, she's just upstairs,' I explained as I pretended to struggle with the bolts.

The door opened inwards on a right-hand hinge, which allowed me to hide the Taser. I lifted the latch, waiting for Adel to push hard against it. She opened it cautiously.

'Adel!' I cried in mock shock.

'Hi, Aubs,' she greeted me casually; she enjoyed the fact that she was unexpected; she seemed to enjoy surprising me on a regular basis. I know she enjoyed carrying the gun and the power it gave her. She brought her right arm up; I aimed the Taser and pressed the button. There was a fizzing sound, the electricity arcing from the two points, looking like devil's ears.

The lightning strike of electricity hit her chest and neck, and split off in different directions from there, a burst of electricity hit her hair and I smelt it burn, like toast. She danced for me, literally threw the gun into the kitchen, her left hand hitting the door with such a thud, I thought either her hand or the door would be broken by the force.

Her legs jumped up and down a few times, then collapsed underneath her as the electric arcs flashed. I was mesmerised. The fizzing soundtrack was hypnotic, but I quickly came to my senses. If I failed to take my hand off the button, she would be dead.

I was tempted I can tell you, but I could not do it. She had used me and betrayed me in every way possible, but I could not kill her. I still loved her. When she passed out, I took my finger off the activator.

She lay on her right side her arms crossed, the left arm lying on top of the right that stretched out as if trying to reach the gun. I plunged the Epi-pen into her upper arm with a savagery that was really not necessary. Her left arm would ache for a few days after, or so I hoped. I had not been a vengeful person up until that point.

Picking up the gun, I examined it; the safety was off, so that was my first concern. We were lucky it had not gone off. It might have taken Kate out of the game if it had accidently fired when it fell. I flicked the safety catch back on before taking a look.

The gun was a Glock G43 pistol, designed to be slim for concealment purposes. It was heavy, a lot heavier than I imagined. It was a beautiful looking weapon, ideal for a woman like Adel. It was a great weapon for defending yourself from anyone and an amazing tool for an assassin. It was discreet and deadly.

Having checked that I had actually put the safety catch on, pressed the magazine release and tossed the magazine into my bag, I checked the chamber for any bullet lurking there. It was empty; she was confident in surprising me and taking me out. She really did have a low opinion of me or perhaps a high opinion of the power she had over men. She had not bothered to put a round in the chamber.

Now was not the time to ask questions. Normally, an assassin holds a bullet in the chamber so that they can fire immediately without having to cock the weapon before pulling the trigger.

The only drawback was that if the safety catch was inadvertently flicked off, you could shoot yourself by mistake. Major Thom had briefed me, showed me similar weapons, and taught me how to handle a gun.

In preparation for this part of the operation, Thom was insistent that we went through all the scenarios and rehearsed the performance repeatedly. We used an old television studio in Wandsworth near the brewery development that had been halted in 2019 due to the property recession.

Over three days, we rehearsed with actors who were almost doubles of Adel and Kate in build and height. I had deliberately contacted Kate and I had known she would bring Adel to her cosy cottage.

Kate had no parents living with her, I had been informed; it was a decoy, designed to allow Kate the ability to have an alibi or a reason to be home. She could keep people at a distance, too.

Adel's spy in the village had to have a convincing cover. If she was caught where she should not be, her mother or father had sent her to fetch something.

If she had someone poking around, they were warned off by the prospect of being chased away by her father and his trusty rusty shotgun.

I was to disarm and knock out both of them. They were aware that Adel might use a knife and they were unsure whether Kate had any violent tendencies. We had rehearsed all possibilities: violent Kate; expressively amorous Kate; and armed with a kitchen knife Kate.

Then, we had rehearsed part two: silent assassin Adel; guns blazing Adel; knife-wielding Adel. I had been trained to survive all scenarios. I was sure that they had not really expected me to survive but they were so desperate to keep their friend Terry on the throne at Poseidon Bay that they would have tried anything.

The gun went in the bag. Heaving the bag on to my shoulder, I took one last look at my sleeping beauties, before I left. I shut the door carefully. I did not want to arouse suspicion if I could avoid doing so.

After four hours, search parties would be sent out for Adel and I did not want to make it obvious that they were there. I had been instructed to leave the cottage very much as I had found it and to get rid of the car as soon as it was humanly possible to do.

The Maserati was waiting patiently outside; it was turned towards the sea where I could have ended up after my reunion with Adel and Kate. I shuddered at the thought or perhaps it was the cold wind that whipped off the sea that day, I was not sure.

Putting my bag on the back seat, I closed the back door and hopped into the front seat. I was immediately hit by the heady scent of Adel's perfume that seeped out of the leather and filled me with a feeling of loss and regret.

I loved the smell of Illuminum White Gardenia Petals.

I shook the thoughts from my mind, determined to see justice done. The key was in the ignition this time, so I pushed the start button and the Maserati fired up with a roar.

I was looking forward to driving the Maserati as much as I was looking forward to seeing Freddie again. The car was a beacon, saying: 'come and get me'. I turned on the radio to pick up local reports of traffic and the gossip from the local radio station. It was easier to drive than the first time, it was more familiar, and I knew about the rocket-like acceleration and the stop-on-a-sixpence brake.

I pushed the accelerator gently to reverse the monster away from the cottage in an arc. The power steering whined as I threaded the steering wheel through my grip. My hands were clammy, but I was impressed with the turning circle of such a large car; a little more acceleration and the whining stopped.

I braked sharply and the tyres skidded on the gravel or sounded like they did. The crunch seemed louder than it was.

Turning the wheel up the hill I eased my foot off the brake and on to the accelerator. It was only then that I realised that I had been really shaken by taking on Adel and Kate. That annoying rivulet of sweat trickled down my flank again. Major Thom had neglected to provide me with a gadget to stop that. I knew Lawless could cure my cold sweats, permanently.

I checked my watch against the clock on the dashboard when I stopped at the junction with the lane and the main road. It was eleven fourteen; I had been told that I had eight hours before the serum wore off and everyone in the county would be looking for me.

Major Thom had told me about the price on my head.

The collar of my white shirt seemed tighter, the black suit and black tie were suitably funereal. Major Thom had bought me a brand-new pair of Loake's Archway, a toecap Oxford shoe in black calf leather with a rubber and studded sole. They felt tight but they were my size. I preferred leather soles, but these had better grip, which would help when I had to drag Freddie's body out of its tomb.

The Lawless mausoleum was the only piece of property that was not guarded. They thought that no one would stoop as low as robbing a grave.

The trade in body parts was still brisk but live organs fetched a good price and there were plenty of people living in doorways to supply the trade. Freddie had died and been laid out in state on a table in an old Methodist chapel that had been established and built in 1784, the year of John Wesley's death.

Cornwall had been a Methodist stronghold back then. These days it was a stronghold for smugglers, drug dealers, thieves and people who would barter their own granny for food, God-fearing to godless in just a few generations.

That was progress.

It had been a chapel until the smugglers took over in 2020. It seemed a fitting and quiet place to allow the villagers to pay their respects to a young man they had known as part of their village community. I wondered how the landlord had managed his Saturday night gig without a bass guitarist.

From the chapel, Freddie's body had been taken in procession to the mausoleum. The mausoleum was not Lawless's originally. An old, titled family, the Mohune family, had owned it. A huge piece of white marble from a quarry in Italy and three days' work by two stonemasons and the job was done.

The Mohune name was expunged and the Lawless name was etched in letters thirty centimetres high.

The crypt stood next to the church of Saint Luke's adjacent to the village green. There was a house on the other side of the green, but it belonged to a merchant sea captain so Major Thom thought I should be able to get in and out unnoticed.

I had been shown a model of the village including the route I should take into the mausoleum and two possible escape routes if things went wrong.

Driving the Maserati to the rendezvous, I wondered if the serum really would ensure Adel and Kate were unable to raise the alarm for a whole eight hours. Within half an hour of knocking them both out, I had arrived at the pickup point where I was going to switch vehicles.

I had argued that if they could arrange for me to pick up the black Ford Transit van, they could have arranged for me to have someone ride shotgun with me. They made up excuses about manpower and the possibility of being caught if there were too many players on the field.

I thought they were talking nonsense, but I was not the intelligence expert, was I? I could have done with more company. That was for sure. I felt vulnerable enough taking on Adel and Kate and driving off in the car.

Stage two of the operation was even more daunting. The thought of driving the van to the mausoleum, collecting Freddie and making it to the rendezvous with the helicopter filled me with dread.

Parking the Maserati, as instructed, next to the wood where the van was parked, I turned off the engine, snipped the wires that connected the transponder and tossed the device into the ferns among the trees. I stood and took a breath; my left leg was trembling. I could feel my heart racing in the silence. My senses were heightened due the adrenaline and Benzedrine in my system: colours seemed more intense, the grass looked greener, the trunks of the silver birches seemed greyer and their browning leaves more khaki.

The Transit looked like the type of vehicle you would transport a corpse from hospital to the coroner's laboratory. The passenger door was unlocked, and the key was sandwiched between the passenger sun visor and the roof of the cab. There was a metal wall between the cabin and the loading platform.

I was relieved – it might limit the stink from Freddie's corpse. He wasn't very fresh though they had told me the saltwater would help to preserve his body. It had been six weeks since his demise, long enough for the maggots to go to work.

The van started first time. I slipped the gear lever into first. I had been driving this same van around a go cart track near Tolworth roundabout for three hours for three days to get used to its handling at speed and in corners particularly.

My instructor Kate Hatch had taught bus drivers, mini-bus drivers and the police. She had encouraged me to use all three mirrors every few seconds, very handy for checking if you are being followed.

She also taught me to work my way quickly through the gears. On the course, I learnt to power-slide, take corners at speed and race through bends, I could drive the Transit like a racing car. She was a great driver and a great instructor; she had to be, there was no margin for error. If I crashed, the whole operation would be compromised, and I would be doubly dead.

The engine had been modified, souped-up by their engineering department. It had been adapted to run on LPG, liquid petroleum gas, which had become the preferred fuel since fracking had taken off in the old mining areas up north. The brakes had been upgraded to match the increased power and the suspension had been firmed up.

All I needed was my racing driver helmet and dark sunglasses and I was ready to go. They sat waiting for me on the passenger seat.

'Clunk-click, every trip,' I mouthed.

The government had tightened up on the seatbelt law and revived an old slogan from the 'Post-Space-Age Dark Age' that was the 1970s.

Those were the years of unrest where strikes had torn the country apart and there only seemed to have been one positive result, a catchy life-saving public announcement. The years when fuel and food prices soared, the years when the poor get poorer, in short, the years before we joined the Common Market and were saved from economic ruin.

Since the legalisation of cannabis, the death rate on the road had quadrupled, people stoned out of their heads driving around, not caring what or who they hit. Most were too out of it to put their seat belts on, so when they did crash into a wall or knock a pedestrian flying, they normally went through the windscreen as well.

There was a public outcry, not at the idiots who drove when spaced out but over them not wearing seat belts and injuring themselves. As a result, we got a full media campaign, scarred faces on posters all over the place and on all our screens. Alongside that, they sent Instagram or Snapchat or WhatsApp messages and tweets saying: 'Clunk-click, every trip'.

I put on the motorcycle helmet and dark glasses before fastening my seat belt. Since I had last driven it, they had added a leather cover to the steering wheel, a nice touch, courtesy of Major Thom, no doubt. For her, the finer things in life mattered. My shoes still pinched but they were shiny and new so I could handle that for a few hours.

Easing out of the forest clearing, I turned on the radio as I passed the abandoned Maserati and hoped Lawless's men spent several fruitless hours looking for Adel in the forest.

The cutting of the wires on the transponder was designed to pique their interest. Their best fix would be where I picked up the van but when they found the transponder ripped out, they would be compelled to search the forest assuming she had escaped on foot. My van had been parked in a tarmac layby, there would be no tell-tale tyre tracks left by me.

That was the plan. While Lawless's men were distracted, trying to find Adel, I could slip away with the body.

Turning on to the main road, I worked my way through the six-speed gearbox and sped towards the family crypt.

Behind the front seats, Major Thom's engineers had housed the LPG cylinder and a reserve petrol tank in case I had to switch over to unleaded at any time. I should be safe once I was out of Poseidon Bay, but I still had enough fuel to drive up to London. Behind the cylinder was the wooden wall, a ply board barrier between living bodies and dead ones.

Attached to the steel floor on the cargo side was the winch that I would use to lift Freddie's remains from the mausoleum. That was what I liked about Thom, attention to detail: metal on his side, varnished wood like a sailboat on my side.

My hands were dry now, the trickle had disappeared; it was just my machine and I making our way along the winding roads and I concentrated on eating up the miles to take me to my destination. We were racing against the clock and I could almost feel its tick-tock.

I watched the rev counter move towards red, the speedometer needle rise towards twelve o'clock, sixty miles an hour, before braking slightly into the right-hand bend and accelerating on the curve. I hit seventy before tapping the brake and lining the van up for a left-hand bend.

The roads of Cornwall snake through the countryside like an old meandering river. I was really enjoying myself. I was going too fast to spot the road signs, but my handy satellite navigation voice had been adapted to give me a countdown. I was thirty miles and half an hour away, more or less.

There were few cars on the road that day, not along my stretch, at least.

A solitary red Nissan Micra driven by a white-haired old lady passed me coming the other way along one of the straights, but she had seen enough delivery vans tearing along the lanes in her time to ignore mine. She must have had some reason to complete her journey. Even though we were exporting huge volumes of LPG from the North Sea, domestic supply of liquid petroleum gas was still scarce and expensive.

I had only received an ample amount due to the fact that I was deemed to have been on government business.

Eventually, I landed up on the outskirts of the village and that was where my driving technique became more measured. I slowed down to the legal limit. Adjusting my speed to match the prevailing speed limit shown on the signs was difficult for someone who had been trained for three days to push the vehicle to its limits.

Haring through the countryside against the clock was necessary to ensure I had ample time to escape and I enjoyed it. Pootling along at thirty or twenty made me feel uneasy.

I was surely wasting valuable time.

However, this was the stealth part of the operation where discretion and subtlety were required. I did not want to draw attention to myself.

As I neared the family crypt, the enormity of my enterprise hit me. There was no turning back. I parked the van in a lane between the church and the mausoleum; it was warm in the van simply because I had the heating on.

I stepped out and shivered.

There was a chill wind blowing off the sea and it felt to me as if someone had 'walked over my grave'. The irony of the expression was not lost on me.

After all, I was resurrecting Freddie.

It was freezing but what do you expect with all the icecaps melting in the North Pole.

In my rush to get going, I hadn't noticed but now I realised what flimsy protection my suit jacket was against the elements. Tiptoeing around to the back of the van for some unknown reason, I opened the double doors as quietly as I could. I was on tenterhooks.

I have yet to encounter a van old or new that does not have creaking doors.

It was like walking into a haunted house and the hairs on my arms stood on end, shocked to attention by the gruesome ghoulish task I had been given.

Stepping into the van a few paces, I unclipped the trolley from its harnesses. There were three orange nylon straps: one held the stretcher to the back wall of the van, the other two kept the trolley from moving left or right. They were clipped on by zinc-plated climbers' clips; quick release, snap-hook carabiners, Major Thom called them.

The trolley or stretcher was the one I had rehearsed with. It had six wheels so I could roll it to the lip of the exit and raise the head of it, so it sat on the middle set of tyres, allowing me to lower the foot on to the ground. It was easy as pie to lower the stretcher from the back, you could do it with one hand, but I used two just to be on the safe side.

I rolled the trolley beyond the doors and fixed the footbrake before returning and closing the doors firmly but quietly. I had been taught to work quickly and quietly in order to minimise the disturbance and draw as little attention to myself as possible. I avoided looking furtive. Respectful and purposeful were the two impressions that I was trying to make, giving off the air of an apprentice to a funeral director competent and confidant.

I pushed the trolley along the road towards the mausoleum and that was when I saw him. At first, I thought it was Terence Lawless visiting his son – expensive brown leather shoes, probably Church's, an expensive camel coat and thick woollen, superior quality charcoal grey suit trousers.

He eyed my sober suit, took in the black tie, looked me straight in the eye and smiled. Clearly, he was inviting me to speak, to justify my presence. I declined his invitation. Instead, I smiled back and continued the journey from van to crypt.

'Excuse me,' he exclaimed, as I continued on my path. There were few places I could be going, the mausoleum or the village green.

'Good morning, can I help?'

'I hope so,' he announced. 'Where are you off to?'

'The crypt, of course, why do you want to know?'

'And you are?'

'Bill and you are?'

'Doctor Richard Reagan, Mr. Lawless's G.P.'

'Bill Sikes pleased to meet you. Reagan that's an Irish name isn't it?'

'Doctors avoided the deportations.'

'No, it's not that! You don't have an Irish accent.'

'Sorry not to pander to your racial stereotyping, should I be carrying a glass of Guinness?'

'Just remarking, you must have been Frederick's doctor.'

'Yes, indeed I was. Very elegant shoes you're wearing.'

'A gift from a kindly uncle, I need smart footwear for this line of work.'

'Generous uncle,' he remarked. He was observant and the sight of a man wearing a poor man's suit and rich man's shoes clearly disturbed him.

'Meaning?' I asked, all innocent.

Although my mind was racing, I tried to seem calm. I wondered how I was going to get rid of this nosy parker. He was slowing down the whole operation.

'Just remarking.'

'I must get on.'

'With what?' he asked, no longer bothering to hide his suspicion.

'I've come to take Frederick Lawless to be properly embalmed.'

'Really? Terry didn't mention it to me,' he observed archly; he was getting more and more curious.

'I'm working on the orders of Abel.'

Thom thought of that one – genius, it made the whole thing more plausible, a slightly miscommunicated name given to a surly subordinate who did not check the spelling over the phone.

'You mean Adel.'

'That's the one. '

'Do you mind if I phone her to confirm?'

'Go ahead. I've got the papers with me.'

'I'd prefer to call; paperwork can be forged. Haven't you heard about the recent scandal surrounding all the forged cannabis prescriptions? It's been all over the news.'

'Just doing my job.'

'In very expensive shoes? Really? Besides, the embalming process should have started weeks ago,' he complained self-righteously.

'You know how it is these days. Besides,' I deliberately copied his tone and vocabulary, 'who would mess with Mr. Lawless, he's well-known for his ferocity, isn't he?'

'He doesn't suffer fools gladly and has to be firm these days.'

'You call Abel and she'll sort it out.'

'I will, thank you.'

We were standing outside the mausoleum, the words 'LAWLESS' almost a foot high persuaded me we were in the right place.

Doctor Reagan began to ring Lawless's secretary, taking his eyes from me as he tapped his phone to bring up the contact details. I pretended to fish around for the paperwork, but I was in fact groping in my inside pocket for a quick way to get the Taser out.

I know that Irish people are famed for their music and their dancing, as well as their sense of humour, but this was really funny. As he scrolled through his address book and was about to press the call button, I took the Taser out and pulled the trigger. I watched with mounting satisfaction as the know-it-all succumbed.

The dear doctor looked as if he were doing a drunken audition for River Dance, his feet crossed and uncrossed and he jigged about before slumping to the ground in a heap. I looked to see if anyone was in sight. Surrounding the oblong mausoleum was a three-foot-high brick wall; a double gate led into the small grass apron around the building.

Opening the gate and dragging him behind the wall, I looked at my watch. The interlude had cost me five minutes when every second counted. Fortunately, he was wearing lace-ups and his shoes were not pulled off, but I was fed up with him and yanked him under the arms, manhandling him roughly and dumping him behind the wall.

Afterwards, I looked up. There was no one around. I left the doctor on the ground. From my pocket, I took my third Epi-pen, jabbed it into his wrist where his shirt cuff had ridden up and pressed the button on the top.

I knew that he would not be discovered until later that evening at the earliest. Lawless did not strike me as a man who might give up a chance to make money in order to pay a visit to his son's final resting place.

According to our intelligence, he would visit on a Sunday, if at all. I guessed he was a creature of habit not prone to sudden sentimental acts.

I simply could not afford to meet many more friends of the family. I was down to my last two tranquiliser Epi-pens, so I took the trolley for a spin to the Mausoleum doors.

The doors were locked but I had a skeleton key. The housing was a black rectangular lock and a metal door strike. It was just like opening a front door, only heavier and this lock looked like the one that you might see in a castle. The key slipped into the keyway as smoothly as a silk shirt slipping off a silk sheet.

My key was black, like the original, I presumed. It had an oval bow that fitted four of my fingers inside. The shank was about eight centimetres long, the collar, throating and pin were plain, but the key wards and bit were indented with square patterns.

A twist anti-clockwise, that I had rehearsed so many times in London, yielded the desired result, a satisfying click of the deadbolt sliding out of the lock. I pushed and the right-hand-side of double-door opened inwards. On the inside of the left-hand door, a bolt had been thrust into the stonework.

A flick and a tug and that barrier unlocked. I was pleased that everything had worked so smoothly so far.

The door creaked on its hinges. I had not rehearsed that.

Military Intelligence had provided doors with well-oiled hinges and rising butts that cleared the concrete floor. This second door was more reluctant than the first. It scraped over the stonework, the wood complaining loudly, sending me into panic.

The sound of wood snagging on stone is disturbing enough. In my situation it made my heart freeze in terror. I would definitely be caught if I made too much noise and sure enough, I was well on my way.

I was meant to be discreet; noises echoing around the crypt might be heard in a house across the green. Then, 'the game would be up', as they say.

I gently moved the stubborn obstacle but only far enough to allow me to get the trolley through the gap unhindered. All sorts of debris and leaves had gathered around the doorway in such a short time. Where all the detritus had come from, I could not tell, centuries of not having a cleaner had not helped my task.

There was a smell of dust, dry leaves and stale air. It was dark and as dry as a coal cellar, the only light came from the door and I was genuinely scared of the dark shadows beyond. My skin crawled. It was spooky there. I felt small and vulnerable and alone.

Freddie's coffin was the only one in the crypt. The daylight from the doorway was sufficient to show me that there was a shelf below where coffins had been stored from the time when the other family, the Mohune gang, had owned the crypt, but their coffins had been removed, leaving dark patches on the light stone.

They must have been removed recently as there was only a thin layer of dust on the shelves. I inspected it with my gloved finger, leaving a stripe in the dust. I was fascinated by the place.

Perhaps my fixation was based around keeping calm; it stopped me from rushing out of there screaming at the top of my lungs. Remain calm and methodical, take in the situation; those were my strict instructions.

Thom knew best. I trusted her. She had saved my life.

Maybe the other coffins had been removed to allow Freddie to have centre stage in the crypt. I was not about to have a philosophical debate about the ethics of their removal, not with the clock ticking and the imminent danger of being discovered. The coffin was at waist height, so it just meant adjusting the trolley slightly and sliding the coffin across.

It was very straightforward in theory. Freddie's coffin was English oak – only the best would do for a Lawless – so it was heavy and difficult to move even when empty. Freddie was a dead weight; ninety kilos I would have thought with all the weightlifting he had done at his gym. When I had last seen him, he was lean and muscular. He had the toned body of a gym bunny and that meant he would make my task more difficult.

I knew things were going too smoothly, there had to be a catch, and this was it. The stone would not give up the coffin without a fight.

Again, I was too weak to help Freddie out. I would have to use the electric winch. It would be noisy but there was no way I would be able to drag that oak coffin over the stone shelf on my own. Four pallbearers sliding the box in had been a tricky enough operation, I imagined; the space was too tight for me to get a purchase.

The winch was at the opposite end of the trolley to Freddie's feet, so I had to walk the two metres back to the head of the bed and unfurl the two steel wires, dragging the hooks to the coffin as the wire unfurled like fishing line on a rod.

There was no point in looking outside; if I was caught, now, the game was up. I put the Taser down to attach the winch but, apart from that, I kept it in my hand, just in case I should need to give anyone else dancing lessons for interfering. I attached the hooks to the handles, hearing the clunks as I did so.

The 'boffins' in London said the winch was the quietest electric motor yet devised and it was almost silent. Almost, like that word, not quite. It was not quite silent enough.

The buzz echoed around a room that had the acoustics of an empty cellar of an old mansion.

To my ears it seemed excruciatingly loud. The noise bounced off all the walls and was amplified by the cavernous space – the winch was whining like a banshee. It sounded as if someone was in great pain. It sounded as if Freddie were haunting his own crypt. It sounded as if I was going to get caught.

I might have got away with it but for the sound that the steel cable made on the winch as it hauled the coffin laboriously on to the trolley. It was like watching a slow-motion movie. Added to the whining was a whirring that hummed along.

I might have got away with it if the coffin had not been so heavy and scraped along the stone; it was like a shovel being dragged across a pavement.

I might have got away with it if all these sounds had not mixed and mingled like voices at a party, getting louder and louder all the time.

I might have got away with it if no one had been close enough to hear. Okay, the rich might not work but this was the hunting season, and it was lunchtime. They all should have been occupied with eating at expensive restaurants or Pilates or Ashtanga Yoga classes or charging after foxes or shooting birds and rabbits.

The cacophony of sound – humming, whirring and scraping – was amplified by the echo chamber that this discordant orchestra was playing in. All my hard work was about to be spoilt; the whole village would be out, wondering what was going on. All the meticulous planning, the success of duping Kate, trapping Adel, knocking them both out, getting to the van undetected and getting rid of the doctor were about to be spoilt.

After three excruciating minutes that might as well have been ten times as long considering the damage it did to my nerves, the coffin was securely mounted on the trolley. I placed my Taser on the lid and pushed the trolley along the dusty floor of the tomb, wheeling the coffin out through the tiny gap into the light of the day.

That was when I saw him. I realised where my Taser was and quickly stuffed it in my pocket. I raced to the gate at the entrance to the apron; he hurried to cut me off from the van. I was aware that the doctor was lying on my side of the wall and if this stranger noticed the body on the ground, I would be in serious trouble.

He was equally aware that if I got the coffin in the van and got into the cab before he arrived, I would get away. We were on a collision course, our paths were converging; at the rate we were going, we would meet just on the other side of the mausoleum perimeter wall and just behind the van.

As he approached at speed, I noticed a brown trilby pulled over grey hair and suspicious penetrating eyes staring unblinkingly at me.

He wore the age-old uniform of a country squire: green Harris Tweed jacket, burgundy cashmere sweater and a white and grey checked Viyella open-necked shirt, grey worsted wool trousers and green Hunter wellingtons. He even had a walking stick, a bark ash crook, which I felt sure he would bludgeon me with if I gave the wrong answers to him.

'What's all the racket,' he demanded without breaking his stride.

He was close enough for me to notice the colour of those gazing eyes.

They were blue; he was a real old Anglo-Saxon, British way back to 999 ADS, I reckoned. I waited for him to blink. Then, I had an idea.

'Works on the crypt, Abel's orders, we've got to take the coffin out while the damp's sorted out.'

'It's a crypt and it's Adel; have you got any paperwork?'

'Of course,' I replied, my voice flat, professional, dignified and respectful like anyone who worked in the funereal business.

I took out the forged letter on fake Lawless notepaper and handed it to the man.

'I'm Bill Sikes,' I offered, giving him the opportunity to be polite back; he did not bother.

He just grunted as he scanned the letter instructing me to remove the coffin and take it to the dockside office. I could see his eyes narrow; he was looking for anything suspicious, but I knew the boffins would have made sure the minutiae were correct. They could forge documentation in their sleep.

I hated my pseudonym, so clearly lifted from *Oliver Twist*; the section in charge of identity had no clue about subterfuge and, clearly, did not have a well-read individual in their team. I would have thought they would have seen the film, but I suppose they were too busy being boffins and inventing stuff to know about the real world.

What surprised me was that this other nosy parker obviously did not know the name either or did not choose to comment on it. Perhaps Sikes was a common name in those parts; Dickens would have had to have got it from somewhere, but I was thinking Broadstairs not Bodmin. Maybe the boffins were not as mad as I had at first thought.

'That all seems in order, carry on,' he barked like a major, which he most probably was, without too much stretch of the imagination. 'I'll tell the others not to worry.'

'Would you mind opening the doors of the van, please?' I asked.

He sighed and complied.

The van doors creaked open. I was an expert in handling the trolley into the back of the truck. Major Thom had made me practise repeatedly against the clock. I had to keep doing it again and again until I got it right in one smooth fluid movement.

I put the brake on the trolley, locked the forward wheels in place in the runners on the floor of the flatbed and pushed. The front of the trolley rose up. I had to make sure I was behind the coffin, so it did not slide off the back.

Then I pushed; the middle wheels locked into the runners; I tipped up my side and the trolley slid all the way home along the track to the end of the runner. The handle of the trolley worked as a brake to the rest of the wheels. I snapped it down and six bars slipped down and forced rubber chocks in place against the wheels.

My second inquisition was over; he was impressed; he made an about-turn and literally marched off towards the houses on the green. You can tell a military man by his gait, he had most probably come out of the army, made a fortune in the city and bought his way into the English gentry.

There were a lot of those about.

We knew about them because they generally shot those poor people who tried to burgle their houses. Manufacturers of shotgun shells saw their shares triple post-Brexit.

Closing the back doors, I walked around to the driver's door and jumped into the cab. Keep calm, I soothed. I willed myself to maintain my composure and carry on as a funeral director might. I started the engine and drove slowly out of the village the way I had come in.

As I drove on to the main road, I saw the Maserati Quattroporte coming towards me at great speed.

I was about to brake and take the gun from the glove box when I realised that it would compound my problems; as far as I was aware, no one had seen the van. No one knew about it except for my most recent inquisitor and he would have only joined the group a few minutes before. There was no way Lawless could react so quickly.

I decided to see if I could recognise the driver. The mausoleum could have been the driver's target, but it was more likely that whoever was driving was heading past the village and taking the car to Lawless for a reward.

The driver turned out to be Major Thom and she drove straight past me without waving, without flashing her lights and without taking her foot off the accelerator.

Chapter Eight

Deliverance or Downfall?

Driving on to the agreed rendezvous, I put on the radio to listen to the pirate radio station.

'Breaking news. Jamaican Joe has landed some superb food for everyone; Totnes marketplace is the place to go. Mention us and you'll get some free Rizla papers.'

'The news headlines follow; profits from fracking in Lancashire have resulted in the county being the first to pay off its county-debt and after deporting those of Scottish ancestry, they can now declare full employment.'

I let the newsreaders drone on and on, listing events and milestones from around the forty-eight counties of England.

There was never any news from abroad.

Most importantly for me, they did not mention my raid on the mausoleum. It could have been a good sign: no one had discovered the trail that I left behind, or it could have been a bad sign – Lawless knew and the net was closing, and they did not want to tip me off. Once I had processed the shock of seeing Major Thom, I went into flight mode, fight or flight, adrenaline coursed through my body. I started to push the van into corners at greater speed.

Major Thom had thought of everything including making me practise with a weighted coffin. I do not recommend it, but you should try driving a van empty, light and nimble and compare that with one loaded with one hundred and ninety-five kilogrammes of weight even if it has four-wheel drive and stiffened suspension.

Such a small difference in weight affects acceleration and braking.

From gunning the van through curves at speed just on the edge of a skid and braking as surefootedly as a horse refusing a jump, I had to adjust my driving. The van laboured through the gears, I had to rev the engine harder and the brakes were like blancmange even though they had been enhanced. The sheer force needed to brake had to be tempered by not allowing the coffin to break free from its moorings.

Despite this, I clipped past the unclipped hedges. Branches scraped the van like someone dragging their fingernails over a board. I knew where I was heading: the Royal Marine Commando base at Lympstone. The only problem was that the whole area outside the perimeter fence of the naval base was controlled by Lawless. The troops were effectively surrounded, but they still had access to the sea and the protection of the Royal Navy. No one had yet dared down a military helicopter, so they had effective communication, just not by road.

They could use the road if they chose to, but nothing would stop Lawless putting up a roadblock or arranging an 'accident' in order to slow up their progress. His son would be leaving by helicopter at a camping and training centre on the B3387 just to the north-west of Newton Abbot. I just had to get there.

I was using the driving techniques drummed into me by my driving instructor, looking at my side mirrors at every bend, ostensibly to check the line of my cornering and make adjustment on any following corner of the same camber, maybe adjusting my road speed or accelerating earlier or later on the bend.

Kate Hatch had been an amazing teacher, so much so that she had made me better than ever. She had gone over everything to ensure I was the best that I could be. I was becoming impressed by my driving skills, but I was not blind to what was going on behind me.

A matt black Land Rover Discovery Sport was suddenly taking up the clear space in each wing mirror. At first, I was relieved; Major Thom had promised an escort through the byroads. Then I wondered why they were not calling me on the phone, which had been fitted to the van. These military types seemed to be overly polite and would always announce their arrival.

Such behaviour limited friendly fire and yet it seemed rude in the extreme not only to be following me so impolitely closely but also to fail to introduce themselves.

My hackles were up, and I knew that any minute now, I would feel that trickle of sweat roll down my flank. When they attempted to overtake on a bend, I definitely decided that these were not the highly disciplined and highly trained troops I had hoped for.

Perhaps, if they were not my deliverance, they had to be my downfall.

I had seen similar vehicles at Lawless's docks. I only saw the grille at first, and had a vague notion of the colour, but on closer inspection they were painted in matt black paint for a reason; it was harder for searchlights to pick out in the dark – glossy or metallic paint shines like diamonds in arc light beams.

At the harbour, I had noticed a reinforced steel joist on the front where the bumper should have been; they too had been painted black, disguising their brutal strength.

I could only see the Land Rover's sidelights in my mirror without shifting in my seat, which I was not prepared to do on such twisty roads. I knew I could not outrun my pursuers, but I might be able to outdrive them. If I could only concentrate on driving effectively into and out of every bend, then I might avoid being overtaken.

I focused wholeheartedly on the task in hand. I set the van up for each bend. The tyres squealed. The body of the van rolled. I fought the wheel. Each of the bends offered a different curve, a slightly different camber to the road and needed a different approach. My brow glistened with cold sweat; that trickle from my underarm broke out in a vengeance and started its journey down my flank.

Five bends in, lining up for the sixth and I was beginning to think that I might enjoy this after all. I almost forgot about the four-by-four breathing down my neck.

I almost forgot that my engine was three times smaller than theirs, almost forgot about the reinforced steel joist below the grille.

When the RSJ made contact with the back of my van, there was such a bang that I jumped out of my skin. I could suddenly feel my heart beating, nineteen to the dozen. If it had been racing before, it now started to sprint. The shock was incredible. It was so unexpected. Forcing me off the road on a bend seemed madness.

The effect on the van was worse, much worse. My steering faltered; the impact smashed the back of the van. The van slewed out, the rear wheels fishtailing as if I had gone into a skid and there was another bend looming.

Trained and trained again, I took my feet away from the pedals and I wrestled with the steering wheel. Steering into the skid, I managed to keep the van on the road. The back end skidded back into place again and I had control. For a full forty seconds, I had control.

I was hit again.

My feet came off all the pedals again. It was like being a billiard ball hit by a cue. I was snookered. The van spun around and around, like a dizzy merry-go-round. Six, seven times, I spun, my neck straining against the centrifugal force. I gripped hold of the steering wheel, hanging on for dear life, ten to two.

When I finally stopped spinning, I was as dizzy as a giddy aunt.

I sighed with relief. I was still alive.

The impact of a moving object on a still object is ten times greater and the effect, twice as bad. They had no mercy. I was hit broadside by a moving mass of one and three-quarter tons. The driver did not brake. There was an ear-splitting thud and crunch, the air bag in the steering wheel inflated and that is all I remember because my head hit the driver's door window and I passed out.

Chapter Nine

Coffin Fit

Waking up seconds later, I heard voices. One was speaking excitedly, talking to someone whose reply was as agitated as the other. My temple throbbed and my shoulder ached, but I was all right; my clothes and hands were covered in talcum powder or whatever it is they put in an airbag to limit the burns, but I was okay.

The deflated air bag lay like a melted football in front of me, the white nylon fabric looking very let down; there was a cloud of smoke and the smell was like rotten eggs. I felt I was in some surreal Salvador Dali painting. My ears were ringing from the bang and my head felt fuzzy.

I read about it later. Air bags are actually inflated by sodium azide and potassium nitrate, which react to produce a large pulse of hot nitrogen gas. This gas inflated the bag, which literally burst out of the steering wheel as it expanded. About a second later, the bag was already deflating because it is designed with tiny holes in it. The smoke was the corn starch they put into the airbag to keep it pliable in storage.

Dazed and confused, I awaited my fate. I could try and start the van; they might shoot me. I could try and run away; they might shoot me, or I could admit defeat and wait for them to drag me from the van; the only trouble with that was, they might shoot me.

Nothing happened. The Land Rover vanished, and the men disappeared, I had heard at least three voices. The voices were angry. There had been a heated debate in a foreign language; it had to have been polish. These men were clearly Lawless's bodyguards.

They had left. Now there was silence.

I decided I would drive on to the rendezvous and find out what had happened. It was all very strange. I turned over the engine and it started first time. Dear old Henry Ford, he knew what the customer wanted, reliability. Before setting off, I stepped out to inspect the damage and as I did so I inspected the tyres. All four were safe.

Despite having a huge, crumbled side, the van could still be driven. I cranked open both windows to get rid of the pungent reagent smell and to keep me awake. Opening the back door, it looked like a rectangular block had been built into the driver's side panel. The coffin was still in place even though the guy ropes on the right-hand side of the trolley were loose.

I did not dare try to tighten them.

Returning to the van, I checked the fuel gauge and turned on the headlights. Only then did I realise what a vulnerable spot I was in, on a bend, on a country road made dim by the overhanging trees that lined the road. I moved off sharpish. Yes, there was little traffic on the road, but I only needed one car to hit me.

Everything seemed enhanced. It might have been the shock of the crash, but the engine seemed louder, the rush of the wind seemed faster – it howled around my ears. The driver's seat felt firmer underneath me and against the back, the lights seemed brighter and the road seemed more convoluted, the bends meandering more sharply. Even my speed felt faster, although a glance at the speedometer reassured me that I was still clipping along between fifty and sixty miles an hour coming out of the bends.

I was half a mile away from the rendezvous point when I heard the sound of a chopper overhead. The helicopter hove into view, a great black Chinook, looking like an ungainly grasshopper. It flew through the air towards the hill. I sped out of the bends and up the straight road of the B3387. It was the quickest part of the journey. I tore up the road at high speed.

Then I saw it. I was sure it was the same one, same matt black paintwork, and same four-man crew, armed to the teeth, same RSJ bumper on the front.

I could not see but I imagined there was some of the paintwork from my van on the reinforced steel joist and I was willing to put money on it.

They weren't interested in me. They were all watching the helicopter as it hovered above the training ground.

I braked, slowed, looked for somewhere off the road that was safe, pulling over into the entrance of a field and parking parallel to the three-bar gate. I doused my headlights, switched off the engine and waited to see what happened.

Helicopters move fast and are efficient methods of transport but when viewed from the ground they are like ponderous whales. I have often driven past planes that appear to be moving backwards but every time I see a helicopter landing or taking off, I have lost interest after the first ten minutes.

'Get on with it!' I hissed impatiently.

It was reassuring to hear my voice. I had spoken to no one for a few hours and three of the people I had spoken to earlier that day were lying in a drug-induced stupor.

Still the invisible rotors spun, still the helicopter lumbered in the sky, still they looked on.

I had no guidance, no way of getting in touch with Major Thom and by the look of the rendezvous site, no way of getting away. The only clue that the helicopter was getting nearer was the thumping of the rotor blades and the growl of its engine becoming louder and louder.

The helicopter landed. The men jumped in and the helicopter took off. I was left stranded.

I had forgotten to listen to the radio, I had been so distracted that I had blocked out the sound; I knew nothing of the latest turn of events. I had been abandoned.

Ringtones are strange things; they are either very personal or generic and ubiquitous. This one I recognised immediately. It was the 'Ride of the Valkyries' and it was the ringtone Major Thom used on her phone. The sound emanated from the glove box.

I pressed the button and let the door fall open.

Taped to the top and glowing vibrantly was the latest iPhone, which I had obviously fingerprinted on my stay in London. I tore the black tape away and pressed the answer button almost letting the phone slip from my fingertips in my eagerness.

'Change of plan, young man!'

It was Thom. The voice was like balm.

'Tell me what to do,' I replied, smiling genuinely for the first time that day.

She said she would not let me down and she had not.

Chapter Ten

In a Two and Eight

I was feeling the cold now. It was suddenly twilight; how that happened, I had no clue. The headlights of the van picked out my new rendezvous point, a deserted hard in a deserted bay off a deserted road. I parked the van where I had been instructed and looked up at the cliffs above, fully expecting the arrival of Lawless's men at any minute.

Then I heard distant roars, one coming from in front of me and the other coming from behind.

Immediately, I twisted around to the sound. The one I did not recognise was emanating from the English Channel. It was more like the sound of a plane, a turboprop, I guessed, the slow drone like a bomber in a movie. The sound from the land, I had recognised instantly, and it made my heart sing – Major Thom was coming.

The exhaust note of a Maserati Quattroporte is unmistakable. As for the sound from the sea, it could be a boat, one of Lawless's smuggling ships; one of the powerboats painted black, but this time it was hunting rather than fleeing capture. I was its quarry; only Major Thom could save me.

The first thing you notice about being alone on an autumnal night is how cold it is without cloud cover to trap any heat from the day; the second is how dark it can be. It was pitch black. Perhaps the moon would help once it rose, but it was reluctant to come out on such a bitter night. I was so cold; I got back into the van and started the engine.

It was not an ecologically or environmentally friendly thing to do, run the engine just to get the air-conditioning working but I needed warming up. It was not good for fuel consumption either. I looked at the fuel gauges: petrol quarter full, LPG half full.

I had done a lot of driving and had driven hard; it was not a surprise. I was determined not to drive the van again if I could help it. Thom could save me and leave Lawless or drive the van herself for all I cared.

The helicopter escape had needed the van; I was not sure how a coffin and two people could be evacuated successfully from a beach. The first problem was getting out to sea; the second problem was getting on to the boat; the third problem was getting past Lawless's sea patrols.

The roar of the fan in the truck, I drowned out by the radio, turning up the volume, hungry for news about the situation. Of course, I was listening to the pirate broadcast, not the BBC. There were still the banal announcements: one about food on offer at certain discount; another advertised a band's gig, which I knew Frederick would have loved to have gone to either as part of the audience or as a player in the group.

My feelings of warmth and of melancholy did not last long; the Quattroporte drove on to the hard, roaring like a bull seal. The headlights blinded me until it drew up alongside the van.

Then I saw her.

Adel was sitting next to Major Thom and she was holding her Glock in her right hand, which she held close to her chest. She could always make an entrance.

I stepped out of the heat and noise on to the concrete 'hard', into the cold wind that whistled between our two vehicles. I zipped up my jacket and listened to the sea lapping against the shale beach beyond. There was nowhere to run to and nowhere to hide.

I just had to bluff my way out if I could. All I could do was wait; I could not outrun a bullet. Fredrick's body would never be used to clear my name and Major Thom, the only person who could save me, was the prisoner of the woman who had tried to poison and drown me.

The engine died along with my hopes of survival.

The headlights were doused and all I could hear from that direction was the slow tick of cooling metal.

I tried to catch their eyes, all three of them, the two in the front and the figure in the back, but they had yet to adjust to the dark, so they peered out at me trying to focus on seeing me against the dark of the van.

Hearing a door open, I tensed.

However, it was the back door that was flung open; a furious figure slammed the door and charged towards me.

I recognised the slim legs of Kate way before I saw her angry face. It was like facing a berserker high on magic mushrooms. She was a dynamo of flailing-arms and her skinny legs were pumping like pistons as she charged towards me.

I was not sure where she would strike.

In the end, she went for a right-handed slap to my face. I blocked her arm, but her left hand came up and hit my cheek with the most stupendous crack. I thought my jaw would break and the blow sent me flying back against the van where I banged the back of my head. The van complained with a tinny thud.

'Hey, Kate, calm down!' I cried, trying to get my balance back.

'You calmed me down all right, I'll show you the bruise I got and give you a matching one,' she threatened, her arms flailing in front of her.

I held my hands up in front of me and felt the blows rain down on my arms.

'It was nothing personal.'

'Yeah, well this is,' she cried.

Pain can be calibrated; on a scale of one to ten, this was a twelve.

Before I knew it, her knee had managed to make contact with the sensitive part of my anatomy. My left gonad throbbed like the walls of a nuclear plant about to explode. I groaned, fell to my knees and rolled over. My hands, which had done nothing to fight off the unexpected blow, now cupped my crotch.

Better late than never. I do not think so.

I rolled around as Kate stood above me, watching me writhe. I felt sure she was just deciding where her next blow should fall.

'That's enough, Kate,' Adel soothed.

'I don't think so; I'm just getting started.'

'It's my turn, now,' Adel added, playfully,

A shiver ran down my spine.

Adel offered me her left hand to help me up; in her right she still held the gun. I knew in my heart of hearts that she was helping me up in order to knock me down. I gripped the hand and she pulled me to my feet though I could not stand up straight yet. I felt winded. She actually helped me to a crouching position. I could not stand up straight such was the pain. I put my hands on my knees and took great gulps of air.

'Thanks,' I gasped as I caught my breath.

'That must have hurt,' she said, laughter in her voice.

'It did,' I assured her, staring up into her eye, my heart jumping for joy despite my animosity towards her and her shenanigans.

'I think you'll live,' she replied.

'Not with you around, I won't,' I thought.

The sound of the engine out to sea brought me back to reality. The cove was filled with the drone of diesel engines. It was too loud for a boat and too low for a plane. It crossed almost four nautical miles in ten minutes. The throbbing diesel Deutz MTU engines echoed around the bay like four German World War Two bombers; it was not a silent arrival.

'Speed not discretion, perfect for our needs,' Thomasina said, her perfect white teeth flashing me a smile of reassurance.

'What is it?' I asked aghast, looking at the hulking monster whose noisy engines were clearly not designed for stealth operations.

The arrival of this strange vessel and the close proximity of Thomasina filled me with hope. I caught a whiff or Dior 'J'adore', which was a pleasant change from diesel, dust and fetid air.

'Wait and see!' she commanded. 'Get in the truck and get ready to drive into the sea.

We all looked out to sea to see. Thirty metres is about ninety foot, a double decker bus is about fifteen metres long. So, this was the length of two double decker buses, and it was fifteen metres wide. I watched as I clambered into the driver's seat, briefly looking over at Kate who had joined me in the passenger seat; she, too was watching the spectacle unfolding in front of the windscreen.

Even coming into the bay, it was a monster. With a low deck at the front and, behind that, a streamlined passenger cabin, it looked like an overgrown landing craft. On the very top of the cabin was the bridge where the pilots and navigational crew sat. Beyond that, at the very back of the boat, were two circular projections looking like an enormous pair of goggles, which housed the propellers that drove the hovercraft forward.

It skimmed over the waves despite its huge bulk. The hovercraft rose up on to the hard like a beached sea monster and cut its engines. The fans slowed and the ship rested on its skirts. A metal bow ramp lowered, and I drove the Transit up and into the steel well deck, stopping opposite the crew cabin. The pilot's cabin was above, looming over me.

I turned the engine off and leapt out into the freezing cold one more time. My mind was spinning with all I had been through. The roar of the Maserati behind me was reassuring and the sports car parked behind the Transit; its engines died as the ramp rose gradually and electronically. The whirs and whines of hydraulics and electrics were drowned by the main engine on the hovercraft, which was still running. I felt the throbbing of the diesel. Idling rhythmically like a beating heart, it belied its massive power and ability to lift and propel this hefty giant not in the sea but above the waves, floating like a magic carpet.

Then the fans of the propellers started to spin faster and faster as if there were two helicopter rotors, spinning and thrumming, more and more quickly. Almost imperceptibly, the skirts plumped up and the machine rose. skimming over the hard in the direction of the sea.

We were slipping backwards towards the cove and escape. The fans spun until they were no longer blades but a blur.

The two pilots checked the port and starboard sides, then turned the vessel around. There were bow thrusters at the front of the craft, which provided control in the yaw that allowed the large craft to manoeuvre in such a tight space. In flight, aircraft will rotate about their centre of gravity; this motion from side to side is the yaw – just so you know.

Within minutes, we were circling around and heading out to sea, the speed increasing incrementally. Before the speed rose above ten knots, we were collected from our vehicles by five unarmed Royal Marine Commandos, dressed in black night exercise fatigues; the only clue that they were RMC was the green beret they wore on their heads, standing out from their dark clothes even in the gathering gloom.

One collected me saying, 'Welcome aboard.'

'I am very relieved,' I said.

'We're not out of the woods yet, Lawless always monitors unusual activity and this little princess is a little too unusual to escape notice. Follow me.'

The other four protected the girls as they fought the wind on the well deck and made their way towards the warmth inside. The well deck was quite sheltered; if we had been elsewhere, I think we would have been blown off the boat.

As we stepped into the passenger cabin, each of us was greeted by a marine who had been allocated to us for the voyage. The other marines disappeared but the difference from them was that our new shepherds wore disruptive pattern trousers with matching jackets and they each wore a khaki webbing belt, which was complete with a holster. The butt of the weapon looked like a Browning or a Glock; it was difficult to tell, I am no expert.

They led us to a mess that was deserted.

'Thank you,' I said as a steward led us to a table where four bowls of steaming soup sat waiting for us. They were standing on place mats that depicted an English hunting scene, something from 'The Irish RM' and silver soupspoons with the Royal Marine crest engraved on them.

We had reached civilisation and they wanted us to realise it. The English did tradition so well even post-Brexit.

'Pleasure,' he replied, indicating that I should take my place.

I waited for the ladies to sit down first – old-fashioned Irish manners.

There were four silver bread knives and a tiny saucer-like bowl filled with creamy yellow butter carved into curly shavings and a wicker breadbasket overflowing with brown bread rolls. I knew instinctively that they would have just come out of the oven and their warm doughy insides would melt the butter.

'What is this machine?' Adel asked, as the marines sat down next to us, encouraging us to tuck in – I did not need to be asked twice. The senior officer, Major Lawrence Stern, explained to us that we were on one of the few remaining hovercrafts in the world.

'Fascinating,' Kate gushed like a flirtatious Jezebel. I could see she liked a man in uniform; she hung on Lawrence's every word. All the nice girls love a sailor, Kate loved marines; I was not sure what that said about her.

'They're produced by Griffon, this one is amazing – British Hovercraft Technology Series, which has a well deck and can take over twenty tonnes of cargo and over forty passengers. Of course, we've modified it for MOD use.'

'Ministry of Defence, Kate,' I added, determined to get my revenge for my sore cheek by showing her up as ignorant.

'I know that, you great M-A-K-B!'

'What? It must mean the most amazing knowledgeable brain.'

'No, morons always know best!'

'Thanks!' I muttered.

I was so incensed I could not think of a decent reply. It was I that was humiliated. The whole crew laughed, all four of them. Later, after supper, on the bridge, Kate wasted no time in flirting with the co-pilot.

'So, tell me, how come this beauty is so fast?'

'You mean the boat. When you said beauty, I thought you meant you,' he said.

'You're a sly fox. Not me. I'm not fast!' she replied, smiling and moving closer towards him, showing behaviour that was at odds with her words.

'Best to take it slow,' he agreed with her, the smooth operator.

It was so obvious what she was doing, the flirt. She had no shame.

'Tell me the technical stuff, my father's a boat builder,' she urged, almost fluttering her eyelashes at him.

'Well for a start the structural design is highly robust with an aluminium transverse rib similar to that used on the wings of aircraft, so it's light.'

'And strong like you!' she enthused. It was sick-making listening to her. 'What's it like when things get rough.'

I could not believe my ears. She suddenly wanted to know how the boat was in a storm. Please, she had no interest in the boat only in talking to sailor boy.

'We are able to operate comfortably in sea state four and wave heights up to two metres, so on a calm night like tonight we can go as fast as you like.'

'Slow and steady is good for me; I feel like I'm floating.'

Floating on a cloud of obsession more like. She was being insufferable; I felt embarrassed for her.

'That's because we have four engines on-board, two for lift and two for forward propulsion.'

'I see.'

'We progress at speeds of up to forty knots.'

'Isn't the ride a bit hard at that speed?' she asked.

'We're floating on a carpet of air, so it's barely noticeable.'

Kate smiled; a broad, cheeky grin played on her face.

'Wafted away on a magic carpet.'

Okay, we all got the point, subtlety was not her forte; she wanted to be swept off her feet by this handsome hunk.

'Something along those lines,' he conceded.

'I'd love to be wafted away myself.'

Did she really have to be so blooming obvious?

'Your wish is my command,' the smooth operator replied.

She was shameless and just trying to make me jealous.

'Just give him your number,' I whispered, seething.

I could feel my face reddening in anger. Thankfully, the cabin lights were dimmed for night sailing – or was its night flying?

'What was that?' the co-pilot asked, running his index finger along the inside collar of his white shirt.

'Just wondered what number of uses it has,' I lied unconvincingly.

'The Canadian Coast Guard used her for search and rescue and ice-breaking duties before it was sold off cheaply to the English Administration.'

'That sounds awesome,' I replied.

In reality, I was thanking him for saving my bacon and he carried on digging me out of my hole.

'There are countless roles; remember, almost fifty passengers and almost twenty tons of cargo can be carried by a boat hovering above the sea.'

'Last time I was out here, I ran out of fuel,' I complained. It was true but secretly I also wanted to stop Jezebel from planning her elopement, marriage and honeymoon. 'What's your range?'

'Safely, we can run for six hours; we took only an hour and a half to get here. It will be about three hours on the way back, roughly, though we have a good tail wind in our favour, so we have an hour and a half cushion,' he replied.

I think he was a little bit overwhelmed by 'Miss Hit-you-over-the-head-with-a-club-and-take-you-back-to- my-cave' and he was relieved to be talking to me.

Of course, I encouraged him.

'I see,' I murmured approvingly, investing as much enthusiasm as I could into my response, maintaining eye contact and nodding avidly.

'It's ninety-one miles, at thirty knots per hour, it should take us no time. You'd be lucky to get that from any surface vessel.'

'That's true,' I agreed. I was never going to let Kate back into the conversation if I could help it.

'We can push it to forty or even forty-five if we come across any of Lawless's crews,' he assured us.

I knew he was only talking to me. Kate had frightened him off and I would block any further attempts at her trying to pressgang him into matrimony.

As if on cue we burst out into the open water and the mirror surface of the sea became a little choppier. The hovercraft seemed to slow as it was battered by the waves, but I watched the pilot push the throttle forward; suddenly we were going more smoothly still.

I guessed that our comfort level must be related to increased upward thrust as well as increased speed. Even thinking that showed I had been paying attention. The boat had less draught in the water and the ride was smoother as a result.

We were all silent as the moon rose, making the black carpet of the sea glimmer like coal in candlelight. The horizon ahead of us was charcoal, the sky above was the darkest blue I had ever seen, like the blue velvet that diamonds are displayed on; so blue as to be almost black.

Looking out to sea, we all noticed two vessels approaching at speed, one from the port bow and one from starboard. They were parallel to the coast, but they were definitely heading towards us.

'Action stations,' said a voice behind me.

I had not noticed a sixth man in the bridge. He was keeping hidden. Had he been standing there in the shadows at the back or had he just stepped up to join us? I was unsure. All I knew was that he was in charge.

'Clarion-call, this is your commander's orders, action stations,' the co-pilot announced, flicking switches and talking into the mouthpiece hanging from his headset.

'Standing by,' the pilot added.

'Action stations, chaps, all crew to action stations. Confirm, action stations,' the co-pilot repeated.

The blue light inside the bridge was doused. A single red light produced a glow that immediately enhanced the lights of the instruments.

Radar swept the horizon in burnt orange concentric circles, mandarin digits revealed our trajectory, speed and height.

The sonar beeped through the speakers and showed fish on a green screen.

Another member of the crew arrived and opened a cupboard at the back of the bridge. Helmets were handed out to all those present; they were like soldiers' helmets with black cotton-cloth covers stretched over them.

Then he disappeared. I could see the red port and green starboard lights of the approaching craft. Each one had a searchlight suspended from an aluminium frame arcing off the boat mid-ships, which lit up the water in front of the craft, a circular disc of white that moved like a spectre across the sea.

The dark green ribs were distinguishable from the sea because of their matt colour and their silhouette. I wondered how we would defend ourselves against a Lawless snatch squad. We were big and bulky; they were nimble and light and deadly, I imagined. Behind them they trailed a churning white plume of wake.

The inflatable dinghies bounced across the surface and the heavily armed crew held their machineguns in front of their chests, ready to raise and fire. Speeding towards us, I looked at the commander of the vessel for some form of reaction. I wondered if he was waiting to see the whites of their eyes.

My mouth felt dry and I felt that rivulet seeping down my side yet again. It made me annoyed but not too annoyed to be frightened. Being blown out of the water at this stage would be extremely annoying; especially after all I had been through.

The boats were closing in on us; still the face of the hovercraft commander was difficult to read; he did not seem to be concerned, I could not see his eyes clearly in the glow of the red lamp, but I could see they were open and staring ahead. His right hand rested on his binoculars. He leant forward and for the first time I felt relieved that he was doing something.

Our hovercraft was less vulnerable to attack than the other craft, but a well-aimed rocket-propelled grenade would see our skirts ruined and the hovercraft would lose its lift and its speed, losing its ability to evade capture.

A few bursts of gunfire would puncture the inflatable sides and ditch the hull, the crew and vehicles into the sea with alacrity. Then we would be a sitting duck.

'Patch me into the lieutenants, please, phones,' he requested, breathing into the microphone suspended from his headset, which he wore under his helmet.

'Patching you through now, sir.'

The voice that belonged to the communications officer, in the bowels below, echoed around the bridge, his words fed through the loudspeakers.

'Echo Papa One Four to Bravo Delta Two, over.'

'Bravo Delta Two to Echo Papa One Four, receiving, over.'

'Is the red carpet spread, Bravo Delta Two? Over.'

'All mosquitoes dispersed by DEET, Echo Papa One Four, over.'

'Bravo Delta Two, come alongside the port bow, over.'

'Port bow position, understood, out.'

The radio operator tuned to the second boat, Bravo Delta Five.

'Echo Papa One Four to Bravo Delta Five, receiving, over.'

'Receiving and awaiting instructions, over.'

'Take up position starboard stern, over.'

'Starboard stern, out.'

I was the only one who did not know that these craft were our escorts across the channel. I felt my face flush and my ears burn but fortunately the red light in the bridge remained lit, so no one saw my embarrassment.

My cold sweat started to dry. Those ribs were the ultimate escort vessel; I felt safer. The others stared out to sea with their own thoughts. Thankfully, that was the last of the excitement for that night. Several patrol ships had scared off any curious craft.

Of course, if they were aware of our cargo, we would not have had such a smooth crossing. It appeared that either the disappearance of the Lawless sarcophagus had not been discovered, or if it had, its unorthodox extraction from Poseidon Bay had not been contemplated. Whatever reason, we were safe and on our way to the Channel Islands.

Relief swept over me. I had almost been caught several times that day and what really happened needed to be explained slowly and carefully to me so that I understood. I was shaken by the fight that I had with the pair at the cottage and by being almost forced off the road.

The soup had warmed me up, the roll had been enough to take the edge off my hunger but all I wanted now was something else to eat and a warm bed. As if reading my mind, the silent sailor reappeared behind me, tapped me on the shoulder and offered a small plate with sandwiches cut into triangular quarters, their crusts cut off: dainty delicacies, two ham and mustard, two cheese and pickle and two cucumber. Tucking into them, I wolfed down half of the quarters in an eighth of second.

Chewing frantically, I lined up the other three beauties, which I would savour, all a different flavour. Looking around me, everyone seemed to have a plate in hand, and they were munching away, too. All you could hear was the sound of the engines. After my cold supper, the silent sailor brought us all some piping hot Bovril in tin enamel mugs, white with a blue rim that must have been from World War Two. I hoped the meat extract inside was fresher than that.

When we arrived, we rose up the concrete hard and stopped next to a huge Hoverlloyd SRN4 Swift GH-2004, which was one of the very first hovercrafts. My parents had taken it from Dover to Boulogne with their car before the divorce.

They had grown up in an era of technology: Concorde, hovercraft, rockets to the moon, fast cars and the self-destruction of British industry by its own workers, OPEC helping the process, and putting the final nail in the coffin. High fuel prices, miners and car workers striking had ruined the economy and turned England into a nation nicknamed, 'The Sick Man of Europe'.

My parents had left Ireland, looking for better prospects and all that they had managed was a trip to the Continent on a Sealink hovercraft, which was considered progress in those days.

However, they had never stolen a body, driven a van at high speed, nor had they escaped in the moonlight on a hovercraft headed for Alderney. We hovered over the slipway, then the engine was cut, and the hovercraft settled on to its skirts.

Troops from 45 Commando frog-marched us from where we had landed, down the ramp, and into a wooden and glass structure that looked like it was a World War Two airfield control tower complete with conning tower. Only the telephone masts and an oversized golf ball that housed the early warning systems put the building in the twenty-first century.

We were greeted by the commander of the base and were all ready for bed; luckily, they understood that without being told. Immediately, a Land Rover Discovery Sport took us to our accommodation. Major Thom, Adel and Kate were in the female barrack and I was in the male barrack. We all had our own rooms: a single bed, a cupboard and a small bedside table with a lamp on the top.

Chapter Eleven

Major Thom Lays It on the Line

The next morning, it was time for the debriefing. I was woken at seven, shown the showers by my shepherd, Lance-Corporal Daly and afterwards we ate breakfast at the canteen with the other marines, sailors and soldiers.

In the briefing room, the walls were vertical tongue and groove wood panels painted cream and every metre there was a framed picture of some aircraft. I recognised a Spitfire, a Vulcan, a Lightning and a Buccaneer. My knowledge was based on the recruitment poster for the RAF and some models that my father left behind as well as 'World War Two' and 'James Bond' movies.

Major Thom was sitting at the head of a table that looked incongruous in such a setting, more befitting a cabinet meeting room. The brown sea of the top shone brightly, reflecting the circular light-emitting diode lamps that were embedded in the false ceiling.

To her left was Adel and to her right was Kate. I paused at the doorway, escorted by my shepherd. I never learnt his first name; he never offered it and I never asked.

'Thank you for looking after our guest, Lance-Corporal,' Major Thom announced, rising from her chair, 'that will be all.'

He clicked his heels together as he came to attention. She bowed her head in acknowledgment.

'Good morning,' I said, addressing my remark to Major Thom, ignoring the smiles from Adel and Kate.

My face was like stone, I wore a scowl for all of them. I was beginning to think I had been taken for a fool.

'Take my seat,' Thom offered lightly, as if sitting in a viper's nest would be what this mongoose would relish.

I had no choice but to comply. All of them, I now realised, could break my neck if they so wished. As I moved towards the hot seat, Major Thom moved down the table and fished a remote control from her top pocket. She pressed the button as I reached the seat, watching the screen come down from the ceiling at the end of the table. When I sat, she flicked off the lights and a projector above the centre of the table hummed into life.

Thom spoke clearly and slowly in order for her words to sink in; she knew I had been through a lot. Adel and Kate patted a thigh each. I felt even more like their plaything – patronising pats and set smiles. How much of a fool did they take me for? I wondered.

'You know Adel, but you won't know that she is in fact a Polish policewoman, who was inserted into Lawless's organisation by our intelligence service. They gave her a plausible back story and a new identity. You also know Kate who is in fact a member of Naval Intelligence. You know me from your extraction from Poseidon Bay on two occasions and a visit to my London home where you were persuaded to help us obtain the evidence, we need to bring Lawless down.'

I was speechless; Adel and Kate were working for Major Thom all along. I could not credit it. How could that be true; they had been so convincing.

'I'm so sorry for your involvement in this,' apologised Adel, sounding sincere. 'You were never meant to be part of this operation.'

I was speechless for the second time, struck dumb by the revelation; she was apologising for almost drowning me.

'I'm sorry, too,' Kate whispered.

She sounded as though she regretted lying to me, but I was not so sure. I was tongue-tied. She was apologising for pretending to like me. I felt that humiliating me on the hovercraft did not show much remorse as far as I was concerned even if I had instigated the fiery exchange. Perhaps she just could not help herself or perhaps I still harboured feelings for her.

'And I'm sorry, too,' Thom added. She was the only one I believed.

I found myself smiling at her despite myself.

'Thom will guide you through what happened and how you got involved in this spider's web. She will explain everything,' Adel assured me.

I waited; I had nowhere to go and nothing to do. I desperately wanted to know what was going on; Thom's explanation, the first time around, had obviously been a tissue of lies.

'Right, well, I'll start from your arrival. Just beforehand, Lawless's son Freddie had somehow got on to the fact Adel was working for us. Hence her decision to send you to Kate's shop so she could ensure you were safe.'

'I was responsible for your safe extraction,' Kate explained.

'And very successful it was, too,' Thom continued, 'Adel had to get rid of Freddie. He was about to expose her to his father. She would have been eliminated immediately; Lawless had ruthlessly exterminated traitors before now. Adel had to kill or be killed. You were never a target; you were never in danger. The two people at the beach were there to add authenticity to our story and to protect you should you have got into further trouble.'

'They certainly fooled me,' I replied.

'And provided you with protection,' Thom insisted.

'If you say so. The man did a great act of trying to prevent me leaving.'

'He was trying to stop you and reassure you, offer you advice.'

'Whatever you say,' I answered sullenly.

'Kate alerted us to your situation, and we were able to dispatch a lifeboat with thermal imaging to find you; not that it was needed as Kate had attached an electronic beacon to your boat. However, we had to send the right craft in case the beacon failed,' Thom explained.

'You think of everything,' I hissed, still seething.

I had been used and horribly abused.

I felt like a pawn in their dangerous chess game. I could be sacrificed at any time to save the queen.

'Once you were out, we had to keep up the deception that Adel and Kate were against us. If you had been caught, you might have talked.'

'I was only in danger of being caught because you had sent me back and there was no need. You had Adel and Kate in place; they could have grabbed Freddie's body.'

'We needed you to collect the body for us without bringing suspicion on to either of our operatives.'

'I was expendable.'

'Dependable,' Thom corrected me.

'Whatever you say,' I replied sulkily. The trickle of cold sweat had returned.

I was unimpressed by all their lies; there had been so much subterfuge and shenanigans, I no longer knew who or what to believe. It was clear to me that the heat had been put on me to divert it from them.

'Lawless was keeping a close eye on Kate. She was the last person to see you and you were never going to leave alive with the insult you had meted out on Freddie. You had insulted his son in front of the whole pub. Did you think he was the type of man to forgive or forget? Adel heard the conversation arranging your assassination.'

'What?' I exclaimed, standing up to leave, unable to control myself. It was preposterous.

I looked into Thom's face, her eyes told me she was telling the truth, so I collapsed back into my chair and prepared to listen to the litany of excuses.

'You would not have been the first person to be eliminated. Let me take you back to events that you were not privy to that I am sure you will forgive us for putting in motion.'

Chapter Twelve

Adel's Story - The Noose Tightens

Adel told all of us what had happened to her. The others knew most of what she told me. It had been in her report, which no doubt they had all discussed before I was ushered to the meeting room. I knew nothing, so it was for my benefit that she told the story.

She had walked into the office on Monday morning three weeks before I arrived. It was a typical day at the office, or should I say hangar. She was wearing a red tartan skirt and navy-blue stockings. She never wore tights. Her white blouse she had tucked into the thick waistband of the skirt. She looked desirable and she knew it.

She enjoyed the power her beauty brought.

Next door, Lawless was at his desk in his white shirt. He insisted on all staff wearing white shirts or blouses and, if not, they had to wear one of the colours of the Union Jack, the specific red or the same shade of blue. He knew about branding and the image he wanted to create.

He himself wore a blue designer suit, the exact colour of the Union Jack; the jacket kept him warm. It was difficult to keep a room the size of an aircraft hangar heated.

A Calor gas cylinder heater on either side of the desk heated his area. Cold wind swirled around the cavernous space. A radiator on either side of the partition wall added to the ambient heat but all it did was keep their hands from freezing. Adel was wearing a white thermal vest under her shirt and Lawless expected her to be wearing red, white and blue; cream was tolerated, as was Sapphire Gin blue and port wine red or a red tartan. Everything had to have shades of empire.

She had managed to hack into his computer a month before and she was gathering enough evidence for him to be arrested should he ever set foot outside Poseidon Bay. Her cover had given her access to Lawless's inner sanctum. She had built up a rapport with him, allowing her to avoid deportation and become a key member of his operation.

Adel arranged his security; all his guards were Polish policeman, undercover. His smuggling affected the trade of several countries. She had done well to infiltrate his organisation and control his security.

She hoped to penetrate his computer system again that week, and download the last of her evidence that she hoped would convict Lawless once he had been captured. Without it, his lawyers would have him back in business within days.

'Good morning, Mr. Lawless, I have your appointments for today. Buccaneer Barbers at ten fifteen, lunchtime meeting with Monsieur Denat at Société Surcouf bistro at twelve, midday, followed by a tour of the black boats at two; that should impress Mark.'

'Thank you, Adel. That's perfect, thank you so much for your help on this; Monsieur Denat has the best Brie in Normandy, worth its weight in gold.'

'And delicious, too,' Adel added.

'Indeed, délicieux and extremely profitable. I think he'll be impressed with the improvements in the fleet. You need to tell him we can make an extra journey every day with the new engines we have fitted. Just drop it into the conversation when I make him wait the customary twenty minutes, which is the time I waited at French customs on my last visit while they gave their own people priority. They did it even when we were part of the EU – chauvinists. Can I have the figures for the shipping from France?'

'Just Denat or all the suppliers?' she asked wondering why the pot was 'calling the kettle'; he was the most chauvinistic person she had ever encountered.

'All the suppliers, we'll hit him with how well the others are doing, pour encouragement.'

'Bien sûr.'

'I reckon we could increase trade with him by twenty per cent.'

'My projections say thirty-five.'

'That reminds me why I love having you work for me. You make me richer all the time. You can have the Maserati as your bonus this month.'

'Thank you Mr. Lawless, but you do not own it yet, the finance firm in London does. We still have eleven months left on the company lease.'

'Yeah, yeah, tax efficiency! Take the keys anyhow. I'll use the Rolls. Tell Trevor to sort it out, give you the keys. He drives it too fast. I can keep an eye on him when he's driving me around.'

'He's been your chauffeur for ten years; I've only just joined the company. Don't you think it would be better to wait until my anniversary and speak to Trevor yourself?'

'I suppose you're right but let's get you into the car. I hate seeing that old Golf in the car park. It's a vintage motor I should think by the look of it.'

'It runs on LPG and it's a GTI.'

'As you well know, all my cars run on LPG, even the Rolls. I won't touch diesel with its poisonous particles and the cost of petrol is an outrage,' he was very sensitive about his 'green credentials'.

No one knew why.

'We all know it,' she sympathised.

'Take the car; you'll be doing me a favour. It's got a bit more poke than a GTI. You deserve it. I'll iron things out with Trevor.'

'Thank you, Mr. Lawless.'

'Pleasure and that's for you.'

He indicated the parcel on the desk.

'Thank you Mr. Lawless, let me guess, another scarlet Victoria Secret's lace thong?'

'Uncanny, you have a natural gift for choosing stocks and shares as well as guessing the gifts you are given.'

'Thank you. I have no excuse not to be wearing the company colours every day.'

'It's not from me, it's from my son. You're having dinner with him, tonight, aren't you?'

'Yes, I want to pump him for information about the logistics chain.'

'Lucky him.'

'Sir?'

'Having an intelligent woman to take to dinner.'

'I enjoy spending time with him.'

'Music to my ears. If I was thirty years younger, I'd marry you myself but as things are, I would love for you both to take over the business.'

'A partnership?'

'Yes, but not business. You could marry.'

'Mr. Lawless, you are shocking.'

'No, I mean it.'

'You hardly know me and yet you want me to be your daughter-in-law.'

'Who else is there?'

'What about Kate, the sweet girl in the sports shop?'

'They tried to make a go of it, but she dumped him.'

'I shall have to pick her brains, then.'

'You just let my son charm you and disarm you. You'll see my idea is a good one.'

'Yes, Mr. Lawless, will that be all?'

'For the time being, we'll look at the diary this afternoon. I need to get to the gym.'

'Of course. Thank you for the thoughtful gift,' she exclaimed, grinning and turning to leave the room.

Lawless rose from his desk and strode over to a hat stand next to a filing cabinet. Slipping on his navy blue Harrods overcoat, he looked around the space with satisfaction, put on a brown trilby hat from Bates and walked towards a side door hidden in the skin of the building.

Pressing a button hidden in the rib of the steel frame, he waited for the door to swing open with a hydraulic gasp. Then he stepped over the lip of the doorframe to his waiting Rolls. Trevor stood with the door open, waiting. Lawless was a creature of habit. The gym was five minutes' drive away at a luxury hotel and spa further up the coast at The Poseidon Grand overlooking Whitsand Bay, which had been renamed Poseidon Bay. Of course, the hotel was owned by Lawless.

As soon as the coast was clear and the automatic door sighed to a close, Adel palmed a memory stick from her inside jacket pocket. Sitting in the warm seat, she plugged the dongle into Lawless's computer and typed in his access code.

The monitor woke up immediately and the desktop showed a myriad of files. She had navigated the screen before and opened the file she wanted, clicking on the mouse to transfer the relevant data on to her device.

The phone rang and she jumped.

'Good Morning, Lawless Enterprises,' she crooned into the receiver, which she had picked up after three rings.

'Adel, Kate here, are you in the hot seat?' the voice asked, sounding anxious.

'Yes, why?'

'Your boyfriend has just left the shop and he's coming to see you.'

'He's not my boyfriend. What's he bought me?'

'A scarlet silk bodice from the lingerie section.'

'Just like his dad, obsessed with red. I thought you were a sports shop.'

'Underwear is considered sportswear these days!'

'Thanks for the tip.'

'I chose the red – love, passion.'

'Yes, danger and blood, too!'

'He'll be there soon.'

'I'll be finished soon.'

'You'll be finished if he finds you.'

Adel heard the security door open. That was quick, she mused; he must have run down here.

'Got to go, see you later.'

'Be careful,' Kate warned.

Adel left her memory stick in Lawless's computer but grabbed the package and dashed out to her workstation just as the door opened. She sat in her seat as Freddie, fresh faced and smiling, appeared in the doorway; she picked up the phone and spoke into the receiver.

'Absoluement, Monsieur Denat. Je bois te parole!' she gushed, glancing up at Freddie, 'Merci, and au revoir.'

Replacing the receiver, she smiled at Freddie with a pained expression.

'Hi, Adel, I'm not disturbing you, am I?' he exclaimed cheerfully, walking over to her desk and sitting in the seat reserved for visitors, a green Chesterfield armchair.

If he thought, he was being a pest he was making a good impression of ignoring that fact.

'Not at all, how are you?' Adel asked casually, as if she had not a care in the world. She was stiffer than normal, ready to pounce but it was imperceptible to poor doe-eyed Freddie.

'I bought you a gift, 'he announced proudly, leaning over and putting the bag on the desk.

'How lovely, a tracksuit for my early morning run?' she suggested, looking at the sports shop logo.

'Not as such.'

'You can come running with me in the morning if you get up early enough.'

'No, thanks, I like my sleep, especially after playing a gig, and the morning after the night before is never the time for a run. I like my midday workout.'

'Each to their own.'

'So, aren't you going to open it?' he gasped.

'Well, I would but I have to prepare for a client of your father who is calling soon. Do I need to open it, now?'

'I was hoping you would wear it tonight.'

'Really?'

'Really.'

'Well, I will be delighted, then.'

'Aren't you curious?'

'That would spoil the surprise.'

'As you wish. I'll just go next door and organise tonight.'

'I'm the PA. Let me.'

'No, it's no trouble.'

'Well, you're not the only one to buy me a present today.'

'Really?'

'Really.'

'Not like my gift.'

'I don't know about your gift but the one on the table next to yours is quite intimate.'

'Who would buy you intimate gifts?' he asked.

'Who indeed.'

'You're trying to make me jealous,' he complained.

'Maybe, are you. Jealous?'

'Not really,' he lied.

He leapt up and tore at the packaging, opening the package and fishing out the thong, which he examined minutely, stretching the elastic waistband and feeling the lacy texture.

'I think you've proved I'm right,' Adel asserted, holding her hand out for its return.

'Who bought it for you?'

'Your father.'

'I see.'

'It's part of my uniform.'

'You should put it on then.'

'I'm wearing one right, now,' she confessed, standing up, 'white shirt, blue skirt, blue stockings, and red knickers. Red, white and blue.'

'Show me.'

'I thought you wanted me to put on your gift. What is it, a bikini?'

'Try it and we'll see if it fits.'

'Why not?' she acquiesced.

There was little choice.

She opened the package with trembling fingers, she told us, trembling because she had to keep him occupied so the download would complete. She was worried that Lawless would only have half an hour of exercise and only a brief sauna, in which case he might open the secret side door without her knowing. If Freddie had kept her at the desk, then Lawless might have returned and noticed the unusual memory stick and she would never know he had discovered her treachery.

That would be the end. It would be curtains for Adel. Her skulduggery would be discovered.

She carried on with her story.

'I had to think fast.'

'If you wait here, I'll go into your father's office and change.'

'Why can't you change here?'

'You need to be romantic; it would take away the mystery.'

She smiled, grabbed the bag, took her jacket from the coat stand, and then swung the door open and walked into Lawless's office. She turned at the door and put up the five fingers of her left hand. He would have to wait five minutes, which would give her enough time. The door shut with a reassuring click. She could see that the transfer of data was complete.

Deftly, she palmed the memory stick into her hand and zipped it up in the inside pocket of her blue jacket. Before she changed, she logged out. Slipping off her jacket, her blouse and struggling out of her vest, she stepped out of her navy high heels and into the camisole, pulling it up and over her shoulders. She kept her knickers and stockings on.

It was cold and her skin grew goose pimples, but she knew Freddie would not leave until he had seen her dressed to kill. She carried her blouse, jacket and skirt folded over her arm. The camisole clung to her body like a second skin. Opening the door slightly, she put a stockinged leg into the reception.

'Close your eyes,' she begged.

'Of course.'

Walking into the room, she draped her clothes over the chair in front of her desk. Moving very slowly and deliberately, knowing from the flutter of Freddie's eyelids that he was peaking and had been since she had asked him to close his eyes.

'You can open them.'

She moved to the side of the desk. She stood legs apart and arms akimbo like a warrior princess proud of her power.

'It fits like a glove.'

'It's a bit tight in some places.'

'Not as far as I'm concerned.'

'I'll keep it on until I see you.'

'I thought you might take it off for me, now.'

'Mr. Denat is arriving in ten minutes at most, I need to be wearing more than this and it's cold in here.'

'I hadn't noticed.'

'That's because you're hot under the collar.'

Adel picked up her clothes, knocking her memory stick off the table.

'What's that?'

'My dongle for my mobile.'

'Really?'

'You are the suspicious type, why not take it with you?'

She held out her hand, offering the memory stick.

'No, it's okay.'

'Take it, seriously. It will help you with your reception, I have a spare at home.'

'Really?'

'Of course, if you don't want it, bring it with you tonight when I see you but give it a go.'

'Okay.'

'Now go!'

Freddie stood up abruptly on hearing the secret door slam, knowing that meant his father was back.

'You haven't seen me.'

'If I don't get changed quickly, we'll both be leaving.'

I interrupted: 'Why did you give him the memory stick?'

'That was the decoy; I told you, I zipped my memory stick into the inside pocket: your listening skills are terrible.'

'I was distracted by what you were saying about the red lingerie.'

'That should have meant you were listening more carefully.'

'I know.'

Chapter Thirteen

Kate's Story – The Plot Thickens

Kate had been working for Adel from the time when Lawless had been careless enough to allow Adel access to his computer, enabling her to hack his files. Adel bought a lot of swimwear from Kate's shop. They were never seen to meet unless it was at the shop in town. Adel would drive down to the cottage in the Golf or the Maserati whenever it was necessary, not regularly enough to cause suspicion.

Kate took up the narrative while Adel helped herself to coffee. I sipped some water.

'Freddie came straight to me after leaving Adel that day.'

Madame Denat was loading up on swimwear and lingerie while her husband negotiated with Lawless.

'Hello, Kate,' Freddie whispered. Coming up close to the checkout desk, he leant over and almost licked my ear, he was that close. 'Why don't you come to my place for lunch?'

'I've already eaten, thanks, Freddie.'

'Who said anything about eating?' he asked – the cheeky sod.

'Freddie, you dirty dog. I thought you were after Adel.'

'What makes you think that?'

'The fact that you just came in and bought some lingerie for her.'

'I'm just trying to keep her sweet.'

'Chocolates would work just as well, I think. Don't you?'

'I only have eyes for you.'

'I'm on my own in the shop and Mrs. Denat is looking at some very high-ticket items. I'll have to pass. I've got to think of my commission.'

'When she goes, you'll be free?'

'You don't give up easily. Okay, I'll call you when I've finished.'

'Kate, do you have this in a size eight? My daughter loves this brand. I think she would just wear the logo,' asked Madame Denat.

'Even better, we have a teenage range. What colour?'

'Blue, please.'

'How old is she?' Freddie asked.

'Seventeen,' Madame Denat replied, sounding worried that Freddie might want her number.

'Madame Denat, you must have had your daughter when you were a teenager yourself,' Freddie exclaimed flirtatiously.

'Freddie, you have made a pass at me every time I have met you, twice in front of my husband. Kate, watch this one. He has only one thing on his mind,' Madame Denat complained.

'Yes, lunch, I'll be in the pub if you both want to join me,' Freddie added hurriedly.

'See you later, Freddie,' I responded dismissively, 'Madame Denat, if you go for the nineteen, in our teenager range, you'll find it will fit her; I remember her as being quite lofty.'

'Lofty?'

'Tall.'

'Long-limbed,' Freddie added from the doorway.

Both of us gave him a stare.

'How will you be paying?' I asked.

'And lovely, as far as I remember,' Freddie could not resist making the last comment.

'Dollars of course,' Mrs. Denat said, ignoring Freddie.

'Of course.'

When I looked up. Freddie was gone.

Kate thought she had fended him off.

However, it appeared Freddie was quite happy to see both Adel and I, waiting for one of us to give in and be his girlfriend. Until then, he showered us both with lingerie, chocolates and flowers. Adel was downloading all the information needed. Then, I transmitted it to London using a secure line that had been set up in the cottage.

The authorities, The Administration, were hoping to turn one of his contacts in order to draw Lawless out of Poseidon Bay and finally put him under arrest. The authorities had waited too long to close down the smuggling rings; a high-profile arrest was needed.

'We tried everything to get him out of his safe haven,' Kate explained. 'We even organised a meeting with JR Murphy & Sons, the biggest booze smugglers in Dublin but someone tipped them off and the meeting was rescheduled to Poseidon Bay, which was a disaster.'

'The revenue reckons they've lost about ten million in duty since that debacle,' Adel explained.

'Wow, that's a lot of money.'

'That's why we have to get Lawless,' Adel insisted.

'Even if I have to die helping you?'

'We won't let that happen,' Kate assured me.

'I wish I could buy that,' I protested, fixing her with the cold stare that I call the death stare.

'We'll protect you,' Adel promised.

'Remind me why you can't go back, please?'

'I killed his son,' Adel reminded me.

'I killed his dog,' Kate confessed, 'Not on purpose, of course. Plus, he discovered I was friends with Adel.'

'So, she was in grave danger, particularly when Lawless found out I had his data,' Kate continued.

'I would ask how that happened, but I know you will tell me. Remember, I stole his son's body,' I insisted.

'Yes, but he does not know.'

'And you can say that with a clear conscience.'

'We've been monitoring his calls.'

'You are forgetting his bodyguards.'

'They were working for us. We evacuated them by helicopter. They had to leave, too. In fact, they took your place and that of the coffin. It was all last minute. Adel had to get her people out after her cover was blown. They were the reason we had to evacuate you by hovercraft.'

'So, they were compromised too.'

'That's about it. They were handpicked by Adel. Once she was exposed as a spy, Lawless would assume that all the bodyguards were working for the British government.'

'And he would have been right,' I added acidly.

'We were keeping a close eye on Lawless and his son.'

'So why did Freddie have to die; flirting with both of you might be annoying, but it is hardly a crime punishable by death?'

'Freddie's death was an accident. There was nothing I could do.'

'What? I was there, the two of us were drugged.'

'Yes, and the two witnesses were meant to see you both go under and report back to Lawless! We had people standing by who were going to save Freddie and you, but your drug had not worked properly so you had more strength, enough strength to try and save Freddie.'

'So, it was my fault was it?'

'In a nutshell, yes.'

'Thank you. I tried to save him.'

'Ultimately, the responsibility is mine of course, it was my idea to take him out.'

'So why include me?'

'Cover.'

'That's great.'

'I was hoping to convince Lawless that you both went too far and were pulled under by strong currents.'

'Really?'

'Really!'

'Sure, it was,' I hissed, hoping the irony in my voice hit home.

'Of course, we had three mini-subs within the bay. The drug was designed to numb. We have carried out similar operations ever since Professor Mark Pigou from the Cousteau Marine Institute completed his research on Alaskan fishermen who fell overboard. The drug replicates the shock you get from hitting ice-cold water.'

'And.'

'The body closes down; the epiglottis stops the victim drowning and the heart can be started up to twenty minutes later without any brain damage. Our subs should have picked you up in a few minutes.'

'So, I was going to drown, too!'

'Only on the surface.'

'Is that a joke?'

'To all intents and purposes, you were both going to drown, we were going to rescue you and pump your lungs, bring you around and use the knowledge you had of Lawless's operation in order to bring him down. Freddie was key to that process.'

'Then, you blundered in,' Kate moaned, 'with your obsession with for Adel. You left her with no choice but to invite you along.'

'Hang on,' I protested, 'that's not fair, I flirted with her a bit.'

'Come off it,' Kate continued, 'you were like a lovesick puppy around her. You should have had as much champagne as Freddie and you would have been doped enough to be swept under and picked up by our divers. You chose to be the hero and drowned him.'

'That's not what happened. I tried to save Freddie.'

'Our report,' Kate argued, 'will show that you were jealous of Freddie and his favoured place as Adel's fiancé and in a drunken rage you pushed him under the water and held him there.'

I saw where all this was leading. I knew I had not deliberately contributed to Freddie's death. They all knew it, too.

I was being told that I had to cooperate, or I would be charged with murder. They would make the charge stick. I felt sick to the pit of my stomach; my heart felt cramped, my mouth was dry. I reached across the table; all eyes in the room were on me.

Grabbing the bottle of fizzy water, I unscrewed the cap and poured a full glass of water. I was going to sip but I ended up gulping down the water, the bubbles exploding on my tongue. Replacing the glass, I sighed, overwhelmed by the whole experience.

'What is it you want me to do?' I asked resigned to the fact that I would be forever under their control.

'We're sending you in again; you'll join a smuggling gang and keep us posted as to Lawless's movements.

'How will I keep in touch?'

'We'll give you a mobile; the signal is much stronger now that Lawless has put in his state-of-the-art cells. Remember, you are the eyes and ears.'

'I can't replace you and Kate, can I?'

'We have no choice; you will inform us when and where we can snatch Lawless. That's your mission, nothing else. No falling in love with girls or grave robbing.'

'Is that another joke?'

'No, what's your answer?'

'No, I'm not putting my life on the line for you lot again, ever.

Chapter Fourteen

Thomasina Town

I was stationed in London while my training went on and I had a lot of time to reflect; I tried to remember when all the racism started, when the fascistic elements first appeared in our society.

It started slowly enough, the insidious 'them and us' attitude that followed Brexit. I was travelling home from the foundry where I worked before Campbell-Lamerton took me on. It was a Saturday, just a month before the place closed for good. The pound had plummeted but not enough for us to compete with Asian steel; we little realised we were in our last few weeks there.

It was about three. I had come off my eight-hour shift and I was heading across the common beside the canal, cycling slowly with my work clothes in a yellow Overboard backpack.

It was a lovely afternoon, a blue sky dappled with cirrus clouds and a robust breeze blew but my helmet kept my head warm and my hair unruffled. A toddler wandered out into the cycle path a few metres ahead of me and I stopped. The mother was dealing with her older child. I called over to her.

'You've almost lost this one,' I exclaimed jovially, watching him weave past me.

'Pardon,' she apologised, I recognised the French accent.

'Pas de problem,' I replied, I knew that much French.

Ting, Ting.

A warning.

It was the sound of an impatient cyclist ringing his bell. We were in the way.

I turned, there were five of them, all of them clad in black bicycle Lycra suits. To say the material was straining to keep them in would be an understatement.

'Are you ringing your bell because I stopped for a toddler?' I asked incredulously but good-naturedly, almost teasing.

'We were just warning the mother she had lost her child,' the fat middle-aged woman asserted.

'But I already told her, before you rang,' I said, noting her mendacity with a raised eyebrow.

'It was the person at the back,' piped up another, a younger thinner woman.

'A bit of an aggressive act for a common wouldn't you say,' I noted archly.

Then it started; the intimidation – pathetic intimidation – but it showed how far things had slipped since Brexit.

'Don't be such a condescending arsehole,' the fat older woman crowed, as they cycled past me.

'I was just saying, it's not a highway, it's a shared space, that's all,' I argued.

'We were having a lovely day until a wanker like you spoilt it,' came her acid reply.

'I'm just trying to get home, I don't want an argument,' I responded meekly. Who would want the responsibility of ruining five riders' day?

'Blah, blah, you shouldn't even be here should you,' the grey-haired older hag said over her shoulder, making a mouthing action with her thumb and fingers.

'You ought to have some lights, mate,' started one of the middle-aged men. He looked frankly ridiculous; he was ridiculous – a weedy MAMIL, Middle Aged Man in Lycra, whose bike was only barely thinner than him. He was short into the bargain, like a boy on a paper round, but he thought that circling around me would intimidate me.

He was on his third loop, just like a fly in my periphery.

They had overtaken me and then slowed to a walking pace and the old hag up ahead kept on braking and stopping deliberately right in front of me, so I had to stop. I had put up with this nonsense for far too long.

'You want me to put my lights on, they're in my bag, but it's light, it doesn't get dark for another few hours,' I complained.

'Leave it, Sam,' she warned, making a beak pincer with her hand again.

Then she put her brakes on hard, so I was forced to skid to a stop.

'Why are you bullying me?'

'You're the bully,' she argued, making the opening and closing of the beak sign before riding off. She looked ridiculous, like some overweight pantomime dame who had been dared to ride a racing bike in her thermal underwear with her pet glove puppet.

'There are five of you,' I laughed, it was becoming more and more bizarre every minute and, unfortunately, it was a long path.

'You're the one causing trouble,' she insisted braking again, the fifth time in so many minutes; no wonder the path seemed longer than usual.

'Why are you circling around me?' I asked the man

'I'm not,' the slim man with the big paunch shouted, circling around me for the fifth time.

They were quite the double act. Then I worked it out, they were slowing me down because I slowed them down; it was a ridiculous case of revenge.

'You are, that's the seventh time you've done it.' I deliberately exaggerated.

'Sixth,' he insisted, 'I'm only doing it because you are being rude to my friend.'

'But she's the one who's been insulting me.'

'We were having such a lovely day until a wanker like you came along and spoilt it,' she complained, neatly illustrating my point.

Then she braked again, I would never get home at this rate.

'Oh, I see you're getting revenge. I held you up and now you're holding me up.'

The woman was incensed. 'Why can't you just piss off!'

'I'm on the way back from work, that's all, you're the one getting heated.'

She had gone rather red, but I couldn't help picturing a pantomime with a duck's beak mouthing something like:

'He's behind you.'

It was difficult to take her seriously when she was stretching her Lycra to splitting point. I should have just stopped but I felt they too would stop and harangue me. I would have passed them, but the large lady had her friend next to her; there were two people directly behind, meaning I was very effectively hemmed in.

There was no escape from my public humiliation. For good measure, the old 'boy wonder' circled on the path and grass; it was a pity he was not wearing yellow with his black, as he would have resembled a wasp around a white wine glass.

I turned off on a side path just before the end of the common.

'You're going to die of a heart attack if you're not careful!' she screamed, going puce like an angry headmaster from a fifties movie.

'Not before you, love,' I replied, shouting back at her for the first time. I was pleased, I was better than them, I did not swear once. However, this sort of gang culture was on the increase and I knew that post-Brexit it would get worse and it did. They had intonated that I should not be here, picking up on my Irish accent even though it was barely noticeable.

First it was people on bicycles being fascistic, running over people on shared paths and in side streets, hospitalising some. Then, it was Lycra clad gangs, wearing Doctor Marten shoes or boots teamed with fitness gear; it was not the black shirts but the black suits. Girls wore strange spandex leggings with see-through panels showing pasty flesh and heavy, clumpy boots designed for kicking.

There were girl gangs who were known for their viciousness; the wrong word, the wrong look or the wrong race and it was curtains. They kicked their victims to death. It was like *A Clockwork Orange*, but with xenophobia included. Anyone who was not blonde and blue-eyed was vulnerable. It was just the beginning.

Polarisation continued: the bikers began to run over dogs and children who got in their way. Pedestrians jumped out at traffic, trying to get run over and win compensation as people became more desperate for money. Cars no longer took turns in narrow village and town streets, one car would give way and a flow of ten cars would piggy-back on the back of the first car, trapping the polite driver. Roads became clogged with cars not prepared to give way.

Homeless people were hired by drivers to ride shotgun and leap out at these self-inflicted traffic jams. Using a tyre jack, they would smash the windscreens of all the cars that stopped the driver from pulling out from the passing space. It was mayhem.

I knew it was getting bad when normally mild-mannered lorry drivers began to get fed up with the drivers and bullied them; the drivers bullied the cyclists and the cyclists, ever the most rebellious of the tribes, bullied each other, cyclists and pedestrians in parks and in the streets. They shot through red lights, rode furiously along pavements, mowing people down if they failed to jump out of the way.

When a report on pollution came out in 2022, people's diesel cars were smashed up. People discovered that it was not the chemicals in the diesel but the microscopic particles that lodged in their lungs and brains and they were angry. The government had meant to ban all diesel and petrol cars and only have hybrids on the road but that did not go to plan. When the government fell and The Administration took over, they had other worries apart from pollution.

The plague arrived in Birmingham and spread like wildfire throughout the country in 2023 and food riots followed. Food banks ran out of food and people raided supermarkets.

The police could not stop the onslaught. It was like a swarm of locusts; everything was stripped bare. Social media allowed people to choose a time and place and attack the place en mass. Ordinary shoppers were swept out of the way by the marauding hordes that stripped the shelves of all food before disappearing. The police managed to grab one or two shoplifters, but the majority got away with their spoils. The weekly shop was replaced by the weekly 'mop-mob' sucking up all the goods from the supermarkets. Adele had lost her eye in Iceland when a 'mop-mob' descended on the freezer shop. People desperate for food fought with frozen lamb legs as clubs and frozen poultry as missiles. Those who were left standing loaded up the trolleys and fled. Adele was hit in the side of the head by a gammon joint and crushed by a pile of customers. Paramedics arrived to treat her, but they could not save her eye.

The rich were forced to pay more taxes to keep the police and health service functioning. It's amazing how willingly they pay more tax to ensure their survival. The amounts helped but still the National Health Service was run on the good will of doctors and nurses prepared to take poor wages to save lives. The ancillary workers managed to negotiate a decent living wage and canteen food.

Flu epidemics, riots, protest marchers and plague – that was our life post-Brexit. I tried to blank out the past. The north was grim. I was down south now. There was no going back. I was part of a new world; Thomasina's privileged enclave was a world away from the violent society we had all become used to.

I was in London that night and I would be seducing Thomasina, or she would be seducing me. Why else would she invite me from the barracks in Knightsbridge to her swish Clapham home? I wondered.

ii

Getting to Thomasina's house in Clapham was an event in itself. Since the first Black Cab Clash of '21, the number of taxis on the streets had halved. Uber sponsored the takeover of the taxi industry, removing the name taxi from the lexicon and replacing it with Uber. I saw a cab with the orange UBER light on; it was fat and squat like all the new electric cars were; the London Taxi Company – LTC – TX5 looked really great, an urban icon already, even if sightings of them were rare. I was looking forward to being in a London taxi for the first time.

I had been in a clapped out TX4 in Birmingham one rainy day; that was in the years Before Brexit, or BB, and I had never been in one After Brexit, AB. The tabloids toyed with Post-Brexit, but it sounded too similar in radio and television broadcasts to catch on in the rest of the media, so AB was adopted.

So, long ago, my mum had hailed that old cab to get us to the station, a once in a lifetime treat. That night, visiting Adel, was going to be my first cab ride that I had paid for, ever. Okay, Thomasina had given me the money; well, a prepaid credit card to be precise. I was excited I must confess. The cab came towards me in the gathering twilight, the orange light glowed in the sombre air; he flicked on his headlights and magically the streetlights came into life as well. It was 'lighting up time', clearly; maybe both vehicle and lamp post were connected to the same computer. I knew the cab was for hire, I stretched out my arm, my hand open in the international signal for hailing cabs – I had seen it on countless movies.

The cab turned its 'for hire' light out and its headlights swept over me as it turned three-sixty degrees and headed off in the opposite direction.

Later, I found out this happened all the time. A mobile customer had outbid me. I had been issued with three phones by

Thomasina's department; all of them had been fingerprint activated by me; the other two were back in the office in Victoria.

The cab had to meter my fare as he picked me up from the street but with the other customers on the phone, he could negotiate a price; taxis were in demand, they were few and far between; these were desperate times.

That was it; I had to walk. Arrival of buses were clearly displayed at bus stops but due to cutbacks they only ran at 7 am, 8 am, 12 pm, 3.30 pm, 6 pm, 7, 8 and 9 pm.

The Administration did not want anyone on the streets after the ten o'clock curfew. They claimed it was too dangerous with 'muggers, murderers and footpads'. They actually used that term, I had to look it up; footpads are not something you put on the soles of your shoes to make you walk more quietly, they are thieves who attack pedestrians.

There were more pedestrians because the rich were the only people that could afford to drive cars; taxi drivers and bosses ruled the streets. Admittedly, they all drove electric vehicles, Tesla and BMW mainly. All vans were LPG or electric, but deliveries could only be made between ten in the morning and four in the afternoon to cut down on congestion and pollution, they said. The Administration pretended it was to cut down on pollution and save a drain on the power stations of the national grid but really it was to cut down on smuggling. Any van on the streets would be impounded and crushed. Amazon and Uber understandably made sure that their vans had a computer chip that switched their vans off between four-fifteen when staggered hours allowed schools out in the afternoon and nine-forty-five in the morning, when deliveries were allowed to recommence.

All the bars had shut by nine. As I passed, a high-end restaurant was about to close its shutters as the diners were ushered out of the Buona Sera. At the end of every street, there was a high gate, one and a half metres high, made of heavy steel. As I approached Shellgate Road, an electric Tesla drove by, the white caps and red jackets of a private security service flashed past my face.

I would wager they wore blue pants. All the security firms accentuated their patriotism. 'Wagers' were back in; 'Brexit bets' were off, and people wagered with all their wages, or with whatever else they could barter in some cases.

At the side of the gates was an intercom with a sign above it: Welcome to Shellgate West. Please ring for attention. I rang Thomasina, her house number punched out in digits followed by the call button.

A camera was mounted on the top of the gate. It loomed over me and dipped its cycloptic eye at me. She picked up, she said nothing, but the lock on the small side door clicked open, I pushed the cold black metal and I walked into a steel cage.

The door shut behind me; three dead bolts shot across the doorjamb. The cage was electrified so I stayed still. A red light was directly overhead and in front of my nose was a sign: Electrified Fence, do not attempt to move until red light is extinguished. Failure to comply could result in a fatal injury.

Welcome to Shellgate Road indeed.

The red light went out; a metallic click made me jump. I was nervous; I had been hit by a Taser during the riots. A voice from a speaker made me jolt again.

'Come on through,' Thomasina soothed.

The gauze gate swung open automatically; I dared not touch it. I knew the house was at the end of the road.

Shellgate was a cul-de-sac, the wall at the end backed on to the cemetery; the wall had a twenty-foot high tensile electrified fence protecting the street. CCTV cameras operated by the security services swept both ways mounted at each end of the fence.

She had twenty-four-hour protection.

I was in the safest place in London except for Buckingham Palace and the MI5 and MI6 buildings. Walking up the street, I was struck by the amount of light emanating from all the windows; the drawing rooms were well lit, unlike all the houses in the country and even the rooms upstairs threw light into the street. These people had money to burn.

It must have been so good not to have to worry about your energy bills. They paraded their wealth by sucking as much electricity as they could from the national grid; this was the national wealth system at work: horde it and flaunt it.

The rich had no curtains so passers-by could view their fantastic furniture and amazing artwork, an advertisement of one's good taste. It was a waste of time when your street is a fortress, I would have thought, but these residents clearly thought that they should have front rooms that displayed their wares; most looked like a sofa shop front window.

They knew the cost of everything and the value of nothing. Maybe they were showing off to their neighbours. Everyone lived in pristine kitchens at the back of the house; the drawing room was their display case. I was fascinated but not in a good way. People were living with candlelight in the rest of the country, eking out their electricity to cook or wash.

As I walked down the street numbers and up the hill, I noted lack of colour coordination, hideous paintings and sofas for staring at not for sitting on. It was great fun, finding fault with everything and looking down my nose at them. It made a change, I can tell you that for nothing.

There was no need for streetlamps, which had been removed and replaced by LED lights on the pavement that were activated when you put your foot on an adjacent flagstone. It was weird hitting a flagstone and the next one lighting up as you went; it was more energy efficient but any gain on the street was negated by the profligate use in the homes of the rich.

It was uphill and a fair distance to Thomasina's house, the last on the block, on the left-hand side, Number One. I was feeling warmed up by the time I reached her threshold.

She opened the door as I approached the railings to her quaint Victorian house. Opposite was a hideous modernist house, painted white; a two-storey block that took up the space left by two bombed houses. They had been destroyed in the Second World War, not the riots.

There were three rectangular windows on the first floor; the ground floor had an enormous black metal double door and a tiny cottage kitchen window; to the right was a garage with a floor above it. I had no doubt that it was packed with Thomasina's men, secret service operatives that would be monitoring my raised temperature and heartbeat.

'Good evening, Aubrey, welcome to Number One, London,' she announced, smiling at me with her perfectly polished teeth. She had been poured into a black dress and had forgotten to say when; she was overflowing from the ruched silk; she had a beautiful face and an amazing body. My heart leapt, I was madly and deeply in lust. My love for Adel was merely dust.

'Good evening, Thomasina, you look more gorgeous than ever,' I replied smoothly. I knew how to impress, even if I was just a lost boy in her eyes.

'Thank you, come on in,' she said.

I smiled and walked towards her, the warning bells chiming in my head. I was reminded of the nursery rhyme: 'Will you walk into my parlour?' said the Spider to the Fly.

I wondered what was on the menu. The excitement of seeing Thomasina was tempered by the sinking feeling that whatever she had in mind for me would be dangerous. Mary Howitt knew about spiders and she knew about danger, especially the danger of listening to flattery.

'Will you walk into my parlour?' said the Spider to the Fly,
''Tis the prettiest little parlour that ever you did spy;
The way into my parlour is up a winding stair,
And I've a many curious things to show when you are there.'

'Oh no, no,' said the little Fly, 'to ask me is in vain,
For who goes up your winding stair can ne'er come down again.'

'I'm sure you must be weary, dear, with soaring up so high;
Will you rest upon my little bed?' said the Spider to the Fly.

'There are pretty curtains drawn around; the sheets are fine and thin, and if you like to rest awhile, I'll snugly tuck you in!'

'Oh no, no,' said the little Fly, 'for I've often heard it said,
They never, never wake again, who sleep upon your bed!'
Said the cunning Spider to the Fly, 'Dear friend what can I do,
To prove the warm affection I've always felt for you?'

I was sure she would prove she liked me, make me feel I took her fancy.

'I have within my pantry, good store of all that's nice;
I'm sure you're very welcome – will you please to take a slice?'

I also knew she would have good food in her great pantry.

'Oh no, no,' said the little Fly, 'kind Sir, that cannot be,
I've heard what's in your pantry, and I do not wish to see!'

There were people starving in the street that I could see, but even I had to know what cost the food would be.

'Sweet creature!' said the Spider, 'you're witty and you're wise,
How handsome are your gauzy wings, how brilliant are your eyes! I've a little looking-glass upon my parlour shelf,
If you'll step in one moment, dear, you shall behold yourself.'

She had made me feel that she fancied me. Could this meeting end in matrimony?

'I thank you, gentle sir', she said, 'for what you're pleased to say, and bidding you good morning now, I'll call another day.'

She had asked me to risk my life and being besotted I took on trouble and strife. I was hoping she would be my wife.

The Spider turned him round about, and went into his den,
For well he knew the silly Fly would soon come back again:
So he wove a subtle web, in a little corner sly,
And set his table ready, to dine upon the Fly.

My instincts had told me to take care; my heart felt they were being unfair.

Then he came out to his door again, and merrily did sing,
'Come hither, hither, pretty Fly, with the pearl and silver wing;
Your robes are green and purple – there's a crest upon your head;
Your eyes are like the diamond bright, but mine are dull as lead!'

She did have the most alluring eyes and I was taken by surprise at how alluring she appeared that evening in her tight dress.

Alas, alas! How very soon this silly little Fly,
Hearing his wily, flattering words, came slowly flitting by;
With buzzing wings she hung aloft, then near and nearer drew,
Thinking only of her brilliant eyes, and green and purple hue –
Thinking only of her crested head – poor foolish thing!

At last, Up jumped the cunning Spider, and fiercely held her fast.
He dragged her up his winding stair, into his dismal den,
Within his little parlour – but she ne'er came out again!'

I knew that I was being unwise, and it might lead to my demise.

And now dear little children, who may this story read,
To idle, silly flattering words, I pray you ne'er give heed:
Unto an evil counsellor, close heart and ear and eye,
And take a lesson from this tale, of the Spider and the Fly.

Mary Botham Howitt had meant that bit; we had listened to that part so many times that we knew most of the verses off by heart. I had learnt the first verse fully for a school assembly. I had not listened to her unfortunately. I had not learnt that particular lesson properly: she was the spider; I was the flea. A gorgeous woman asks me to put my life in danger and I just nod meekly and agree.

Chapter Fifteen

Into the Lion's Den

The shiny black car drove up, the electric tinted window wound down. I leant down to speak to the driver. Rainwater had collected around the rim of the hood of my raincoat and it dripped on to the grass at my feet. My trainers were soaked, my jeans sodden and the nylon on my waterproof jacket shone like new shoes.

I was freezing; I had been waiting over an hour for a lift.

I wondered at the sanity of the authorities dropping me at a fast food outlet in Amesbury on the wettest day of the year. I had made it from there to Mere, a mere twenty-four miles.

I was still between a hundred and twenty or a hundred and forty miles from Poseidon Bay, depending on the route. It was at least five hours away and it was midday.

Hunger was gnawing at my stomach when my misery was dispelled by the arrival of that shiny black Jaguar.

'Where are you heading?' asked the driver; a blast of warm air grazed my frozen fingers.

'Anywhere out of the rain,' I replied.

'I'm on my way to Wells,' he confessed.

'Great.'

'Throw the bag in the boot,' he ordered.

'Perfect,' I agreed

I rushed to the boot and tossed my yellow Overboard thirty-litre backpack into the boot, which the driver had popped open for me. It was too wet to worry about who was driving.

If he was a weirdo, I could fight my way out of the car and get some gear from the boot.

Major Thom had chosen my equipment for the mission, of course.

As I closed the boot, I panicked, wondering if he would drive off with my bag. It happened a lot these days. We had all heard horrific stories of people losing their worldly possessions in a puff of exhaust fumes or with the sound of an electric whirr.

I rushed back to the front of the car.

'Hop in, then,' he added.

I opened the passenger door and slipped into the warm environment. The driver had thrown a massive beach towel over the leather seat.

'Where are you from?' he asked.

'Up north, originally, but from London just now!'

'You boys up north like to carry your cudgels, wrenches and tyre irons; it's not our style. I've got my own persuader in the cubby hole next to my hand so no funny business.'

'Don't worry, I'm too wet and cold to do anything but sit and thaw out!'

'We can be violent too, if necessary.'

'I wouldn't mess with you.'

I would definitely avoid fighting this bear of a man. Any blows would bounce off him and his arms looked like bulging bags of barley. He was in his fifties but looked like a sergeant major, fit and dangerous.

People often underestimate how fit and strong fifty-year-olds can be. A decade later you could push them over with your index finger but until then, if they looked after themselves, they were tough cookies, and I didn't want my teeth broken on this one.

'Good, down here we rely more on cunning and skill; we load barrels with just enough weight to sink them, toss over a camouflage net and anchor it to the shallows.'

'Clever.'

'Hey presto, instant warehouse out of sight of the authorities. All the tobacco is packed in waterproof wrapping.'

'That's very, very clever.'

'We put false keels and bottoms in our boats, as well.'

'I'm sticking with you guys,' I laughed.

'Don't suppose any invitation has been extended. This is where I turn off.'

'But you said you'd take me to Wells?' I complained, staring at him in disbelief, struggling to keep my jaw from dropping onto my lap.

'I lied, I'm a smuggler, we never tell the truth, you know that,' he argued convincingly. He pulled over and stopped the car.

'So why did you pick me up?'

'I wanted to check the waterproofing on the seats worked.'

'Seriously, why?'

'Why do you think?'

'You hate people, so you like to torture them? It's tipping it down out there. I was only just starting to thaw out and you're going to put me back into the cold and rain?'

'I picked you up because you are a stranger in these parts, aren't you?'

'Your observational powers match your cruelty.'

'You could be in the pay of the authorities. Who's to say you're not working for The Administration.'

'If I was would I wander in during a rainstorm, the forecast is fair for tomorrow, I'd come, then, wouldn't I?'

'How do you know?'

'Television at the Fried Food Express, Amesbury; I saw it when I caught a lift from there to Mere.'

'Well, there's plenty enough people who would take the king's shilling to get out of poverty and starvation.'

'I guess there are. I suppose you have to be careful of strangers, but look,' I added fishing in my wallet.

'Put it on the dashboard for me to see,' he ordered.

'I'm a salesman for a silver ingot dealer. You can ring my boss if you think I stole the cards. Aubrey East, pleased to meet you.'

'Sam Newton charmed I'm sure. Now hop out before I get the wrench that's in the side cubby by my right hand.'

'Okay, okay, I'll leave my card if you ever think of exchanging cash for something more solid.'

I stepped out into the rain and shivered as drips of cold rain trickled down my neck, it seemed to be colder and heavier than ever. I shut the door, resisting the temptation to slam it; Sam might yet prove useful, an ally on my way back out of the area.

As I reached the back of the car, the red lights glowed like two pairs of devilish eyes, then one pair faded. I heard a roar. Sam drove away. I watched him pull out. I thought that it was the last that I would see of my bag, losing it had not been a very good start to the operation.

He accelerated away and then braked sharply. As he started to reverse, I started to run.

We met halfway and I was just grabbing the handle to the passenger door when a van rushed towards us, drove through a puddle, splashing water just behind me and at the last minute, it overtook us. If it was not for the Jag, shielding me, I would have been drenched.

Sooner than you could say 'that was close', I was sitting in the passenger seat and slamming the door.

'I'm prepared to give you the benefit of the doubt,' Sam confessed, indicating and pulling out on to the empty road.

'Thank you, it's good to be in the dry again. Tell me your story and I'll tell you mine.'

'Might make the journey go faster,' he admitted.

'Don't you listen to Poseidon Bay Radio?' I asked, ostensibly to check how informed he was.

'What do you know about PBR?' he asked. He was a sly cove, answering a question with a question. I was none the wiser. It was time to charm.

'Only what Lawless told me.'

'How do you know him?'

'I tried to sell him some silver.'

'And?'

'He wanted gold'

'Ha, that sounds about right,' he chortled.

'I thought you were going to tell me your story first.'

'Maybe later, let's eat up some miles first.'

It was clear my taciturn torturer was dreaming up some more humiliation for me or deciding whether to kill me or whether to let me go.

I had to sit it out, quite literally.

We drove along the A303; the car was in sixth gear, humming happily.

The rain was drumming on the roof; the tyres were splashing into roadside puddles; the windscreen wipers were sweeping furiously to clear the windscreen. The silence between us became natural after ten minutes. We passed Sparkford; I found myself no more enlightened by my driver.

'We're heading for Exeter.'

'That's ideal, my next port of call.'

That was brilliant, if it was true. I could stay overnight and be in Poseidon Bay by Tuesday.

It was a simple route: A303, to A34. I could sleep in Exeter, then eat in Torquay and then get a lift to the Tamar Bridge, the border of Poseidon Bay.

'Okay, so you want me to fill the time. Up until Brexit, I worked for an Italian food company.'

'Ouch!'

'Yep, the pound's plummet put paid to that.'

'So, what do you do, now?'

'As Brexit broke, we hoped the pound would bounce back and then came the recession and the repatriation.'

'My mother was sent home to Ireland and she had been here since the seventies.'

'I'm sorry to hear it; you managed to stay?'

'Only because my boss said I was vital for the running of the company; I was his only salesman. We had to beg the British Border Force. My father was English – is English – wherever he is.'

'The BBF? I was arrested by them!'

'Why?'

'I objected to the way they rough handled some Romanians.'

'That was dangerous!' I gasped; you did not mess with the BBF, ever.

'We used to take our delivery van to be washed at one of those hand car wash depots; the BBF arrived just as they were literally polishing off my van.

'The car wash boys were lovely guys; we knew them well, they worked hard and always did a good job. Anyway, they immediately put their hands up; they weren't going to argue with immigration. They knew they would be deported; no one would argue with someone dressed up and armed like a starship trooper.'

'They have a reputation for being rough.'

'Well deserved, too. I objected to them being so rough and the police, who were with them, arrested me for obstruction. Cuffed me there and then and put me in the back of the van with everyone else. At least they let me out; the others were sent to the processing centre at Bristol.'

'Terrible.'

'Tip of the iceberg wasn't it.'

'Sadly,' I agreed.

Europeans first, Muslims next and with each set of deportation things got worse. The smaller the population the more our productivity slumped and the more the pound dived and the more difficult it was for us all to survive.

'I remember and that was before the Plague.'

'2021 was when Portwrinkle annexed itself and Whitsand Bay became Poseidon Bay.'

'Followed by Southampton and Bristol.'

'The south-west was followed by your lot; first the north-west, Cumbria if I remember; there was a lot of unemployment up there even before Brexit. Then the north-east suffered.'

'Our biggest market is the annexed territories,' I admitted; it was true after all.

'Well, the wealth is still in Wessex, Sussex, Norfolk, Suffolk and Surrey and of course Berkshire and Oxfordshire; the South-East Hub.'

'They all want gold or platinum there.'

'Sod them, we don't need them.'

'You're right there.'

'What were you doing up in London.'

'A little smuggling myself.'

'And you're going to Poseidon Bay for a holiday?'

'Ha, very funny, I'm going to see the Poseidon Dolphins play hockey against the Bristol Pirates.'

'Really?'

'No, I've got to go and see Lawless to sell him some more silver; the London client didn't take as much as my boss wanted.'

'You're good, you lie like a smuggler.'

'I'd rather live like one!'

'Why would you want to do that, surely not the glamour?'

'No, I know the squalid life they live and it's not for the unlimited supply of cannabis – that stuff messes with your brain.'

'Why, then?' he asked.

'My mum needs money to survive. She has no job, and her rent is high; they confiscated her home in the Immigrant Purge. I can't get a job in Ireland, so I'm stuck here.'

'You're on commission; you look like you do all right.'

'Looks are everything in sales: shiny shoes, seven years old, newly resoled, a suit that needs dry cleaning in my bag; don't get me wrong, I've got some nice stuff at mum's in Ireland, but I've sent everything over there.'

'You must do well.'

'I used to get commission but not anymore.'

'That's common enough; bosses with squeezed margins keep back wages.'

'He gives me just enough to function for him and not starve.'

'Your flat?'

'A room at the back of his office!'

'So, what's stopping you?'

'Doing what? Going to Ireland?'

'No, becoming a smuggler.'

'If I go to Poseidon Bay Lawless will tell my boss and that will be it for me, my boss would track me down and kill me; actually he would pay someone to kill me just to teach me a lesson.'

'Can you swim?'

I tried not to hesitate before I replied.

'Of course.'

'Good, you can help me.'

'Where are we going?'

'Beer.'

'Not for me thanks it's a bit early, I'd love something to eat though.'

'No, not ale; Beer the place, I've no food but there are some mints in the glove-box.'

'I'm that hungry,' I admitted, 'I think I will have a mint or two.'

I had eaten a good breakfast, but my metabolism means I am constantly hungry. I had never imagined mints might be food but as they say big buggers can't be choosers.

'Help yourself.'

It was as simple as that.

I was in.

According to the blurb on the net, which I looked at on my phone as we drove, I would soon be arriving in a pleasant backwater.

I knew better.

'Beer is a picturesque ancient fishing village with stunning coastal walks and a fascinating past that includes smuggling, lacemaking, and Beer stone'.

Lacemaking and smuggling has made a comeback and the Beer stone is snapped up by a Chinese wholesaler, cheap as chips, they reckon; the lingerie sells well all over the world.

'Beer nestles in a narrow valley that opens out into a natural bay sheltered by towering Beer Head'.

We smugglers like sheltered bays as they offer protection in the storm; the valley offers storage for ill-gotten gains.

'Its name is not derived from the drink, but from the old Anglo-Saxon word 'bearu' meaning grove, which referred to the forest that surrounded the settlement.'

A new forest had been planted years ago to help with flooding; it was hoped the roots would help in binding the soil together and the new trees were something to tie our swag against.

'Walk the glorious South-West Coast Path at Beer for sea breezes and far reaching views'. You will be beaten senseless by armed men who carry baseball and cricket bats as cudgels who patrol the area twenty-four hours a day.

'Hire a motorboat for one of the best views from the sea of this stretch of Jurassic coast', and be blown out of the water by the stolen Royal Artillery 45-pounder field gun that is sited on Beer Head.

'Beer's long fishing heritage is still very much alive today, with a colourful population of fishing boats, fresh fish and Beer crab for sale, and mackerel fishing trips.'

This colourful population is pressed into service to smuggle tobacco, booze and clothes in boxes, barrels and bags, all sealed in impermeable sacks with saltwater resistant tape.

'In the past Beer was equally well known as a smuggling base and the home of notorious Devon smuggler, Jack Rattenbury.'

Now it is under the control of nefarious, infamous and ruthless Robert Mercury, obviously a made-up name and a fan of Queen, the pop group. Known as Big Bob, RM, his moniker led people to believe he was a Royal Marine.

'It was also famous for fine lace including the lace flounce for Queen Victoria's wedding dress crafted in Beer by Miss Jane Bidney and her team of 200 workers.'

Now, it is famous for fine lace again, but this is for lacy knickers, bras and stockings. The sex industry and poor pound help to drive a decent quality and quantity of exports, mostly naughty underwear.

This is used as 'contra'; we exchange lace for liquor, tights for tobacco and bras for booze.

'Modern bartering started in the eighties in Totnes and spread to the rest of Devon; this enclave on the Dorset border embraced its resurgence.'

'Although small, easy to control, Beer's pleasant flint-studded buildings include interesting shops and galleries, and excellent places to eat' and to store all the contraband.

'In Beer where life has always centred on the sea, it is not surprising that the most important date in the events calendar is the annual Beer Regatta.'

'In August, the distinctive Beer luggers, with striking red sails, are always an imposing sight. Another popular event in Beer is the annual Beer Rhythm & Blues Festival in October.'

I had missed them both. Those luggers were big buggers and took tonnes of tobacco and bundles of bras, back and forth each night and each day, every time using a different route.

Still, I had a joke about beer, which I told Big Bob in the car.

'What do you call a woman with a tray of beer on her head?' I asked, relaxing into the seat, the mints were surprisingly successful in suppressing my hunger pangs.

'You're going to tell me, aren't you?' he answered my question with a question, which was annoying but even I realised it was best to let it go in Big Bob's case.

'Beatrix!'

'Very good, beer tricks, ha,' he laughed, not loud but I had read his file and he was rumoured never to smile.

'What do you call a woman with a try on her head who is playing pool?'

'Dunno,' he said.

'Beatrix Potter.'

'Very good,' he gasped in between guffawing. He really liked the joke.

'Beatrix Potter, very funny,' he wheezed, 'the writer. I had a girlfriend, Jemima, used to call her "puddle-ducks". She would have loved that joke, dear old Jemima Puddleducks.'

'You didn't marry her, then?'

'No,' he replied.

'Why not?'

'She died.'

'Oh, I'm sorry to hear that. What happened?'

'I made her walk the plank,' he said deadpan, as if he were announcing the price of fish. I gulped unintentionally, I didn't mean to, but I could not help myself.

I was feeling relaxed and then he dropped that bombshell.

'What would he do to me if he found out about me?' I wondered.

My mouth went dry, as dry as Beer stone, but I managed to speak, albeit with a cracking voice.

'Why?'

'She looked at another man.'

'Could she swim?'

'Yes, she was school champion.'

'Is that why you asked me if I could swim?'

'No, though she did do diving for me; that's the project you'll be in charge of as it happens.'

'Sounds straightforward.'

'Oh, it is. You'll be diving down anchor ropes on our smuggling buoys and releasing the goods from their moorings.'

'So, she could swim well, so it was a punishment; did she make it across the bay to Dorset?'

'Sadly, she couldn't swim very well when she had her hands handcuffed behind her back.'

The silence that followed allowed me to tune into the noises of the car again.

ii

Beer Full of Cheer

The beach at Beer is golden sand in summer sunshine; in the winter it looks like a golden retriever's coat after a duck shoot – shabby, dirty and dull.

Beer was seventy-eight miles away on one route, taking one hour and forty-one minutes on the A30; that was on a good day. The other route was eighty-nine-point-five miles and would take two hours on the A38.

Either way, if I wanted to get back to Poseidon Bay, I had to get through Exmouth, but it was one of the Triangular Towns: Exmouth, Lympstone and Budleigh Salterton were in the 'Southern Triangle', a government stronghold established to police the area. It was twenty miles from Beer.

Also, there was a 'Triangle' at Tiverton to the north-east, Minehead to the north of that and Torquay to the south-west, a thin triangular line of fortress towns full of rich people protected by Royal Marines, the Special Boat Service and Special Forces Police. There were pockets of government influence all over the country, protected by local regiments. The Special Air Service in Hereford in the west, the Royal Green Jackets in the east – they had been sent up from their base near Salisbury Plain.

The north was Scotland, so no English troops were wasted there; the so-called 'soft border' had been sealed by the Scottish Nationalist Army. They had a reputation for violently ejecting any southerners who tried to steal across the border. The Scots, naturally, did not want smuggling upsetting their Honorary Membership of the European Union and Common Market nor did they want any worthless sterling, diluting the euro. Smiling Scots took our worthless pounds in such quantities that the wad was called a brick, it matched the size of a house brick and would buy you a coffee; ten pounds notes piled up into fifty-five-millimetres-high blocks.

Rich people filled their boots with brick walls to buy a bottle of malt Scotch. Walls came in ten by five bricks that sat in clear plastic trays that could be stacked up one upon the other.

Ten-pound denominations were the only accepted currency; all other notes had withered and dropped out of circulation. It was easier for us smugglers to barter goods, only rich people dealt in bricks and walls. Our cars were too small to take enough cash in the boot to pay for a full tank of petrol.

The rich had credit cards and debit cards. We did not speak on our hour-and-a-half journey from silence to the seaside. It was a bleak day, a bleak beach and a bleak outlook for me.

Accepting the lift from the local 'Mr. Big' had made me indebted to him; he knew where I was heading so I had the prospect of being in the sea, wearing a dry-suit and releasing packages from their hiding places, letting them bob to the surface where they would be collected by rubber dinghies with outboard motors and loaded into waiting luggers.

'Well, here we are,' announced the driver.

'Thank you, so much,' I enthused, trying desperately to show how grateful I was and hoping I would not be forced to work a week in return for the lift.

'Actually,' he said, 'you can take a package to the Tamar Toll Bridge for me.'

My heart sank; smuggling was punishable by up to twenty years in prison. I was going to pass through a government stronghold. Smugglers avoided the Triangular Towns for this reason; the authorities turned their back on smuggling outside the Triangular Towns but try and take anything into these wealthy strongholds and you were going to have the law book thrown at you. Lawyers and law officers still operated in these middle-class enclaves, but these tended to be in towns or cities. There were no such luxuries elsewhere.

The countryside had been taken over by the populace. The nearby military bases provided troops on the streets of urban areas in army Land Rovers, painted grey like the ones in Northern Ireland.

They also had sniffer dogs.

The countryside was the domain of the starving people. It was the law of the jungle in the countryside; life was uncannily like *Lord of the Flies*. The motorways and towns were where the police and military patrolled. Cutbacks meant that there was not enough of either to patrol the whole country. I might get away with delivering the package, but if I were caught, the sentence that I could receive for delivering his package would be eye-watering.

Smuggling carried a sentence of twenty years; charges would include: trying to pervert the economy, twenty years; attempting to influence or corrupt the population, twenty years; for evading customs duty on goods, twenty-five years, and those are just the ones I knew about off hand. I could be in jail for a century.

'I think I'd prefer the diving.'

'With your hands cuffed?'

'How big is the package?'

'That's the spirit,' he replied, parking in the high street. There were few cars around, fuel being so expensive and thieves being prevalent.

'Aren't you worried about leaving the car here?' I wondered.

'No one would steal my car; there are three cars in this town: the doctor's, the mayor's and mine. Look over there and you'll see what happens to anyone who tries to take from me.'

Following the direction of his finger, I looked across to a war memorial. A man sat on the pavement propped up against the steps and leaning his head on the base of the cross. His body was wrapped in fishing netting, crisscrossing his body in long strands that cut into the flesh. It looked excruciatingly painful; the marks would last for months; I supposed that was the idea.

'What happened to him?' I asked, really not wanting the answer but succumbing to a morbid curiosity.

'Spirogyra.'

'Spirogyra?'

'Spirogyra fired from a harpoon gun.'

'Those strands came from a gun?'

'Fishermen's wire arranged in helical threads. It twists and turns in the air wrapping itself around the body.'

'Helical?'

'A spiral arrangement.'

'I see.'

'We used to call spirogyra, water silk or mermaid's tresses; that poor bugger is trussed up in tresses of nylon thread.'

Having once got some nylon cord wrapped around my leg on a climbing wall, I knew how painful it was to have that digging into your skin. I could not imagine how much it would hurt having so much wire cutting into your skin.

'I think I might like it here in Beer,' I remarked leaving my deliberate irony floating in the fug in the car.

'As I said to my former wife, the one who drowned, it's the Hotel California, you can check out, but you can never leave.'

That sounded ominous. He said it with true feeling, too,

'I think I might like a beer here,' I added, letting my word-play prance about the odour of stale cheap cologne that seeped through the leather in the car.

It was stifling in the car, but I dared not say anything in case I ended up back in the rain, or worse, ended up taking a dive with my hands tied behind my back. My host would not put the air conditioning on as it would use up too much fuel and he would not open the windows because that would add to fuel consumption.

The fan was set on one, which meant the putrid perfume was merely wafted around the interior. The windscreen wipers tried to hypnotise me to sleep with their slow sweep. I know it was a car, but it felt like a room, a room with no windows and a smelly teenager in there.

I surreptitiously sniffed my shoulder to check that I had sprayed the cologne Major Thom had given me effectively enough.

I was rewarded with a waft of Moroccan Myrrh; the fragrance of myrrh that was blended with lively notes of bergamot and cardamom, black pepper, petitgrain, geranium, lavender, amber, guaiac wood; it was in Thomasina's words: 'simply divine'.

A few minutes later, we came to a stop outside a pub. Throwing open the passenger door, I was rewarded by a cool draft of coastal breeze, a salty tang and ozone overtones, so much better than the smell of the stink tank that I had inhabited for the past few hours.

'Can I buy you a beer, Bob?' I asked, gulping in great draughts of air.

The rain seemed to have eased off; my clothes were dry from being in the hot house, so I did not mind the splashes or rain on my thigh. It would only be a short dash from the car to the pub.

'I won't say no,' he said.

'Good, I'd like to thank you for having pity on me,' I added, moving to the back of the car and grabbing my bag from the boot.

He waited while I did so, eyeing my bag suspiciously. If he only he knew what Major Thom had put inside.

'Having mercy on you,' he corrected me, slamming his door and locking the car with the key and not the electronic fob; batteries were notoriously difficult to get hold of and prohibitively expensive.

Walking together towards the benches that stood outside, we noticed a group of people about my age, early twenties, smoking cannabis, but this was Spice and the guys looked like they were half asleep even though it was early afternoon. Cannabis was rife but only the most evil smugglers kept their people on Spice.

They looked like dipsomaniacs emerging from an alcohol-induced coma.

It would have been frightening if they had been sitting there with knives, but it was petrifying because each one of them had a harpoon gun slung on their back; the blunt end of a spirogyra was sticking out where the harpoon tip should have been.

They eyed us suspiciously through blood-shot eyes. Then an extraordinary thing happened. As we walked through the aisle towards the doorway of the inn, they all stood up and started clapping. Some cheered.

There were choruses of: 'Bob the Nob!'

These people clearly loved my smelly driver. They adored him. I took it as a nob meaning a posh person; I do not think Bob would have smiled if they were referring to him as a knob.

Chapter Sixteen

Trapped

'What would you like, Bob?'

'I wouldn't trust the beer here,' he noted.

My heart sank when I thought he might go for wine or, worse, a spirit. Whisky imported from Scotland was exorbitant, vodka imported from Ireland was exorbitant and gin imported from London was exorbitant.

'I'll have a cider,' he decided.

'Great idea,' I agreed readily, it had to be cheap. Thom had given me gadgets but not much money. It would have been suspicious. 'Two pints of your finest cider, please, landlord.'

It had to be cheap.

'We've only got the local scrumpy. It's dry, it's still and it's got a kick like a racehorse.'

'Sounds wonderful.'

I put my bag on the floor and carried two pints of the pub's finest scrumpy from the bar and out to the tables. I did not smoke but I liked the smell, and you could get a bit high just breathing in the fumes. When I went back to get my bag, it was gone. I was not worried. I had the key to a lock that sealed the top and Bob would get the bag back to me.

Bob the knob and I were about to enjoy a pint together while I told him about my bag when I heard a phut and then I heard strands of fish wire whirring around my ears and body; it was like there were fifteen freshwater fishermen casting at the same time. Reel after reel of thick fishing line spiralled around me. Then I heard a click and that meant the loops had been completed.

The spirogyra motors hummed as the loop lines were spun back around the reel wheel.

The wires tightened around me and dug into my flesh. I was trapped; the wire criss-crossed my body, pinning my limbs together, stopping me from moving anything bar my feet and hands but with my arms pinned to my side at the bicep and forearm and wrist, it was impossible to use them.

Trussed up like a chicken, I was reminded of Mary Botham Howitt: 'At last, Up jumped the cunning Spider, and fiercely held her fast. He dragged her up his winding stair, into his dismal den,
Within his little parlour – but she ne'er came out again!'

The wire that spiralled around my body bit into my flesh, I dared not move for fear that the nylon would actually pierce my flesh. I had carried plastic bags for my mother and the handles had cut into my hand – this was worse.

I could feel the bonds digging into my skin, my nerves jangled with the web that weaved itself around my body. The wire dug into my thighs and calves, my waist, my chest, my biceps and forearms.

My legs were pinned together, a strand dug into my buttocks, my arms were stuck to my sides. I might as well have been a statue for all the movement that I was capable of making. It was an effort to breathe.

I looked up and saw the landlord. He was standing over me, holding a harpoon gun in one hand and the yellow bag in the other. He had only gone and cut the top off it and had a good rummage around inside. Before I could say anything, four figures picked me up and manhandled me behind the bar and down the steep steps to where the beer was kept.

It was cold and dark there.

Lying on my side, I felt my shoulder going numb; the concrete-hard cellar floor was unforgiving.

I needed forgiveness, forgiveness for being so naïve as to think that I could take on any smuggler and win, let alone Lawless with all his influence and ingenuity.

I needed forgiveness for putting Adel and Thom on a pedestal and falling in love with them.

I needed forgiveness for getting myself into this situation, for promising my mother that I would see her again.

I was frightened; for the first time I was fearful, not of danger but of my own death. I would have shouted but only people who despised the authorities would hear me. There was no way they would help me. I was a spy, a mole, a traitor to the working man, the smuggler, the barterer, the coster or costermonger who sold his possessions to provide food for his family.

It was clear that I had betrayed those who had been let down by The Administration and whose only crime was to try and put bread on the table. In their eyes, I was the evil one and I was beginning to think they were right.

Just as I was beginning to think how cold and quiet it was in the cellar; I heard the sound.

A hiss like a snake came from the bottom of the step. I craned my neck to try and see. My body was cooling rapidly; I dreaded the point where my shivering might make the bonds cut more deeply into my flesh. The sound reminded me of urination and made me want to go for a pee.

I could not see, so with a supreme effort I rolled on to my back. I felt the nylon cable straining and digging into my limbs; my left hand enjoyed the relief.

Twisting my hips, I managed to move my legs on to the other side and wriggling painfully I managed to get my shoulders and head to face the right way. I could now see the doorway through which the dim light fell, and the wooden steps, and the source of the sound. I expected to be faced by an adder, cobra or rattlesnake. It was a common form of execution in some smuggling circles. Poisonous snakes were a growth import.

What I saw was much worse. It was a yellow hose. I could see it trailing down the stairway and the black hole was spouting water, which spread like spilt paint across the floor. The island of water grew. The hole in the pipe spewed out liquid. Death by drowning was my fate after all.

If I thought I was uncomfortable lying in the spirogyra net, I had only tasted the beginning. The shock of freezing-cold water seeping into the cuff of my right hand and oozing into my shoe and up my right trouser leg sent a shiver up my spine.

I could not imagine how anyone could make things much worse than they were. I would have wriggled in distress if I could have moved. There was no rush to drown me. I wondered how many hours it would take for me to die.

My mind raced even though I was in no position to move much. The bonds around my body meant movement of any kind was impossible. I was just like a fly in a spider's web; there was no room for manoeuvre.

My choices were simple: lie on my right side, lie on my left side, or lie on my back. Lying on my back was the most comfortable and put my nose further above the water, which I could feel spreading over the floor where my body lay; my hair and right ear became moist.

Another huge effort to twist my hips resulted in my legs moving, with the nylon threads cutting into my torso; I managed to roll on to my back. The icy water made me gasp.

Despite my prone position, my heart joined my mind and started racing too, even though I had willed myself to remain calm, telling myself to think of a solution. There had to be a way out, I would not give up hope.

I could feel the water creeping over my body, millimetre by millimetre. I knew there was no escape.

Then I remembered the story of a man in the floods of twenty-two; he had his foot trapped by a collapsed wall, they tried to cut him free, but he refused amputation.

Eventually, the water rose up to his nose and he drowned horribly. It was an excruciating and horrendous way to die. There was no way that I could avoid a similar fate. All I could hope for was a reprieve but mercy, dispensed by smugglers, was in short supply. I remembered poor Freddie and the poor smuggler's wife having difficulty swimming with her hands tied behind her back.

I cursed my foolishness in foul language that I no longer cared to moderate. I mourned the fact that I would never see my mother again; I would never see Adel, or Thom. I had only loved two women in my life, and they had sent me to my premature death; it was just too much to take.

Drowning, of all things, after all the experiences I had endured, filled me with horror. I remembered Freddie's face so clearly. The expression of hope it wore even though he had been doped. He had wanted to cling on to life. The water had swallowed him up. It was my turn next. I wondered for the first time how I had survived that dreadful day.

Still the hose hissed in the stairwell, and the water welled up in the cellar. I rotated my eyes, first left, then right, looking for any route out, a chink in the wall, but there was nothing.

The walls were well rendered, damp-proofed, freshly painted, well maintained as any beer or wine cellar should be. The water rose a millimetre more; my whole body was convulsing with cold. The flow was freezing. I wondered if hypothermia would claim my life before the water had a chance to cover my mouth and nostrils.

Inspiration came as I felt every millimetre of my back soaking up the water. The wool of my jumper – the lovely lambswool, charcoal grey sweater that Major Thom bought me – absorbed the chill fluid. The navy cotton chinos from John Lewis sucked up the solution from the floor, absorbing the chill moisture and transferring it to my goose-pimpled skin.

I was stunned by what suddenly seemed relevant, gifts I received seemed important. I ached to have the St Jude medallion that my mother had given me. My shoes, those elegant brogues from Loake, would need baling out soon.

I could feel the water find its way into my socks and seep deep down into the heel of each shoe. It was torture; the cold water seemed to be chilling my bones.

The idea I came up with was to let them think that I had information that would be useful to them.

All I needed to do was think of something that might appeal to them enough to let me live. I had to think fast; I wondered whether they would be able to hear my shouts from the bowels of the building. I shuddered, spluttering as the water rose up towards my mouth and nose. I grasped at some ideas but dismissed them. I could confess to working for The Administration, but they would surely let me die.

What did they have to fear; they knew all military efforts were being used to protect the king and the wealthy, the only ones who actually could afford to pay tax and actually paid tax. As long as the poor bartered and smuggled, taxpayers' money did not need to be spent on welfare benefits.

The law forbidding any non-taxpayer from receiving the dole, housing benefit, food stamps or treatment in hospital had absolved The Administration of any duty of care. I had been treated in a charity hospital financed by altruistic industrialists and philanthropic businesspeople. Working for the government was worse than murder.

Still the water rose, soaking my shoulder, my flank, and my thigh, drenching my Achilles heel. I had to find theirs.

I could offer them nothing. There was no way out. Struggling was useless.

Chapter Seventeen

Super Supper, Ego Flatterer

My mind drifted back to that evening where I had agreed to work for Thomasina again.

'Good evening,' she sang, her voice was so sweet to my ears, as smooth as silk; then she smiled, and my heart melted.

Thomasina was wearing a black dress that hugged her figure; it looked like she had been poured into that dress and had forgotten to say when.

'You look stunning,' I murmured, trying to sound both mysterious and sophisticated and failing on all counts.

'And you are still the most handsome man I know,' she replied, looking me up and down appreciatively.

I flushed, genuinely embarrassed. Little did I know this was her training talking, she knew how to seduce someone, make them feel at ease, make them confess, make them do her bidding. Calling me a man worked a treat; most people dismiss me with the word boy, and it appeared I was a man in her eyes and a desirable one at that. How gullible I was.

'I'm not used to having a woman open the door in a black dress,' I stammered.

'Darling, if I had a door in this dress, I would open it for you,' she quipped.

I gawped as I processed that salacious comment. There was an awkward silence.

'Sorry, that was too forward of me; I was just kidding, trying to break the ice,' she apologised.

'I think the ice cap has melted,' I responded feebly.

'Come and have a drink; what would you like, a Martello Tower?' she asked.

'I've never had one but that sounds great.'

'It's a long drink, you look thirsty.'

I was hungry too, like a wolf, and I wanted to devour her.

'Thank you,' I whispered nonchalantly.

She brought over two highball glasses with ice and a fizzy brown drink that looked like whisky and soda.

'It's brandy; it will bring your blood pressure down and it will mean you can enjoy the wine at supper without worrying about mixing grape and grain.'

'It really helps the blood pressure.'

'But of course, St Bernard dogs always carried it in the mountains; you want the heart rate to remain low, no sudden shock to the injured. Whisky is the one to get your heart rate up, if someone has a heart attack and you want to bring the blood pressure up, give them whisky – remember that.'

'It could come in useful, I suppose,' I agreed reticently. I wanted frivolous conversation and flirtation, not a science lesson.

'It will do. Lawless has a heart condition and a cholesterol level that invites a cardiac arrest.'

'Lawless? You're not sending me back there, I've escaped twice.'

'Third time lucky.'

'Yes, for them! They'll catch me this time.'

'I'll look after you.'

'Please, Thomasina, don't send me back, I beg of you.'

'Darling, we won't do anything that is not strictly necessary. Let's have supper and talk about it later.'

I saw a shadow appear in the doorway.

'Supper will be served in fifteen minutes, Ma'am,' announced Corporal Jessop.

He was standing at the door wearing a navy and white striped apron over charcoal grey trousers and an immaculate white shirt.

'Thank you, Corporal, have you had a drink?'

'I poured myself some of the Bourgogne Aligoté, to try it as you asked, Ma'am,' he confessed.

'How was it?'

'Delicious.'

'I'm glad, save some for us, please,' she joked. 'And the red?'

'Your favourite, Nuits St George.'

'Perfect.'

My heart sank; I was to be wooed tonight. I could see the evening unfolding: she would fill me with wonderful food, prepared by her expert cook and batman, Jessop, then she would flirt outrageously with me; then she would ply me with fine wines; and then I would agree to do anything she asked.

All dreams of a mad passionate night evaporated with my revelation. The brandy did lower my heart rate, but it also sapped my strength. I knocked it back and put the glass on the table. Jessop had a refill in my hand sooner than you could say: 'Where's my drink gone?'

He was complicit in the plot, too. There was no way out.

Chapter Eighteen

Survival

There was no way out of the cellar and no service that I could sell in order to save my skin.

The last thing Thomasina said to me before I left her that night was: 'I'll look after you.' How hollow those words seemed at that moment.

I was freezing. I was not shivering but convulsing with cold; my flesh felt like water and the nylon spirogyra chords cut deeper and deeper as I wriggled like a fish caught on a line. It was a huge effort to hold my head above water, my neck was straining, and my shoulder muscles were trembling with the effort of holding up my head. I would die of hypothermia or drown like Freddie in minutes.

Suddenly, the water stopped rising. I knew because I had been warily watching the water level rise up the brickwork, working out how long I had before I would die.

The door opened and there was my captor. His voice boomed around what was to all intents and purposes, a massive indoor pool. He stood on the step just above the waterline, if I could have moved, I would have kicked him off that podium before he made the inevitable speech.

'I'm not sure if you're good or bad; a threat or an asset but I am tripping over people who want to help me and I cannot afford any negative attention, particularly from the "Snatch Squads" so it's goodbye. You seemed like a nice guy, but my sixth sense warned me against trusting you. I liked you but I smelt a rat. I'm sorry you had to go this way, just like Freddie.'

So, he knew; there was not much chance of him changing his mind now, was there? I had just about heard everything but only dimly.

I had managed to piece together his rambling farewell through guesswork, but I was damned if I was going to give him the satisfaction of explaining my murder to me.

With a herculean effort I lifted my mouth out of the water, took a deep breath and shouted, 'I can't hear you!'

'Never mind,' he gasped in frustration.

I knew it bothered him and, besides, I never liked him and cursed my judgement for choosing to hitchhike on such a rainy day and I cursed my misfortune at being picked up by him. I cursed Thomasina for forcing me back into danger. My wonderful Major Thom had not sent the Snatch Squad to save me.

The Snatch Squad, The Administration's secret weapon that was no longer a secret. The squads would drop into smugglers' territories and capture the figurehead. They dared not attempt such a trick on Lawless; he was far too well protected. The lesser criminals were the perfect targets for being snatched and taken away. The squads were not going to waste their time saving me.

My neck finally gave way, and my nose and mouth sank under the water. I lay like that quivering with cold, waiting for my last gasp, waiting for the life force to leave my body and leave behind a petrified corpse.

'How long would my frozen body take to stiffen?' I wondered. 'Do cold bodies stiffen into rigor mortis more quickly?'

Chapter Nineteen

Sending Me to the Denouement

I must have passed out because I remember having a dream.

Lawless stood in the cavernous space that was his lair; the hangar seemed even bigger than before. He was armed with a spirogyra harpoon gun.

'Give it up, Lawless,' I demanded, moving towards him with all the confidence of a man who was on the winning side, 'you're completely surrounded by Number 45 Commando!'

I heard a phut and then I heard strands of fish wire whirring around my ears and body; it was like there were fifteen freshwater fishermen casting at the same time. Reel after reel of thick fishing line spiralled around me. Then I heard a click and that meant the loops had been completed.

The spirogyra motors hummed as the loop lines were spun back around the reel wheel. The wires tightened around me and dug into my flesh.

I was trapped; the wire criss-crossed my body, pinning me limbs together, stopping me from moving anything bar my feet and hands but with my arms pinned to my side at the bicep and forearm and wrist, it was impossible to use them.

Again, I tried to keep my balance but ending up falling over. This time I fell on my face, which was held in position by a rogue strand of spirogyra wire.

My face hit the floor and my chin almost knocked my teeth out.

'So, you killed my son and you wanted to imprison me; you're lucky my Magnum .44 is in the Rolls!'

I was lucky but not that lucky.

Lawless marched across to me and swinging his right leg back he planted the thick leather toecap of his Church black brogue right into my family jewels. As I tried to curl into a ball, he turned on his heels and walked to the desk.

I thought *this is it*; Lawless must be going for a gun hidden in the drawer.

Instead, he pressed a button and sat on the enormous La-Z-Boy chair between the desk and the sofa. I saw the roof of the hangar slide open.

There was a tremendous explosion, louder than a gunshot – more like a grenade exploding – and the chair shot up through the hole and into the sky. I could not see where it was headed. All I could do was wriggle in agony, it was like someone had crushed one of my gonads; it ached like a broken bone and I felt an ache in the pit of my stomach,

I gasped in pain, gulping in a mouthful of the noxious smoke that Lawless's ejector seat had emitted and which floated and spread across the floor. It tasted of gunpowder and chemicals that explode in the laboratory and leave behind an unhealthy stench.

I heard that rattle of gunfire. I assumed it was 45 Commando laying down a barrage, but I was wrong. The firing was coming from the bay, covering Lawless's escape.

Not only had I failed in my mission, Lawless was still at large and after me.

I later learnt that a zero-zero ejection seat is designed to safely extract upward and land its occupant from a grounded stationary specifically from aircraft cockpits.

The zero-zero capability was developed to help aircrews escape upward from unrecoverable emergencies during low-altitude or low-speed flight, as well as ground mishaps.

Parachutes require a minimum altitude for opening, to give time for deceleration to a safe landing speed, so zero-zero technology uses small rockets to propel the seat upward to an adequate altitude and a small explosive charge to open the canopy quickly for a successful parachute descent.

The seat cannon clears the seat from the aircraft, then the under-seat rocket pack fires to lift the seat to altitude. As the rockets fire for longer than the cannon, they do not require the same high forces. The zero-zero rocket seats also reduced forces on the pilot during any ejection, reducing injuries and spinal compression.

I had to act fast; I had to stop Lawless getting away. But I was helpless.

Some commandoes burst into the room.

Within minutes they had cut me out of the spirogyra net. I knew where he was heading or at least suspected it.

'What happened?' I asked.

'Lawless shot through the roof, we had been instructed only to fire if we were fired upon. He landed in the water. We had two ribs standing by but when they arrived all that was remaining was the parachute canopy.'

'Where did he go?'

'We suspect it was a submarine.'

'A small one?'

'Yes, to get into a shallow harbour like this.'

'Can you send your boys to Kate's cottage, The Rover's Rest?'

'Of course, you ought to get yourself checked out,' he warned.

'No time for that!'

Outside my super-scooter stood in the car park. My fingerprint recognition system was on, so I picked up the handlebars, which were resting on the seat.

The electric motor clicked into life.

Stepping over the seat, I sat down and twisted the accelerator. The commandoes watched as I rode my bike down the sloping hard that led into the harbour. I moved the handlebars forward and leant my body over the front wheel. As I did so some hems rose around my feet.

With a splash, the scooter hit the water and the wheels locked; the rear jets pushed the scooter through the water.

My waterproof boots kept my feet dry, but my jeans and jacket were swamped in seawater within seconds. I had expected the chilled water to make me gasp but I was so focused on getting to Kate's place before Lawless's midget submarine, I did not notice.

His craft was about fifteen metres long and almost two metres in diameter. It displaced 27 tons surfaced and 30 tons submerged.

The maximum speed was five knots submerged and, on the surface, about ten or twelve knots. My adapted jet ski could do thirty knots, driven flat out, and I was on full-throttle.

The cottage was fifteen miles away, I was sure I could catch up. The windscreen protected me from the sea at the front but not at the side. I was drenched but, squinting through half-closed eyes, I shot through the water like a torpedo.

Then, I woke up.

Chapter Twenty

Deliverance

Coming to my senses, I realised why I had dreamt of cold water. The cellar was flooded still but my head was no longer underwater. I was not sure what had happened at first, but my mouth and nose were no longer submerged. The cellar was being drained. I choked. Water had run into my nostrils and I had almost drowned, despite keeping my mouth tightly shut. I was not sure if my mouth had opened when I fell unconscious. It fell open when I slept but I wanted to know if my willpower had been strong enough to save me.

Why was Bob the Nob giving me a second chance?

I knew that once he had managed to look inside my bag, he would know I was an agent for The Administration. Who else would carry all those gadgets? Thomasina had supplied me with survival equipment as well as a Taser, Glock and Epi-pen along with other goodies. In short, there was a foil sleeping bag worth hundreds, cereal bars, vitamin drinks and all the stuff I had used to take out Adel and Kate last time I was in Poseidon Bay.

Giving me the bag fitted with a lock to stop prying eyes and thieving hands had not been such a good idea after all. Still, who could have envisaged someone splitting it open with a machete? I wondered why a landlord would have such a dangerous weapon on the premises but then I remembered the customers high as kites. I think I would have had something to scare them off. In their paranoid state, seeing a long-handled knife with a huge blade would have petrified them.

I wondered how many fingers the publican had severed to secure the pub.

Running a bar was difficult enough; cash could go missing, booze could be drunk without the bar staff taking payment, or they might give free drinks to their friends. Food could be stolen.

My mind wandered as the water gurgled down the drain. It was a sound that I relished. I was only in a few centimetres of water, shivering still, but I was relieved that I was safe. My dream was some sort of wish to be in control; it seemed all the women called the shots and I just did as I was told. Fat lot of good it did me. I had almost been drowned.

Then I began to wonder about the sudden reprieve I had received. Why was the water level dropping and who had decided that I should live? I heard two sets of footsteps coming down the stairs. It was Bob the Nob; I imagined it was the landlord behind him, judging by the thump of heavy boots.

'If you would kindly cut through the netting, unlock the cuffs, you might say, Bobby Boy, I will see if we can show you some clemency,' she said.

I recognised the mellifluous tones of Major Thom. She had kept her word, she had looked after me, and she had come to me in my hour of need, just as she said she would.

My heart leapt. I was glad to see Bob the knob only because he was going to undo the fishing tackle handcuffs that imprisoned me. He grunted as he came down to my level; he even got his trousers wet when he knelt on the damp cellar floor. The next sound I heard was the sound of the fish net being cut. Several snicks, the knife slicing through fabric as he released me from my nylon bonds. He was not very gentle with my arms, he was downright rough, and I heard Thom cough, a warning 'ahem'.

'I've released your boyfriend', he sneered as he rose to his feet, 'you keep your part of the bargain.'

'My boyfriend? Darling, I'm engaged to a cavalry officer in the Horse Guards, his horse is worth more than your house.'

'Rot in hell!' he screamed defiantly.

'We know about the swimming lessons you gave your wife. This is for mistreating my "boyfriend" you hound,' she whispered.

Thomasina hissed the words at him. Then she fired her Taser. Bob danced like a drunken Morris Dancer.

It was wonderful to see how agile such a corpulent man could be. The electricity arced from his damp trousers to his chest. I looked at his pained expression and I have to admit, I felt no remorse at watching him suffer.

Thomasina enjoyed the show too; she had a sadistic side that she revealed only when she was dealing with worms like Bob. She hated bullies and clearly Bob was a bully as well as a murdering so and so.

How he danced and pranced like a show pony, a Lipizzaner at the Spanish Riding School in Vienna. Watching the pained expression on his face, like a tortured thespian playing Odysseus tormented by the Sirens, and seeing how he folded like a drunken sailor, and clattered to the cement cellar floor, like a sack full of oysters, filled me with glee. It was a satisfactory revenge and provided an opportunity for the use of lots of nautical similes for me to imagine. They whirled through my mind. There had been a television show about the wonderful white horses my dad had made me watch and Bob's footwork might have got him an audition as stand-in for one of those beautiful creatures.

As he lay unconscious on the still damp ground, Thom flashed me a smile and I fell in love with her yet again.

I was beginning to wonder why everyone I ever fell for always seemed to be engaged already. It was one of the perils of admiring the older woman, I suppose. They were ready to settle down after their adventures, yet I was ready to start my first.

'Right, boyfriend,' Thom joshed, 'time to get you on the move, again, and get you to meet up with Terence.'

'After almost drowning, you want me to carry on the mission?' I asked, hoping my gaping mouth would communicate my incredulity.

'Of course, Terence has to be stopped,' she responded as if this was some axiomatic fact. I read a lot when I was younger and prefer the word to self-evident.

'This is the second time I have almost drowned,' I complained.

I was soaked, my clothes were drenched, and I was hoping that my rage would stop my teeth from chattering and my body being wracked by shivering.

'Each time, I have saved you,' Thom reminded me.

'Of course, but you haven't saved me from the psychological repercussions of each event; both times I almost died of hypothermia by the time I was rescued,' I argued.

As if on cue, a soldier rumbled down the wooden stairs and wrapped a tinfoil survival blanket around my shoulders.

'There we are,' he soothed, I felt like he was treating me like one of the horses from the Household Cavalry.

Thom had taken me to see the barracks at Knightsbridge, bristling with machine guns and missiles since Brexit. It was one of my breaks from training. The beautiful heavy hunters were brought into the stables and covered in horse blankets. Just like the groom who had said encouraging words to the horses then abruptly disappeared at some signal from Thom, the soldier left the room, and we were alone. She was good at creating situations where we were alone, but nothing ever happened. Nothing, except I got excited and even more confused than I already had been.

Clearly, I was Thomasina's horse, just like poor Boxer, in *Animal Farm*; I was going to be sold off to the glue factory.

'We need you, Aubrey, do this for Adel, do this for Kate and do this for me,' she implored, her eyes locking on mine.

I looked into those almond pools. I looked at those lascivious lips. She licked them with her tongue. I thought she was going to kiss me. She had kissed me once already; it had been on that night when she convinced me to go back and pick up Freddie's body.

That was then, and this was now, as far as I was concerned. When the kiss promised further reward, I was on board. Now that I knew she had a fiancé; I was no longer prepared to be used anymore.

'I think you can do it on your own, you don't need me,' I assured her.

I turned on my heel and stomped up the stairs my feet squelching in my socks, my shoes still brim-full of water. It was difficult to show how annoyed with her I was with little quacking noises coming from my footwear.

An army field ambulance was waiting for me outside. I noted the benches were empty and assumed my 'Spice' girls and boys had been rounded up and were being taken handcuffed up to London on the M3. Stretcher-bearers moved towards the pub, probably to pick up Bob. I hoped they left him clothed so he woke up soaked to the skin. Hopping up into the back of the ambulance, I came across a sweet-looking nurse – not my type and about nineteen. She was sitting on the bench seat.

'Hi, I'm Aubrey,' I said.

'I'm Sarah,' she replied.

'Can you pass me a towel?' I asked.

I let my tinfoil cover and my trousers drop, peeled off my shirt and underpants. I have a good body and have never been shy about taking my clothes off. Sarah handed me a couple of bath towels, thick, officer quality; they were white, but I would not have been surprised if they had been khaki.

'Get yourself dry and we'll give you something to help with the pain,' she said.

I smiled and wrapped my torso in one towel and wrapped the other over my shoulders.

'Thanks, morphine again, I cannot wait,' I joked.

She gave me two Paracetamol. I looked at her in disgust.

'Nothing more unless Major Thom gives me the say-so,' she explained, smiling sweetly.

'So, she's putting the pressure on, thinking I'll crack. I don't need my opium fix that badly. I'm not some heroin addict.'

'Why not take your pills and lie down on the bed for a few minutes. I'll leave you to get yourself dry,' she whispered.

I was shattered after my ordeal. Her voice was like balm. I sat on the bed and she moved past me and through to the tailgate, shutting it behind her. I was alone with my thoughts and two fairly fluffy towels, which were already making me feel warmer.

My teeth started chattering yet again. I could just not get warm; I was not suffering from hypothermia, but I was close enough to it. I lay down on the bed wrapped up. As I drifted off to sleep, I smelt fresh soap and apple shampoo; my administering angel, Sarah, had returned and as Morpheus once more embraced me, I felt her drape a cotton blanket over me.

Then she put a brown woollen blanket over that. It smelt of horse. I wondered if she had picked it up from the stables behind the pub.

I was Boxer – I certainly felt like the horse doing all the work. I thought of the irony of it and my mind went blank. Apparently, I snored like a trooper. When I woke up, I was in a hospital bed at the Fleet Air Arm Museum in Ilchester near Yeovil. I could see the big hangars where the aircraft and helicopters from the twentieth century were stored.

When I was well enough, I was given a tour. I saw the Swordfish that sunk the Italian navy, a helicopter from the Queen's Flight, Harrier Jump Jets with Bristol Pegasus engines and Blackburn Buccaneers with Rolls-Royce Spey engines. These days the Buccaneers had taken over Wessex and Cornwall, Essex and Yorkshire, Lancashire and Rhyl.

I had been in bed two days, sleeping solidly from the time we drove down the A303 from Beer until Tuesday. The same nurse was with me. I was becoming institutionalised, wondering if most of my life was going to be spent with brief interludes outside hospital.

'Hello, again,' Sarah said smiling, sticking a thermometer in my open mouth as I started to speak.

I mumbled, 'Where am I?'

It sounded indistinct with the glass tube in my mouth, but she understood.

'Just south-east of Ilchester,' Sarah explained and seeing my confused frown, she illuminated me further. 'You're at the Fleet Air Arm Museum, part of which was turned into a hospital during the Virulent Virus. We're next to one of The Administration's military bases, the Royal Naval Air Station Yeovilton.'

'How far is that from Poseidon Bay?' I asked once she slipped the thermometer from between my lips.

'Portwrinkle is about 100 miles away,' she remarked casually, 'about the same distance as Exeter from Plymouth.'

'I've got further away, not closer, it will take forever to get there,' I complained.

'Not by helicopter,' Sarah noted.

I looked at her askance, I said: 'Curiouser and curiouser.'

ii

I decided the best idea would be to hitch a ride on the B3151 that ran past us; grab a lift on a delivery truck, then on to the A303, followed by the A30 and A38. That would get me to Plymouth. How I would get over the Tamar, I did not know. Lawless controlled the toll bridge with frightening security measures. His patrols policed the waters below. He could afford a huge defence force.

His territory stretched from Boscastle and Crackington Haven in the north, to St. Germans in the south and spread west encompassing Bodmin, bordered by Newquay and St. Austell. The rest of Cornwall was shared between several smuggling gangs, The Administration controlling St. Ives, Falmouth, Penzance and Mousehole.

That was my decision, but I was not in charge, what I had plotted counted for nothing.

I was dressing on the third morning of conscious awareness, looking forward to the tour my angelic nurse had offered me when there was a knock at the door. The door swung open before I could ask the intruder to wait. I was hopping around on one foot trying to put my last sock on when Thom swept into the room like a tornado. Like a magician she palmed the door behind her, and it slammed shut.

Her smile, her perfume, her gorgeous looks and a uniform that clung to her like a second skin almost seduced me into falling in love with her again. My emotions were kept in check by my imaginings of the ever-so tall, ever-so handsome and ever-so rich fiancé who awaited her in London.

'Good morning, Aubrey. Fully recovered from your baptism?' she joked.

I stared at her, giving her the dirtiest look that I could muster.

'Fully, thank you, though morphine would have helped me recover quicker,' I opined, pulling on my jeans whose drainpipe style necessitated putting my socks on first. They were long socks bought by Thom. I pictured her handsome hunk wearing such.

'Good, good, we thought Paracetamol would suffice, we don't want you being dependent, do we?'

'Dependent on you or dependent on drugs?' I quipped, slipping on the light blue Hilditch & Key Sea Island cotton shirt that she had bought for me. It fitted like a glove.

'Ever been in a helicopter?' she asked nonchalantly.

I admired the way she changed subject without a blush.

'Not yet,' I admitted.

'Good, thirteen fifty, you will be collected from the mess, your bag will be packed, just be ready to leave. Enjoy your tour of the facility and your lunch.'

About-turn, a balletic palming of the door, open and shut, then I was left in the silence that would have followed her if it could walk through walls. I still liked my plan more but since everyone at the base was on Thom's side, I thought it prudent to obey her wishes for the time being.

The arrival of my nurse reminded me that I was institutionalised, resistance was useless, I just had to go along with what everyone else wanted. I had to be a patently patient patient. Putting on my patent leather Loake shoes, I sat on the bed and waited to be picked up by my attractive nurse. I wondered if she was engaged or married.

I should have picked up the courage to ask her.

She gave me a tour and I think she liked me. I was going to ask for her number and suggest we meet up after this ordeal was over.

My heart was filling with love for her until I realised she was just keeping me busy. All my suggestions of a reunion were rebuffed. Any efforts at deeper conversation were dismissed. Still, we enjoyed a vegan lunch together – salad and couscous.

When we came out of the mess, I could hear the distinctive sound of a helicopter engine in the distance and there was a short-wheelbase Land Rover waiting for me. It was open to the elements. Thomasina sat in the back; there were two marine commandoes, one next to her, the other, the driver, sat in front of her. The passenger door was open, an invitation for me to jump in.

'Thanks for the tour,' I said, coolly.

'I was hoping for a thank you kiss,' she replied.

My bad mood lifted, and my heart melted.

I turned and kissed her on the cheek. A farewell.

'I'll give you a proper one if I get back,' I promised.

She smiled; it might have been sympathy, or it might have been orders; she was either very shy or a great actress. Knowing what I know now, the latter would be my bet.

Clambering into the four-by-four, I ironically saluted her, and she sweetly waved back. Maybe she did like me after all. I was sick of being used by women; my stomach churned, and my heart grew heavy. Was this what being in love was like? I couldn't make up my mind between any of the girls I had met. I loved them all but not one of them loved me.

Adel was a treacherous viper; Kate hated me for what I had done to her; Thom was engaged; and my lovely nurse, Sarah, was only nice to me because she was following Thom's orders. By the time I had processed all this, we were well on our way and I decided to enjoy the ride as much as I could with my heart broken in so many places by so many women.

The Land Rover had a throaty V8 engine and it roared through the space between the hangars. The military never had to worry about fuel rationing; they could get what they wanted. Their mechanics had carte blanche to mix fuels and supercharge.

The driver acted as if he was rushing to put out a fire and when we broke out on to the tarmac runway, I really felt he was aiming to take off. The stripped-down vehicle had a windscreen, and the only two windows were wound down.

The wind whipped through my hair. Of course, the others were unperturbed because they were wearing their green berets. Thomasina had on her black beret with the silver badge of the Royal Green Jackets. All the disbanded regiments had been reintroduced into the British Army but located in the Commonwealth countries, their officers sent to Sandhurst for training. Her hair was tied in a bun behind her head. She had told me their motto was 'Celer et Audax' meaning 'Swift and Bold'. She had certainly asked her driver to be quick in getting us to the helicopter. 'Tempus fugit', clearly, as my dear old mammy used to say.

It was a weird experience; the growl of the engine was drowned out by the wind in my ears and that noise was swallowed up by the sound of the rotors and the engine. The Westland Wessex was a museum piece; I think they must have wheeled it out from one of the exhibits.

It looked like someone had infected a bee and the injected body had swollen – the antennae were whirling around, the 'Ocelli' was swollen to make the top of the cabin, the compound eye was the glass of the cockpit; the swollen abdomen was the cargo bay, and the spinning sting was the rear rotor; its forelegs and hind legs had been replaced by wheels that looked so tiny compared to the gargantuan body. It was an image I tried to put together, but it did not work. Suffice to say, the pilot sat above and in front of the cargo hold and the propellers were on top.

My hair was windswept, and my ears were smarting from the sound. The Land Rover screeched to a halt. The engine died, not that you would notice with the racket of the helicopter engines. A mechanic in light grey RAF overalls that were smeared with oil jumped down from the cargo deck and, crouching to avoid the blades, hurtled towards the driver, a spanner in hand.

Exchanging only smiles and positions, the mechanic sat in the driver's seat and the marine darted towards the helicopter.

Not waiting for me to open the door, Thom and her bodyguard leapt over the side and ran towards the aircraft. The mechanic transferred his spanner to his left hand and slotted it into the dashboard shelf. He wore an aviator's cap with ear protectors built in. I was not going to get any conversation from him, so I opened the door and left him.

Following the others, I crouched low as I tried to run to the helicopter. It was not as easy as it looked. They were like fleeting shadows, moving like smoke over the tarmac and I was way behind them.

The sound of the rotors and the Rolls-Royce 'Gnome' engines was deafening, and I was heading for the epicentre; the engine was directly overhead. We would be sitting in the cargo bay where the sound was worst. However, following Thom in her super-tight trousers and watching her jump into the helicopter and squat down made me fall in love with her again.

She had the most amazing body, lithe and fit but curvy and feminine. I was intoxicated until I remembered the fiancé.

Reluctantly, I offered my elbows to the two marines who held out their hands and hauled me up into the space. The sparse cabin offered few creature comforts. A steel deck and four DPM camouflaged British Army ninety-litre short-back Bergen backpacks.

The three amigos sat on theirs, so I decided to do the same with mine, wishing I had the sort of padding that Thom had, or the iron discipline of my marine friends.

I sat in sullen silence, staring at the feet of the pilots. There was no barrier between cockpit and hold. I could see the instruments, one of the pilot's hands on one of the two joysticks and his feet suspended in what looked like stirrups, pedals that actually controlled the yaw of the aircraft.

I was handed a headset, a microphone and a pair of ear-defenders that did little to dispel the rising crescendo of the thundering engines. Hurriedly, I put them on and wired myself for sound.

The pitch rose, along with the volume, and it was like hearing screaming banshees against a backdrop of crashing waves in a thunderstorm, all turned up to full volume on surround sound.

The more violently the engine growled, the more the vibrations shook the whole cabin and the more my chest cavity heaved and trembled. I was conscious of the rotors and looking out of the doorway, I could see a darkening of the grass in a circle; it was not quite dark enough to be a shadow.

The others sat on their Bergens and stared out of the massive cargo doorways, I thought health and safety concerns might encourage them to slide the doors shut but clearly the marines and Green Jackets had not received that memo.

As we lifted off the ground, the movement of the port-side pilot left me transfixed. My eyes followed as his feet danced before my eyes and he pushed the joystick forward and as if by magic we rose in the air. From the corner of my eye, I could see the shadow of the helicopter, the grass getting further and further away and the shadow getting smaller and smaller. It was a miracle; six souls and tonnes of metal were leaving the field behind. We hurtled forwards and upwards, the nose of our waspy craft bowing as it took to the air.

I had been expecting to move upwards and then forwards, not both at the same time. We flew straight and fast like an arrow and the wind whistled through the cabin. We were aware of that noise and the sound of the motors and rotors almost drowned it out. Fortunately, it was made slightly duller when heard through our headphones.

Thom filled the radio silence.

'Around 55 Westland Wessex HU5s participated in the Falklands War, fighting in the South Atlantic in 1982. Their primary role was the landing, and moving forward, of Rapier missiles, fuel, artillery and ammunition,' she explained.

'And you're still flying this?' I asked incredulously, I knew the 'chopper' was old, I didn't know it was ancient.

'It's had various refits and it's been well-maintained,' she retorted, almost sounding hurt.

I did not share her faith in the mechanics on the ground or the mechanics in the air. My mother had regaled me with stories of my feckless dad spending weekends trying to fix some old jalopy. My mother's legacy was a love of literature, from George Elliot, through Graham Greene to Tom Wolfe; yes, she read him; quotations from Shakespeare, Keats and Yates and sound distrust of any machine from a hairdryer to an aircraft carrier. She apparently prayed all the way to Calais and back on the hovercraft and put a bottle of holy water in the glove box of any car my dad possessed.

'That's a relief, then, but will it get to Poseidon Bay?'

'That's not our destination. We're heading for Lympstone where we'll meet up with the SBS.'

'SBS?' I asked.

'Special Boat Service,' she replied, 'they'll train us in the use of canoes.'

'Canoes?'

'It's not obligatory to answer my explanations with repeating the last word I said as a question, Aubrey.'

I blushed.

'Okay, so we're going to sneak in using canoes.'

'Very good.'

'I've seen *The Cockleshell Heroes*, my Dad forced me to watch when I was six, seven, eight, nine, ten and twelve. I'm sure Lawless has seen the movie, too.'

'No doubt, but he'll be too busy dealing with the distraction organised by 45 Commando.'

'Why don't we provide the distraction and 45 go in?'

She laughed heartily. I loved her laugh, I loved her, and I laughed with her.

'Because,' she laughed.

'Because,' I laughed.

'Because, he has Adel and Kate as hostage, and he will kill them immediately we launch a direct assault on him.'

Neither of us laughed. I sat in stunned silence. The silence lasted a good five minutes as I processed the information.

'Any other questions, Aubrey?' she wondered after she had gauged that I had recovered from the shock.

'How?'

'Of course, we launched two operations. Adel and Kate were to sneak into the Whitsand Bay Hotel, sorry, the Poseidon Palace Hotel. All went well, they crossed the border on Triumph Tigers and the helmets stopped them from being recognised. Sadly, Lawless caught them just as they went in, recognised Adel immediately.'

'Poor Adel.'

I was back in love with her. I imagined that she didn't have a fiancé with a heavy hunter worth as much as a house. I was also a little in love with Kate despite the fact she had been in a bate. It was emotionally draining being in love with so many people at the same time. I was just glad that I wasn't going out with any of them, it would have been exhausting.

Unsurprisingly, we spent the next hour or so in silence. In silence is just a loose term. We did not talk but there was no silence from the whirlybird. I was aware why they called it a 'chopper'; even with my headset on I could hear the constant thud of the propellers like an axe on wood.

It was like being at a lumberjack festival, a constant cacophony of sound. The rotors shattered the silence with their thwump, thwump, thwump. The engine sounded strained all the time and the vibrations made me feel like I was being shaken in a Nutri-Bullet or food mixer. While I was like Elvis, all shook up, the marines slept like babies; their heads were nestled on their Bergens. Thomasina had her eyes closed but I knew that she must have been dreaming of her knight in super splendour, strutting around Horse Guards Parade, she was not in as deep a sleep as the commandoes though. I dreaded to think what filled their dreams.

I was left to my thoughts and they whirled around my head as quickly as the rotors spun above us. We were flying in an antique, but I was not afraid to die. I have never been afraid; St Jude has always looked after me.

Maybe, I had been afraid when I left the pub, when I was on the beach after Freddie died and when I was out to sea and when I went to raid Freddie's grave. However, I had never thought of actually dying except for when I was laid out on the pub cellar floor with water flooding in.

The last few years had been hellish. I would like to have a few stern words with the guy who said: 'May you live in interesting times.' Brexit had resulted in England becoming 'The Sick Man of Europe' yet again. Feckless groups of disenfranchised young men and women my age roamed the streets spitting hate and mugging indiscriminately.

The police were completely and utterly overwhelmed because government 'cutbacks' in the police, fire service and the National Health Service had decimated the force.

After the government collapsed and no party could form an administration, we had another interregnum. People had to fend for themselves, rents and rates were not collected, fences around running tracks were torn down and turnstiles at leisure centres were pinned back. Small areas of the country formed themselves into semi-autonomous collectives, some decided they could afford to maintain services, others decided to drain the pools and let the parks become wild.

These collectives or 'Communards' might comprise anything from half a street of residents to a small village. The patchwork of councils was replaced by smaller administrative sections, all solving their local problems in their own unique way. I lived and worked in the foundry until it closed; my British passport saved me from deportation. At first, the deportations were not based on race; if you had a British passport you stayed, if you had European, Asian or American citizenship you went. It was a difficult time; whole communities were torn apart; it was like the First and Second World War again. The population was decimated.

While Europe made a deal with North Africa, the 'Solar and Wind for Water Deal' of 2022, England continued to use diesel ships to transport materials. An American shipping company had come up with a great idea: they would swap fresh water for solar-powered electricity. Their electric ships would dock and pump the water onshore and charged batteries would be slotted into the hold once it had dried out over the day.

These battery packs turned the boats into massive charging stations, huge chargers that would download their energy at a generating facility located by the sea, boosting its capacity. It was an excellent idea. They were already turning the Sahara into fertile land like the Egyptians did with the Nile. The solar panels shaded the ground and crops could be grown using the imported water. The engineering projects and opportunities resulting from them led to a brain drain.

Skilled and unskilled workers joined to make their fortunes. They lived in privileged ex-pat communities, living off the fat of the land in hotels built along the coast of northern Africa.

The financial services sector, insurance and the law were the only thriving areas in the economy. Engineers left in their droves and industry dwindled with the spiralling costs of raw materials and the lack of unskilled and skilled workers.

Chapter Twenty-One

Before the Brexit Wrecked It

As those thoughts whirled around my mind, like the rotor blades, I became used to the racket and the cold wind on my face, the blistering of my ears. I shivered and shrugged my shoulders to bury my neck further in the collar of my lightweight Belgian Congo pattern camouflage jacket. It smelt clean and starched against my skin, the lapels smelt of soap.

Fatigue overcame me even though I had slept so much in hospital. I dreamed of my mother as if she was still here. We were back in our old home, not where I was born but the small, terraced slum house my mum was forced to live in when my dad moved out.

She worked at a local school; we had them back then before The Administration decided they could save money by producing a 'Virtual Curriculum' and selling the schools off to property developers. Old Victorian triple-deck schools became loft apartments with mezzanine floors and steel staircases.

It was before the property collapse.

More modern schools became Bauhaus spaces with minimalist furniture and views on to the playground, which was turned into six-storey shared ownership, brick built New York style blocks of flats.

We were in a tenement house with two tiny bedrooms; it was a two-up-two-down with an outside toilet and a back yard backing on to a lane. It was basic but my mum kept it clean. She held down three jobs to pay the rent and feed me.

We had no television but lots of books, five pence each from the closing library. My mum got a barrow-load. I accessed the 'Virtual Curriculum' through a second-hand iPad.

In my dream, I was sitting in the kitchen reading the stockade scene from *Treasure Island*, while my dear, old Mammy made a stew on the gas hob. It was vegetable stock, leeks and carrots, my favourite. She was listening as she chopped and prepared. We were blissfully happy; we enjoyed each other's company and we loved *Treasure Island*.

As I read, I noticed she was in a dream world as she poured boiling water from the kettle into a stainless-steel saucepan and, starting with crushing the cheap stock cube, she added the other ingredients.

It was always the best time.

Lunch was a luxury read about in books, breakfast was a cup of tea, supper or dinner was our main meal. In between my mother's jobs, she would take time out to cook me a meal. She was always working otherwise: cleaning an estate agent's office in the morning, working at the hospital in administration, and her evening job was waitressing at an upmarket restaurant where she was given some left-over vegetables to take home at the end of each shift.

This was bliss, half an hour before we ate, reading, then, sitting down to a hot meal and half an hour chatting about what I had learnt and any stories from her colleagues at the hospital or at the bistro. They were tough times but happy times. We were talking about the first deportations and my mother prophetically decided that we should prepare for her deportation. I had a British passport; she had one from the Republic of Ireland.

Her Irish connections meant she had organised carrots and leeks to be delivered from the allotment of a man from Sligo. Rationing had not yet been brought in but, with the pound so weak, the farmers pushed up prices so they could afford fertilisers and pesticides. All foods became prohibitively expensive.

Inflation had taken off and pay packets were squeezed; having cash coming in was infinitely more preferable than having a higher wage. Cash flow was the key to survival, trying to keep as much money flowing into the account as going out. Survival was the only concern.

Bartering and smuggling came to the fore; it allowed people to live a little better, no longer rats on a treadmill, but able to enjoy a little luxury, not much but a little more than just surviving.

My dream was of the simple time just before things got really bad; a time when my mother shared time with me and worried about putting food on the table, paying the rent and surviving. A time before she was deported.

Chapter Twenty-Two

Special Boat Service

The chopper was landing when I woke up. It might have been the feeling of sinking or it might have the rise in pitch and volume of the engine noise that jolted me from my short repose.

I watched the helicopter land, noticing first that no one else except the pilot was interested in the manoeuvre and, secondly, that we were by the sea. I could smell seaweed, salty water and aviation fuel. Frighteningly, it looked like we were planning on landing on a small 'H' surrounded by a circle, which looked no bigger than a tablecloth from where I sat.

Landing and take-off are the most dangerous moments of any flight. The marines took up their positions. I noticed they had unhooked a Colt M4 Carbine each from the gun rack. It was the latest version of the M16 assault rifle manufactured by ArmaLite.

One took the port door, the other the starboard.

Meanwhile, Thom took her Glock 17M from its holster that hung from the belt that accentuated her slim waist. I have always been a bit of a weapons boffin. My dad bought me a book on guns just before he left.

These were momentary distractions. They were obviously preparing to be shot at by smugglers. The ground was moving towards us at an alarming rate and we had a pair of car tyres at the front and a wheel for a caravan tow bar at the back.

Just as I prepared to hit the deck at speed and see the craft broken into hundreds of pieces, we started to float above the ground as if we were on a magic carpet and after hanging there suspended for a few minutes, the pilot plopped the helicopter on the deck as daintily as a ballerina taking a curtsey.

The engine still roared above our heads.

If we had incoming gunfire, we might have to take off again; the marines scanned the hills looking for snipers or rocket launchers. A helicopter had almost been lost to a rocket-propelled grenade or RPG the week before. Bad aim and poor concealment led to a hole in the fence, a ten-metre-round ditch that was already almost full of water and one dead anti-Administration terrorist. The Administration called them terrorists; locals called them rebels. It was a case of your point of view.

Anyone who attacked the military – mercenaries, civilians or smugglers or barterers protecting their territories – they were all considered terrorists by the powers that be. Thom had told me that the dead man was most definitely employed by Terry Lawless.

The smugglers kept the military in their bases, unwilling to move in case they escalated the conflict. Collateral damage, civilian losses that would inevitably result from any clash, would not be conducive to public relations.

'The boys from 3 Commando will pick us up and take us to the barracks,' Thom assured us over our headsets.

Wearing the same disruptive pattern uniform as the other two marines from 45 Commando, who were providing us with an umbrella of covering fire, our escort arrived; their shoulder flashes were black with a red anchor while a red Thompson machine gun and red eagle fought for space in the dark background.

They saluted Major Thom, quickest way up and the quickest way down, naval fashion. Without speaking, twelve men surrounded the aircraft. Two of them escorted me, three of them escorted Thom; we all ducked our heads to avoid the spinning rotors even though they were high above our heads. They led us into a barrack room.

The silence once the door was shut was uncanny.

My ears were ringing like I had spent a night at a pop concert or pub gig but with the base speakers by my ear. There was an electric clock on the wall, a flex trailing from it chased into the cream paint. It ticked noisily and that was all you could hear.

Seven souls were in the room and just the beating of our hearts and the gentle sound of inhaling and exhaling was the only other sound, but my numb and aching ears could not detect that. After a minute or two, we were ushered through a doorway and into another room by six men dressed in black overalls and wearing boots. I knew they were Special Boat Service before I saw their SBS, shoulder flashes: a silver sword and two blue waves along with a motto in silver 'By Strength and Guile' fought against a black background. These Royal Marine Commandoes, highly trained, special service troops, were going to take us into the lion's den, Lawless's hotel at Whitsand Bay, the Poseidon Palace.

Chapter Twenty-Three

The Poseidon Bay Hotel

The full moon was due to rise far later that night, so it was a perfect evening to mount an assault of Whitsand Bay. The plan was for some fast boats to speed past the Bay from east to west seemingly in pursuit of a smuggler's ship. The vessels were, of course, provided by The Administration. Once past the bay, the boats would slow to a stop, release the ribs with our commando canoes, then speed off into the channel.

All went well.

We travelled past Dawlish, Teignmouth, to Torquay and Paignton, Brixham, Dartmouth, Salcombe, Bantham, Wembury, Mount Batten and Rame Head in a fast frigate.

I was shown the chart by Thom. I was little interested in the whole business, but the alternative was playing whiff-whaff on the flight deck next to the Merlin helicopter; ping-pong had never been my sport, all top-spin and hitting the ball as hard as you can, sometimes hitting your opponent.

Although Thom was promised to someone else, I loved being near her, smelling her expensive perfume, watching her move, hearing her voice, imagining the two of us together doing more than just holding hands.

'Won't we pose a very large target cruising along the coast,' I asked innocently, looking at the map and standing so close to her that I had goose bumps on my arm and a delightful frisson frisked up my spine. I was about to ask her to kiss me when I came to my senses.

'The Administration vessels have been mounting these intimidating operations for years,' she explained.

'Patrols to upset the smugglers? Why?' I asked, knowing that if I turned my head to make eye contact our lips would be centimetres away.

I steadfastly studied the map, engaged in a casual conversation as my heart hit one hundred on the speedo.

'To let the smugglers, know the king is not pleased with their goings-on and hopefully to seize some goods from the smugglers.'

'To resell to help pay for administration costs,' I scoffed.

'To pay for consultants like me,' she quipped, turning her head so I could feel her breath on my ear.

I turned to meet her eyes. I looked deeply into them and I saw desire or the reflection of the bridge windows, one or the other. Our lips could brush if I just leant into her a little more, bowed towards her, worshipped her, as she deserved.

I smelt coffee and heard an explosion in my ears. It was the liaison officer, invading my space and cramping my style.

'The old frigate took a while to come up to speed but we're cruising at about twenty knots,' he announced.

'They told me it was capable of twenty-six knots, but I'm quite happy hurtling along on a top-heavy ship at this speed,' I responded jovially. I had to pretend to be urbane and charming, otherwise how would Thom fall in love with me?

'What's our ETA?' Thom asked, immediately averting her face. Her voice sounded slightly affected by our close encounter, or she had a frog in her throat.

'It's about fifty-five nautical miles from Exmouth to the drop-off point so we should have you in the canoes by sixteen hundred hours at the latest,' he answered officiously.

'Just in time for tea,' she noted, 'I love the ship, so smooth and so beautiful.'

I almost jumped in to say something like 'just like you' but I stopped myself.

'Yes, she's a beauty. HMS *Glasgow* was the first Type 26 Frigate launched in 2020; it was meant to have two sister ships *Cardiff* and *Belfast*, but they were scrapped on the slipway in the FMR.'

The FMR was an acronym for the first major recession. It was basically a depression brought on by a weak pound. The dollar and euro became the main currency; the pound was worthless. Manufacturers could not afford to buy raw materials, factories closed in their hundreds and imports became prohibitively expensive.

The whole economy stalled.

The first major recession was a disaster. House prices collapsed, banks started charging interest on current accounts and The Administration declared immigration illegal and that all immigration had been counterproductive. Hence there was a rise in smuggling and the deportation of anyone who had not already been thrown out of the country.

Under three hours later, we were passing the point where two high speed ribs equipped with two canoes would be released into the water and we would make up part of the two-man crew. Each rib had an additional crewmember, the pilot who would get our flimsy fibreglass boats within striking distance of the little harbour at Portwrinkle village.

The hotel loomed over the coast there but there was enough cover from the village for us to get into the grounds of the hotel. Whether we would be gunned down as we raced across the lawn was another matter.

Lowering the boats from the frigate necessitated stopping the ship and I was surprised to see how manoeuvrable it was, stopping on a dime. The SBS ushered us along the corridors and out on to the assault deck. Just as we came out into the hangar, the Merlin helicopter took off, ostensibly on patrols. That was our cover. The racket was terrible.

Urged into the rib, we were winched down the side of the ship. Thom and I were lowered so quickly into the sea it felt like we were in an express lift. We dropped like a stone. I think the propeller was spinning before we hit the water, I could hear the motor thudding like an excited heart.

Our two marines unhitched the cables, and the pilot twisted the throttle and the engine roared as we shot forwards, our wake slapping the side of the ship; its grey hull loomed above us.

As we broke past the stern, the second rib could be seen to our port, giving us cover and running parallel. The Merlin helicopter was dropping cluster bombs near the decoy vessel that I was not even aware had been launched. It was a stealth rib with an electric engine.

They were putting on quite a firework display in the sombre light east of Looe, causing enough noise to drown the noise of the ribs. At the headland, which led into Britain Cove, our two marines unstrapped the two canoes. One would take Thom and one would take me. In the boat to our port, four marines would lead the way in their two canoes.

Stepping from one boat to the next in darkness when one has a rubber hide and the other had a fibreglass skin made the danger of slipping almost impossible to avoid, My marine sat in the back, prepared to paddle me on his own. I was manhandled into the hole at the front by the pilot. These professionals never slipped yet I might. I was mollycoddled all the way.

Major Thom had been given her double-bladed paddle and moved from one boat to the other in a fluid movement like a cat, practically twirling the shaft like a majorette twirling a baton as she completed the treacherous transfer – the show-off.

We were on our way.

I sat impotently in the front as the marine behind me craned his neck to see around me and paddled almost silently, deftly swapping the blades from up to down, left to right. The two marine canoes led the way for us, ready to take on any tracer or gunfire on our behalf.

In turn, Thom and her subordinate went next; my mate and I followed her in our boat like we were her shadow.

I could see very little.

The fireworks put on for our arrival was the last thing I saw in detail or heard beyond the lapping of the water against our hull. I'm sure the other boats made noise, but I could not hear it. The paddles carved their way through the water but made no sound that was discernible above the swish of the waves.

The sombre landscape was undulating hills and billowing waves. I could make out a vague outline of some shapes ahead of me, moving in the water – the other canoeists – and I could only see the harbour wall and the outline of the village once I was practically right on top of them.

The coastline was black, shrouded in a darkness so complete that distinguishing the sea from the land became impossible. My eyes had adjusted to the dark but without the moon and with no lights on shore it was like being at the bottom of a black cauldron. We might not have been going fast, three or four knots, but the way the canoes carved their way through the sea so smoothly, it felt like we were flying.

I was getting stiff and my bottom was aching, someone had forgotten to provide a silk cushion for Thom's London derriere. I had a hard wooden seat too and so hummed a 'Londonderry Air' in my head. I went on to 'The Wild Rover', 'Molly Malone' and all the tunes my mother had taught me. I thought of her and a lump rose to my throat. My heart filled with anxiety, the sure sign of love and loss; I had experienced that a lot since I had come down south.

I never met girls up north, too busy working and too poor to get to the pubs, what was left of them. Clubbing, the only opportunity to meet girls, was way out of my price range and the girls way out of my league. I had been to rock concerts where the rich took drugs and transmitted diseases but not on the inside. My mates and I experienced live performances outside the perimeter fence; the speakers were still able to make our chests shake and our ears ache. We never, ever met the girls who were inside.

My mother always wrote once a month, mainly to thank me for the money but also asking if I had a girlfriend yet. I would always tell her I was too busy. I had to send her the money, she needed it, she had stood by me when Dad had left, it was the least I could have done. I could have ended up in care.

The exchange rate meant it was nothing compared to what it could have been; ten cents to the pound was a poor exchange rate and the bank's charges for sending the amount was twenty per cent of the total – daylight robbery but we all paid.

She needed a thousand euros a month and received no pension from The Administration and was entitled to none from the Irish government.

I was going to start sobbing but my Dad had left me one legacy, a brief piece of advice for a fifteen-year-old: 'Never blub, you're a man.' That and an old grubby vest was all he left. I confess to having cried into that tatty old garment, wondering what I had done to drive him away.

The sound of the sea breaking and wombing on the shore came as a shock. It took me out of my reverie and delivered me back on to that freezing canoe, barely above the icy waters, that emanated a chill that clawed its way into the gaps in my clothing. My heart began to race. I could feel blood pumping through my veins. My hearing and sight seemed to be on red alert. We were heading into danger and the realisation and the adrenaline swept over me like a wild wave.

I could see the Whitsand Bay Hotel on the cliff top. In red lighting, which was not quite visible from where we lay, Lawless had emblazoned the words Poseidon Palace Hotel. At the distance we were from the shore, it was merely a scarlet smear, but it showed that we were near. The beach at Poseidon Bay was shale but a concrete stairway led up to the hotel.

Our escort headed off to secure that area, while we headed for Poseidon Head, a tiny fishing harbour previously known as Portwrinkle. Concrete cancer had left the sea walls mottled and pockmarked, revealing the gravel under the lining. We slipped into the pen like silk off a sword.

The waves lapped against the shore, the paddles slapped against the sea, as the marines manoeuvred their hulls about; no one would have been able to differentiate between the two sounds. The moon had begun to rise by this time and the advantage of complete darkness disappeared with its ascent into the night sky, turning it from black to midnight blue and giving us all a shape and silhouette.

Barely camouflaged by the night but almost undetectable due to our stealthy movements, we moved forward.

Retreat was not an option.

The commandoes brought us right up against the hard. The tide was high, and the moon was just beginning to rise above the hills behind the harbour. Following Thom, as ever, trying to get a view of her gorgeous body, as usual, I scrambled out of the boat and followed that beautiful behind as she crept along the harbour wall and ducked, signalling for me to do the same. I looked behind me to thank the two commandoes with a wave, but they had disappeared. They had other tasks to perform.

It was just Thom and I now.

I noticed she had not given me a weapon. Was it because she did not want me to shoot Lawless? Or was it because she did not trust me to not shoot her? I wondered and it disturbed me. She had told me stories of officers who were shot in the back by their men. It was a trait that disturbed her. I was feeling small and vulnerable. I had been scared before, now I was terrified. Who would protect me if she got hit?

I had no time to wonder any further, as she broke cover and ran across the road to the other side of the slip road. All the buildings looked ghostly white in the ghoulish glow from the moon; it looked like a galleon straight from the Alfred Noyes poem, 'The Highwayman'.

Having little choice, I followed her; the crepe soles of our boots helped us to move as soundlessly as smoke. She led the way past the first cottage and the second without stopping. Then she froze, I stood as still as a statue. She sensed danger. She was waiting for the other marines to arrive. One or the other, we had to wait. We progressed at this painfully slow pace – two houses, pause, listen, wait – until we reached the car park and viewing point just below the bank that sloped up to the hotel.

My heart was pounding, I felt like I had run one hundred metres. If I stayed where I was Lawless's patrols would catch me and he would gut me like a fish when I was brought to him. My safest bet was to stick with Major Thom. It did not feel like the best option from where I crouched but I figured that the trigger-happy guards would fell her first and then I could take her weapon.

It is extraordinary what goes through your mind when you are in danger. Above us, at the peak, there was more illumination, this time coming from the glowing yellow lights shining through the ground-floor windows flooding the lawn in front of the hotel. A seaward-side assault was clearly out of the question. Thom was standing as still as a stone as far as I could see and believe you me, I was keeping a close eye on my bodyguard.

She was the only person who would stand between Lawless and me. He would 'want my guts for garters' as my dear mammy used to say.

I was just thinking about what choice demise my friend Terence might have in mind for me when I felt a gloved hand close around my mouth and I was about to bite it when I heard a whisper in my ear.

'It's okay, mate, it's your boarding party,' a familiar voice hissed so close to my ear that I flinched, his breath in my ear canal made me shiver.

Out of the darkness, three other figures surrounded us. Their close proximity was the only clue that they were more than midnight mist. Their faces were covered in camouflage cream. I could only see the whites of their eyes. I was released and with a nod of his head we went up the left-hand side of the slope towards the swimming pool. The light was more subdued, soft lighting, and we would have more of a chance of sneaking in there or through the back where the kitchens were.

The grass was surprisingly slippery, the evening dew had settled, and we all had to concentrate on keeping our footing. The five professionals scampered up the hill like mountain goats playing a game of chase. I slid and tripped making my trousers wet and getting my gloves soaked.

The whole situation was miserable. We had not even entered the lion's den. I had no idea why we were doing this cloak and dagger raid. I suspected it was because Major Thom enjoyed it. We scurried along like squirrels; the marines knew about the movement-sensitive searchlights.

A team of sappers had preceded us, debilitating all the security systems that Lawless had laboriously installed and meticulously maintained. It was just like the days before infrared cameras, touch-sensitive alarms and photosensitive triggers. I felt like I was in a film, but I was sure that Lawless's bodyguards would use real bullets in order to protect their lord and master.

I was not sure if I was in a film about the D-Day landings or one about the First World War. Would this be our Gallipoli or *A Bridge Too Far*? Whatever, I knew what a backbreaking task crouching, and creeping could be. I am considered tall, six foot three; bending down for prolonged periods strained my long back.

I just hoped that the marines next to me would give me covering fire as I stretched to get my spine back into place.

In the darkness, lit by the few lights in the hotel, we crawled across the lawn like snails. It was cold and I shivered. I could feel the whispering wind trying to find gaps in my clothing. I was reminded of the night I had spent out at sea and it filled me with dread.

My ears were attuned to our surroundings just as my eyesight had adjusted to the night. I could hear our crepe-soled, boots stomping along the parched lawn. At least it was not winter, but the spring evening did not bode well for summer temperatures. The sea breeze was bringing Atlantic Ocean temperatures. I could not wait to get inside the building.

Finally, we made it to the pool room, an extension to the main house with folding concertina doors, which buckled under the onslaught of our marine escort. We were in. The swimming pool glistened in the dim lighting. Within seconds the stealth squadron were at the archway leading into the changing rooms.

On the other side of the showers, a pine door barred our way. Covering each other, one of the marines slowly pushed the door open and, establishing the coast was clear, we bustled along the corridor in single file. So far, we had evaded detection. There was another fire door at the end of the corridor and then steps up to the ground floor.

It was like I was in a dream and watching this all happen; I was moved along with the throng without really registering what we were doing. I had followed the briefing before the operation where we had looked at a model of the hotel and had followed our route, which had already been trod by a masseur who used a hidden Go-Pro to film her journey from the treatment room, opposite the changing room, to the exit.

The marines sandwiched Major Thom and I between them and, covering front and back, we progressed through the basement in a minutely choreographed procession. I felt like the President of the United States being bustled through a hotel kitchen after an assassination attempt. It all seemed so easy, too easy.

Thom had told me how other groups had made the hotel secure.

'They had cleared up the mess,' the marine who had paddled me across Poseidon Bay told me.

No one was specific but I gleaned the different details: Royal Electrical and Mechanical Engineers or the 'RE-ME' had taken down the telephone lines, jammed the routers and blocked the signal from local cell masts.

Basically, no one could phone in or out so there was no danger of reinforcements.

The guards on the golf course and on the cliffs had been 'neutralised' whatever that meant. I wanted to hazard a guess but all I needed to know was that the dangers had been minimised. It was a need-to-know basis, yet again. I was kept in the dark more often than a mushroom.

I scarcely had time to blink or draw breath before we were moving up the stairs. I was swept along by the hurried activity. We burst out on to the landing through a fire door with an automatic release linked to the fire alarm, which I guessed had been disarmed like the rest of the computer system.

One marine broke left and hid himself in the doorjamb, covering the bottom of the stairs that led into the lounge. Another at his shoulder covered the lounge itself. The third had moved from the back to be just ahead of Thom and overtook us all as he shot down the corridor towards the deserted dining room.

I noticed a torch on his German machine gun. The beam cut through the darkness of the corridor. The other two burst past me as Thom flattened me to the wall with her body. So close and yet so far – 'plus ça change' as they say. I enjoyed the moment and dwelt on the positive side as I smelt her perfume and felt her hot breath on my neck.

It lasted a minute; two of the marines at the back followed, broke right and backed up their comrade who was clearing the dining room.

I thought 'chaque jour, c'est un combat' and cursed the fact that we had lived next door to a Frenchwoman who had taught me to speak fluent French and introduced me to Voltaire and Balzac.

The third marine ran straight across to the beautiful walnut wall, throwing himself manfully against the panelling, which buckled against his weight and sprang back as he crouched and raised his Heckler Koch, aiming it at Terence Lawless's heart.

ii

'Welcome to the Hotel California; you can check out but never leave,' chortled Terence Lawless.

He was standing under the stained-glass window on the first landing of the huge oak staircase. The stairs creaked ominously as he walked down into the lounge that overlooked Whitsand Bay. The windows were dark mirrors in the night; a warm golden glow emanated from the side lamps placed on the side tables next to each of the chintz sofas. The floral fabric was brand new and depicted the Rose of Lancashire and the Rose of York on a cream background.

'Good evening, Mr. Lawless,' Major Thom replied, 'I hope you have some pink champagne on ice.'

'A cheeky little Bollinger Rosé should suffice. Major Mutesa, you don't mind if I call you Thomasina, do you?'

'Thom's fine, of course,' she acquiesced.

'I do despise the diminutive. Thomasina is your name in full and I shall use it; please, call me Terence but, I beg you, not Terry. I see you bought annoying Aubrey with you.'

'He insisted, you know, how it is,' she exclaimed.

'No, I don't, actually; never mind it's not important.'

'Well, it's good to meet finally,' Thom offered, extending the olive branch.

'I'm always charmed by meeting beautiful women, not so by seeing the boy who drowned my son. Still, you seem to have control of the situation, so I need to be noble in defeat.'

'Like Napoleon,' I added, helpfully.

'I have always admired Napoleon and he was not so gallant each time he was arrested. However, I wish to be offered a similar exile.'

'Elba and Saint Helena belong to other states and you have little choice but to cooperate with us,' Thomasina insisted.

'Oh, I know, there is no one left here to protect me. When the communications went, I kept sending out my men to investigate and when they did not return, I sent out more. I think I realised it was you when *they* did not come back. I was hoping for exile in Bermuda or the Bahamas.'

He smirked, revelling in his own mistake.

'You've been expecting us?' She sounded surprised; she had him figured as an egotistical maniac who would do anything to keep his power.

'Every day since I started my operation. How The Administration tolerated my behaviour, I will never know,' he admitted.

As he spoke, he moved towards the door, his claret suede slippers slapping the floorboards; the floor was oak as well, stained a warm walnut colour, it was highly polished. Lawless walked to the left, over to yet another panelled room, the library, which was just to the right of the door. Thomasina and I following like sheep.

The marines aimed three guns at Lawless just in case he should make a run for the exit where I suddenly saw two black-clad SBS marines framed in the hallway.

'There's much to discuss,' Thomasina exclaimed, I think she felt sorry for this man who seemed so broken.

'Indeed, there is,' sighed Lawless, sounding like a broken man. My hackles rose, this was not the ruthless man I knew from old. Was it the death of his son or the ease with which the Special Forces had brought his empire to its knees? At the doorway to the library, he turned.

'What is it?' asked Thomasina.

'We'll leave the boy out of our discussions. There's a pool downstairs, perhaps he'd like to take a swim?'

My heart froze. Lawless really knew how to intimidate and embarrass, he was manipulation personified and I wondered what trick he would pull to get him out of this situation. Then I remembered Major Thom was in charge. He would not be wriggling out of this one.

'As you wish,' she agreed reluctantly, giving me a slight nod and catching my eyes to reassure me.

The door closed and I was left outside in the cold.

Terence and Thomasina were going to have a chat without me.

I did not object. After all, Thomasina had said she would be leaving me out at this crucial stage to appease Terence. It was refreshing to think that for the first time she was being honest with me. That was the true revelation. I was apparently needed later though, again. I think she was just showing off, either to me or to Lawless, I was not sure. She had her reasons, but I could not fathom them out.

Then I heard four gunshots.

Chapter Twenty-Four

Don't Leave Me, Thom

I pulled the doors open and Thom staggered towards me.

'Help me,' she whispered as she stumbled across the room. I rushed to catch her in my arms. She collapsed into me and I pressed forward against her shoulders to stop her toppling me over; it was like dealing with a dead weight, trying to hold up a drunk who had barged into me in the street.

We folded together to the ground; I collapsed on to my left thigh while Thom slumped to her knees. Then we rolled together, moving her on to her side. Once she was stable and still, I looked for the wounds. Four shots from a Magnum – that would be the end of anyone.

I heard the sound of an automatic pistol being cocked. I recognised the noise from my training days in London. I looked up and saw Terry hiding behind the desk. His hands, perfectly manicured, appeared first, crawling over the leather top, followed by his tanned face. He obviously thought I was armed. I knew the Magnum .44, the most powerful hand gun in the world, carried six shots; perhaps he had saved the last two for me.

At this range and with Thom in my lap, it would be possible to kill me with one bullet, or he might just shoot off my kneecap, paralysing me for life, or maybe, if he was a poor shot, he would end up shattering my shoulder.

'Thom, talk to me,' I begged as I searched for her wounds.

As I tried to get a response from her, I heard Terry swipe a paperweight off the table and his elbow appeared from behind the desk, levering his body to his feet. He looked at me with horror on his face and hatred in eyes. I stared in disbelief; he was more indestructible than me.

As he rose, I saw that in his other hand he held his gun.

My heart stopped; there was nothing I could do.

Still Terry rose until he was almost standing, leaning on the desk, the gun flat on the surface, his other hand gripped the table as if he were gathering his thoughts.

I noticed his shirt was drenched with blood; Thom had managed to get off a shot, at least. I hoped it hurt. He gasped with pain as if he wanted to confirm that I was right.

Then, he toppled forward; there were three thuds and I saw his head bouncing off the desk, twice, before it settled. His arms spread across the desk; the gun was no longer there. It must have slipped out of his hand – that would have accounted for the third thud.

I looked down at Thom; I felt blood on the arm that was cradling her head. It was warm and sticky; it seemed to be coming from the back of her head. I searched her body for any other wounds, praying that her troops would arrive soon; I knew they had a medic with them. There was no point ringing for an ambulance. The guests had been escorted to the pubs in the nearby village of Finnygook; there was no point in asking if there was a doctor amongst them.

After a while, I noticed two holes in her jacket, revealing a black material and when I tapped on the surface, it resonated like a plastic sandwich box. She was wearing a bulletproof vest. Thom had survived being shot; the rounds were somewhere inside her armour and she must have hit her head on some furniture when Lawless shot her. She must have been thrown back by the impact, struck a hard object but still struggled to her feet before collapsing into my arms. At least she had had loosed off two rounds in return.

Reaching over to a sofa, I took a flowery cream cushion off the seat and lay it under her head. I needed to get some material to stem the blood that was oozing down the back of her neck. As I passed the desk, I took one last look at Terence Lawless.

His mouth was gaping in surprise and his eyes looked like marbles, staring lifelessly; it looked like they were examining a picture on the wall behind me.

There was no doubt that he was dead. I recognised the pallor of a dead man. I had seen enough bodies after the food riots and after the Plague or Virulent Virus as it was called. Death was all around, and it had finally visited its most unlikely victim.

Lawless was potentially bulletproof; protected by wealth and bodyguards, he had the propensity to outlive most of the population. He was in one of the top one per cent in the country and yet there he was slumped over the polished top of an old Victorian writing desk. Behind me, Thom groaned with pain, I needed to get some towels and dishcloths form the kitchen. My mother had been a nurse when she was younger. I knew I had to stem the bleeding.

Adel and Kate arrived with the Royal Marine Commando reinforcements; they had been held upstairs as bargaining chips, but their guards had surrendered as soon as they realised the building had been stormed by troops. They administered first aid as I looked on. We were all silent; I was praying that Thomasina would survive.

Thom was taken off in an ambulance and the rest of the guests – those not evacuated before, a handful of rich pensioners who had been protected in an annexe – were escorted off the premises as the forensic team came in.

I was interrogated – sorry, questioned – by the Royal Military Police, as this was a military operation. During my interrogation the forensic team left; they were swift and efficient. After the interview, the lieutenant left, and I was left alone on the sofa.

Their questions had gone on forever, long enough I reasoned for Thom to get to the military hospital at Lympstone. Eventually, Lieutenant Branston returned and handed me a room key. It was on the first floor and I staggered upstairs glad to have a bed on which to lay my head. I was exhausted, physically drained by the helicopter ride, the ship and the kayak, plus crawling around in the dead of night.

Emotionally, I was wiped out by seeing another Lawless dead and Thom injured. Mentally, I could not process anymore, and my poor brain shut down ready to reboot the next day.

At eleven the next day, I woke up, showered and walked down into the lobby at the bottom of the stairs. Meanwhile, everyone had returned to the hotel and life continued as normal apart from the lounge and the dining room being cordoned off. Golfers came into the small bar for the midday meal. I saw them gathering at the door and surmised they would know where to get something to eat now the dining room was out of bounds.

I followed them into the panelled room. It was at the entrance opposite the library that was now locked up. Banquettes lined the walls and windows. A bar against the wall on the left of the doorway served drinks and took orders for food. Light flooded through the lofty windows, it was overcast but bright, a Cornish winter's morning or a summer's morning – there seems to be more weather than climate in the West Country.

Adel and Kate were sitting there, drinking amontillado sherry with a dashing military man who I recognised from the previous evening. My two friends treated themselves to a lunch of soup, grilled fish and cheese and biscuits, while I was given a cheese sandwich and a cup of coffee, picked for me from the lounge menu by the investigating officer, Lieutenant Branston, the RMP who had grilled me the night before. I knew I was in a pickle but all the people I knew and loved were safe.

Thom had been treated for slight bruising and a cut on her neck. She was on her way to the MI6 station just up the coast in Fort Monckton.

We had an enjoyable lunch. Knowing Thom was safe, we avoided conversation about the operation. We indulged in polite discourse about the food and the weather.

'Back to mine, then,' Kate said as she swigged the last of her white wine and Adel drained her glass of red. They both looked satisfied after their three-course meal. Their good moods suggested they had consumed two or three sherries before I joined them. They shared both their bottles while I was there.

'I thought you would never ask,' I managed to quip, despite my worry over Thom.

I am Aubrey East, the comedy beast.

'You can drive the Masser,' Adel promised, 'we were going to get a taxi, but you have saved us the trouble!'

That was why they had ordered coffee for me. Therefore, they could drink as much as they liked; I was the designated driver. By now I was used to being used and hoped that driving a sports car might eventually become a pleasure, the third time. I did not need to be asked twice so we hurriedly said goodbye to my interrogator and sauntered out into the daylight and the car, which was crouching in the shadows as the building loomed over it. The leather seats were cool, and I breathed in Adel's unmistakable perfume.

The poor lieutenant looked upset; I think he was betting on one of them spending the afternoon with him. Still, he had their details so he could engineer a walk along the coastal path with one of them at a later date.

I enjoyed breathing in the Illuminum White Gardenia Petals this time around. I felt a wave of relief wash over me. Thinking back to my arrival in Poseidon Bay and Freddie and Adel and Kate, I realised how much had happened in such a brief amount of time.

Over a cup of tea and carrot cake at the cottage, which Kate lived in still, we discussed our adventures. Kate said I should write a book about everything that happened.

So, I did.

Afterword

Three years after it all, 2032, Adel and I are running Lawless Enterprises from the Rover's Rest. Kate has gone to live with her parents in Lincolnshire; we set her up with a few porkers and she enjoys pig farming and smoking bacon. She comes down to visit us occasionally. The cottage is her home as much as ours.

Business is good, the twins are thriving. Adel wears a patch over her eye now and she tells the girls lots of pirate stories; she cannot wait to take them to *The Pirates of Penzance* when it performed in Polperro; she plays the soundtrack constantly in the house.

Adel and I wasted no time at all.

She's expecting a baby boy and we're going to call him Freddie. It was a shame about the way Terence went but 'That's Life', I suppose.

We regularly meet our employees at The Captain Benbow, taking them upstairs to the new dining room. We recently secured a supply of fresh fish from a Spanish trawler that passes by on the way to the North Sea, so we always have fish and chips.

The weather can be harsh but driving to work in a new electric Jaguar has its benefits, including a good air conditioning unit, the luxury of leather seats and the heady aroma of Adel's perfume, Illuminum White Gardenia Petals; it makes me feel I am taking her everywhere with me.

She still swims in the sea and has taken up surfing with the two strangers from the beach. Her tan lasts all year round. I have not been back into the sea since the last time with Freddie.

As for Adel and me, we see eye to eye on most things.

I never drink champagne unless I am the one to open the bottle myself and keep hold of the glass.

I could have left but I would have had heartache for the rest of my days. Poseidon Bay was renamed Whitsand Bay. I realised, just in time I suppose that the old maxim still rings true: 'If you can't beat them join them.'

Other Books

We hope you have enjoyed the story. You might like to consider the following books by the same author:

The Clapham Common Caper is a story set in 1959, this Jo Murphy Mystery introduces Doctor Jo Murphy a pathologist and General Practitioner who lived in Clapham. This is her adventure as told by her mentor and friend Detective Inspector Richard Regan

The Taint Gallery is the story of two normal people who allow passion to destroy their peace and tranquillity. This is an explicit portrayal of sexual attraction and deteriorating relationships.

Switch is a dark thriller; Chandler meets *Fifty Shades of Grey* – a nightmare comes true!

Waterwitch, a sailing adventure: two brothers sailing a boat around the Mediterranean during the Falklands War, resulting in disastrous consequences.

Major Bruton's Safari or *Uganda Palaver* is a witty account of a coronation and safari in Uganda. As a guest of the Ugandan people, a group of disparate people experience Africa with a caustic commentator, critical not of the continent but of his own friends and family.

Innocent Proven Guilty is a thriller on the lines of *The 39 Steps*. A teacher discovers his brother dead in a pool of blood; he wants to find the murderer, but he has left his footprints behind.

Seveny Seven is a 'Punk Portrait' The story of growing up in London during the punk era, a whimsical autobiography that explodes the myth that 'Punk' was an angry working-class movement.

Carom is a thriller about an art theft and drug smuggling. Finn McHugh and his team pursue Didier Pourchaire, a vicious art thief. The action moves between London, Paris, Helsinki and St Petersburg. Everyone wants to catch the villain resulting in a messy bagatelle. Carom is an Indian board game.

One also called *Ad Bec* is a dish best eaten cold; a schoolboy takes revenge on a bully. Stephen is a late arrival at a prep school in the depths of Shropshire. He is challenged to do a 'tunnel dare' by the school bully.

When the tunnel collapses on the bully, Stephen has to solve the dilemma: tell no one and be free or rescue the bully.

The story is set in a seventies progressive preparatory school.

Remember the Fifth is the true story of Guy Fawkes; it shows how Robert Cecil tried to destroy all opposition to his power and make himself the hero of the hour.

Karoly's Hungarian Tragedy is Michael's first departure into historical biography. This is the story of Karoly Ellenbacher taken into captivity and used as a human shield by Romanian soldiers during the war; arrested during the communist era and sent down a coal mine, he escaped to England in 1956. His story of survival is barely credible.

Michael Fitzalan has written four plays:

Veni, Vidi, Vicky: a story of a failed love affair.

George and the Dragon: a painter discovers a cache of bonds and sovereigns in a cellar, not knowing that it belongs to a vicious gang. Thankfully his niece's friend is a star lawyer and can help him return the money before it is too late… or can she?

Symposium for Severine is a modern version of Plato's *Symposium* but with women the philosophers instead of men.

Superstar is a play that sees Thomas Dowting meeting Jesus in the temple, travelling to Angel to meet his girlfriend Gabrielle. They convince Thomas to volunteer for work abroad. Three weeks later J C Goodman takes over Thomas's job and moves in with Gabrielle.

Switch and *Major Bruton's Safari* have been turned into scripts.

Michael is working on a script, which he may turn into a novel: *M.O.D.*, Mark O'Dwyer, Master of Disguise – a private detective agency. Francis Barber Investigators, is retained to find out why a model was defenestrated from a Bond Street building.

Michael is working on a script, which he may turn into a novel: M.O.D, Mark O'Dwyer, Master of Disguise, a private detective agency, Francis Barber Investigators, is retained to find out why a model was defenestrated from a Bond Street building.

Printed in Great Britain
by Amazon